SILENT WITNESSES

AN ARLINGTON & MCCURLEY MYSTERY

ANNELIE WENDEBERG

ANNELIE'S BOOKSTORE

ART & MAGIC
THIS WAY

PROLOGUE

Only two people in this world know my name.
I am one.
The other is believed dead.

If there is a memory that best describes those balmy weeks of late May and early June, it is that of a small, silent child sitting under a mulberry bush.

Nothing seemed to escape her notice, those sharp grey eyes she inherited from her father. She would watch Zachary's every move — how his black hands grew paler as a dusting of loamy soil covered his skin, how his sun-bleached shirt darkened along his spine as he plucked and dug and mowed. How his large brown eyes twinkled in the shadow of his straw hat.

Whenever I think back to those days, I see myself standing at the bay window, gazing out into the garden, watching my daughter and her fascination with the world, and wondering what it was that made her so quiet.

She was two and a half years old and had not spoken a word.

It was the time of late spring cleaning. Margery excessively aired out the house, washed the lace curtains, knocked the dust out of mattresses and rugs, and polished tables, cupboards, and floors until our home smelled of beeswax and linseed oil, with a faint bite of turpentine.

Those were our days of peace and quiet, a time that was much too short and far away.

With each day closer to Klara's third birthday, my fear of Moran grew. The man had hacked off my index finger with sadistic pleasure, shot me in the shoulder and very nearly killed me.

He was a constant itch at the back of my neck. There was not a night I didn't lie awake going through all the precautions I had taken over these last years. And I always came to the same conclusions: Anna Kronberg had disappeared. Moran would not find us. My daughter and I were safe.

How blind I was.

THE FIRST VICTIM

1

All the silent witnesses ... the place, the body, the prints ... can speak if one knows how to properly interrogate them.

Alexandre Lacassagne

*C*orey Hill clipped the sun in half. Houses lining the embankment were painted orange, and a fiery red was bouncing off their windows. The Charles River swept past me. A crew of rowers stroked the calm water, their boat as sleek and white as a tern.

I shut my eyes, inhaled the scents of muck and burning coal, and could almost picture the Thames. And the city I'd once called home. The men I'd loved and left.

The air was growing chill. It was time to go.

I slung my bag over my back, and mounted my bicycle. The brisk ride through the Common, across the channel, and down Dorchester Avenue pumped heat through my body as darkness began to descend on Boston.

I turned into Savin Hill Avenue and trundled to a halt some distance from a freight train. For a heartbeat, I thought it abandoned — an old toy forgotten in the middle of the road. But there was movement, lights and noise. Lanterns danced like fireflies around the engine's snout. Cries pierced the rising fog, and farther east, a ship's horn blew.

Cold sweat broke out along my spine, goose flesh followed. My heart kicked my ribs as my mind hollered, *Not Klara! Not Klara!* Despite the unlikeliness of a small child climbing a picket fence and walking two hundred yards through the neighbourhood unnoticed.

But even the strongest logic could not put a damper on the fear I had cultivated for years.

I dropped my bicycle by the side of the road, and ran up to a clump of people waving their arms and throwing harsh words at one another. I squeezed past two burly men, asking what had happened. Irritated murmurs and an elbow to my side were the only replies. Eventually, they parted, and my gaze fell on a man who sat folded in on himself. Head between his knees, he heaved and wept. His hat lay in the grass.

I crouched down and touched his shoulder. 'What happened?'

'I…I…'

I waited, but that was all he managed.

'He saw her too late. Couldn't stop the train. She was… I mean…we *think* it's a woman.'

I looked up at the man who had spoken. The bruised sky reflected off his spectacles — two flecks of dark violet in a soot-covered face. 'He's the driver?'

The man nodded.

'He ran over a person?'

Another nod.

'And you are?'

'Name's Smith.'

'Dr Arlington. I'm a physician. When did this happen?'

'Um… A few minutes ago?' He cleared his throat and pulled at a small chain that dangled from his trouser pocket. 'Eleven minutes.' There was a click as he snapped his watch shut.

'Have the police and the coroner been informed?

'I…' He blinked. 'I'm only the stoker, Miss.'

'Summon them. And point me to the victim, please.'

'Which…part do you want to see first?'

Throats were cleared, eyes dropped. The stoker's gaze stumbled up along the railway.

'I need a lantern,' I said, snatched it from one of the bystanders, and walked away before he could protest.

I had only ever seen one railway accident — a collision of a passenger train and a costermonger's cart. The man had died on the spot. His screaming horse had had to be shot. That train hadn't been going fast. But this…this was a disaster.

I forbade myself to think too deeply about the shreds of white fabric snowflaking the grass, the dark liquid spattering steel and snowflakes and earth. The gloom leaching all colour from the blood.

The muttering of onlookers faded, the snatches of enquiries of who, when, and why.

My gaze snagged on something golden, a wisp of silk wrapped around a wheel. I bent down and held the lantern close to it. A lock of fair hair. Blood.

Klara's hair was dark and short. I pressed a fist to my heart, gulped a lungful of air, and made my way toward the engine.

Bits of scalp trailing long hair splattered track ballast and anchors ahead of me. I almost stumbled over a bump covered with a dark, checkered blanket.

More than a decade of medical training and still my

stomach dropped at the sight. I directed light to the blanket, picked at a corner, and pulled.

It was barely recognisable as a head.

The lower jaw was missing, as was half the scalp, the skin of chin and cheeks, and one ear. Moths fluttered in the beam of my lantern. One caught its powdery wings on the victim's lashes. The forehead was badly abraded, eyebrows shaved off. Blood crawled from the neck wound.

I knelt and inspected her eyes. She'd died with her eyes open. They were clouded, her pupils constricted, the whites bloodshot. I touched my finger against one eyeball. It felt cold.

Carefully, I turned the head face down. The vertebrae had been ripped off, and the large foramen was visible. I slipped two fingers through the opening and into the cavity. The brain was lukewarm.

Frowning, I wiped my hands on the grass and shrugged off my bag.

I WAS FOUND several minutes later. Or rather my legs poking out from beneath the engine were found.

'May I ask what you are doing here, Miss?'

An overly authoritative voice. He must be a police officer. I inched back out and heard the fabric of my jacket crackling against rock. A seam gave.

I wiped my palms on a handful of grass, brushed off my knickerbockers, and stood.

'PC Lyons, Boston Police Department.' The man had yet to extract his hands from his pockets, lift his hat in greeting, or abandon the cigarette that hung from the corner of his mouth.

'Dr Arlington. I was about to examine the torso.'

A lazy lift of his eyebrows. His gaze slid down to the mangled shoulder joint peeking out between two wheels.

I shone the lantern onto the mess. 'She was dragged quite a distance before the train came to a halt. Her head lies about ten yards farther down. One foot was severed as well, and is on the other side of the tracks. I need to move her to reach her rectum. Perhaps you could assist me?'

He stopped chewing his smoke. 'Excuse me?'

'I measured the temperature in her brain, and found it to be sixteen degrees too low. I need to take her rectal temperature for comparison.'

'You…what?'

'As I said, I'm a physician.'

He took the lantern from me and knelt down to peek under the train. 'Why were you taking the temperature of the…dear God!' The light wobbled as he pressed his face into the bend of his elbow.

Before he could drop the lantern, I took it from him. 'Has the coroner been notified?'

'Umpf,' he squeezed into his sleeve.

'The core temperature was twenty-eight degrees Celsius. Or eighty-two degrees Fahrenheit. Whichever you prefer. Body temperature lowers by approximately one and a half degrees Celsius per hour after death. The accident occurred less than fifteen minutes before I took the temperature of the brain. The neck wound indicates that the head was severed by the train — meaning the head hadn't had time to cool down faster than the rest of the body. But I need to make sure that the temperatures do match before I draw my conclusions.'

PC Lyons had regained some of his control. He stood, slid a hand into his pocket and pulled out a fresh cigarette. With trembling fingers, he struck a match and lit his smoke. The flare gave his eyes a devilish glint. 'Meaning to say?'

I refrained from asking whether the police didn't educate its officers on the most basic post-mortem procedures, or whether he'd slept through it.

'It means that the victim must have died around noon,' I explained. 'She must have been placed on the tracks when darkness fell. The train schedule should narrow it down for you. Is a post-mortem surgeon on the way?'

'The coroner has been informed,' PC Lyons said and sucked at the cigarette as if his life depended on it.

I couldn't interpret the flat tone of his voice. Perhaps he was trying to appear hardened, but I found it useless to ponder the matter. 'Would you help me move the body so that I can take the rectal temperature?'

The ember pinprick near his mouth flared and quivered.

'Well,' I said. 'Two people won't fit under there anyway.'

I crouched down. 'Should anyone wish to move the train, I'd be much obliged if you would stop them.'

The track ballast crunched and shifted under Lyons' boots. 'Should have told them yourself *before* you placed yourself in harm's way,' he muttered.

Again I squeezed between train and sleepers, the track ballast cutting sharply into my elbows, hips, and knees. I placed the lantern next to the body, calmed my breath, and let my eyes roam.

She wore the pitiful leftovers of a chemise and stockings. Skin was torn from her belly, breasts, and hips. Bones protruded through flesh. A kneecap hung limply from her leg. Blood was everywhere, and yet the total amount could only be a pint. And much of it had clotted before the force of the impact ripped her open.

'Well, then,' I muttered and got to work.

Upon my huffing and grunting, PC Lyons grew worried and peeked under the engine. Seeing that I was tugging on a bloody thigh, his pale face disappeared at once. 'What are you doing?' he hissed.

'I'm moving her so that I can take her temperature. She's on her back and I can't reach her rectum without the risk of breaking the thermometer, so I will measure inside her vagina instead.' That was probably a bit of information too delicate to share with the good constable.

'Her eyes are cloudy,' I continued. 'And her blood has already clotted. More evidence that her death occurred several hours earlier.'

Lyons said nothing.

'Aha!' I said more to myself than to Lyons. 'The temperature in the vag...of the two body parts is identical.'

I wiped off my thermometer, stuck it back into its cardboard cylinder, and into my bag.

Then I touched the victim's lower abdomen, pushed bits of intact skin around, and pressed into her flesh. 'It appears she was pregnant. I mean...with child. Possibly fifth or sixth month. From the state of her skin, I'm guessing her to be between twenty-five and thirty-five. Rigor mortis present in the extremities was released by the impact of the train.'

I examined her limbs down to her clenched fists. 'Her hands are cold, as one would expect in this season...' Unfurling the stiff fingers of her right hand took some effort. 'No blood or skin under her fingernails as far as I can see.'

Rocks crunched as Lyons shifted his weight from one foot to the other. 'It would be best to wait for the coroner.'

'I'm qualified to perform post-mortems, Constable Lyons. It is imperative to examine the body as soon as possible. If you would write down the address of the coroner, I will send him my report tomorrow morning.' I bent back the fingers of her left hand. Something white — or yellow? — was stuck to her palm.

I picked at it and held it close to the light. 'I've found a flower petal in her left hand. Hmm. From a rose, I believe. Yes, definitely, a yellow rose. A bit early for roses, isn't it? But it might have been grown in a hothouse.'

I directed the light toward Lyons' boots. 'It would be best to block off the area, and ask that the train not be moved until all evidence can be collected in daylight.'

2

I scrubbed the blood off my skin, and dropped my clothes into soap water. Shivering, I wrapped myself in nightgown and robe, and slipped into my bedroom.

An oil lamp silhouetted Klara and Zachary — he on the floor with his back against the bed frame, legs stretched out, a toe sticking through a hole in his sock, and she in my bed, her chin resting on his shoulder, and her hair a frizzly halo.

Both looked up from a book as I clicked the door shut.

'We fought a cobra,' he said.

'Oh?' I knelt on the bed and kissed Klara's head. She ducked, showed me her claws and teeth, and hissed. I poked my finger into her belly. 'Are you the vicious mongoose and I the poor snake?'

Her eyes flared. She shook her head.

'All right. I'm the mongoose.' I grinned and nipped at her throat. She wiggled and squealed, making my ears ring. 'And now you are wide awake. In the middle of the night.'

Zach pushed off the floor and placed the book on the nightstand. 'Have you eaten?'

'I'm fine.'

At that, Klara jumped up, her small face brimming with expectation. 'Poh!' she said, bouncing on the mattress.

'Ah, the mongoose is hungry, I see. Perhaps, we can find cobra casserole in the kitchen?' He held out his hand, she grasped it and slipped from the bed.

'In that case, I'll have some too,' I said and followed.

I LEARNED from the morning papers that the railway had not been blocked for further investigation. Had I been male, PC Lyons might have agreed with my suggestions. Possessing a modicum of diplomatic talent might have helped as well. Nor was I well versed in the womanly art of making men believe that my superior idea had been theirs.

The police arrested a tramp. The man had neither name nor papers. He'd been one of the bystanders, the short article read, and had yet to speak a sensible word.

Not one of these developments surprised me.

I sipped my coffee. The wool blanket itched at the back of my neck, and the old wicker chair poked a stray twig into my backside. I twisted and scooted about until a somewhat comfortable position was found. Then I shut my eyes and tipped my face toward the morning sun.

With the warmth of spring soaking my skin, and the sounds of birds and soft wind in my ears, London couldn't have felt farther away. Two and a half years ago, on a grey November day, I'd stepped off a train from New York. From the shelter of my arms, Klara had blinked her blue-grey eyes up at me. Weary from a two-week journey across the Atlantic, I hadn't even found the energy to smile at her.

And right there and then, a furious northeast tempest had slammed into us, ripping off my hat, upturning my umbrella, and driving a torrent of icy rain in Klara's face. We were soaked to the bone within the few short moments it took me to wave down a cab. Klara hollered until we reached our hotel, and had drawn a bath to warm our frozen limbs. That same night she fell ill. We spent more than a week in bed, her feverish body curled against mine, her hunger ravenous.

Boston couldn't have been more unwelcoming. And yet, despite that cold first embrace, it felt like returning home.

I lowered the coffee cup to my lap and squinted at the gently sloping garden — the grass kissed by dew, spiderwebs, and golden light. There was a flutter in my stomach, and I asked myself why I had ever left Boston. And for what?

Eight years ago, my reasons had been clear enough: It had made little difference then whether I worked in Boston or in some antiquated European country. I'd lived disguised as a man, so the countless restrictions women were facing hadn't applied to me. But that life had come with a price: I couldn't make friends, for they would ask questions that were too private and impossible for me to answer. Even more awkward were the young ladies unsubtly hinting I might take them to social events. They had worried me to death.

I huffed a laugh. *Dr Anton Kronberg was reportedly chased across the Atlantic by wanton girls.* Wouldn't that make an interesting headline.

Now, everything had changed. Medical schools for women had sprung up in the American North, and I could live without the need to bind my breasts and sneak from one hiding place to another. I could simply do my work and talk openly — as a woman! — about patients, surgeries, and cures. It was delicious.

Addictive, even.

What turns would my life have taken had I stayed in Boston and not left for London?

A gentle *tap tap* of small feet behind me was the answer: I wouldn't have met the man who'd fathered Klara, wouldn't have thought it possible for me to conceive, and I wouldn't have murdered my husband. Nor would I have met the two men who came to mean so much to me. One, a thief and gentle giant. The other as sharp as he was sensitive — a man who feared intimacy more than his own death.

Strange, how moments of happiness always brought back dark memories. Stranger yet, that I occasionally wondered about the "what-ifs." Where was the need for that? I was happy with what I had and what I was.

Perhaps that was just how my mind worked. Possibilities and impossibilities wanted to be analysed. Wasn't that how one learned? By reflecting upon the past, on the errors and successes — all melting into one another, changing with time, experience, and perspective? Only with reflection had I felt able to grow, to make peace with what had happened and what I had done, hoping that one day I would be a little wiser.

Tap tap.

I pretended to be oblivious to Klara sneaking up on me. I placed the cup on the floor and began to snore softly. She was very close now.

Tap tap.

I snored louder.

She attacked with a high-pitched scream that made me worry about the window panes. I shot out my arm and poked her in the stomach, showed my fangs, and produced my best and most evil snake hiss. Then I grabbed her and wrestled her onto my lap (she was a rather noisy and wiggly mongoose), and blew a raspberry against her cheek. She twisted and bit my neck in retaliation.

'I love you, my little monster,' I said and brushed my nose against hers.

The fast report of heels on floorboards announced Margery's approach. 'God's nightgown!' Her bosom was pumping dramatically. 'Did someone stick a pig on our porch?'

'It was a mongoose catching a cobra. And the wicker chair is coming apart. Either that or I'm sitting on a hedgehog.' I rose with Klara in my arms, who seemed undecided whether her physical form was that of a mongoose or a clingy octopus. 'Do we still have some of that delicious cobra casserole in the larder?'

Margery narrowed her eyes. 'Just don't say the *gardener* did the cooking.'

WE TOOK breakfast in the kitchen (*sans* cobra casserole). It was the first room to catch the early morning sun, the first to be warm in winter. It was the place where we ate and talked, and shared our silence.

Klara sat on my lap, dismembering a slice of bread until only a ring of crust remained. She placed it on her head like a crown, then blew bubbles in her milk. A heartbeat later, she spat milk across the table.

'Well, now, young lady!' Margery said sharply.

Crying, Klara hid her face in my shirt. On some days, she reverted back to the maturity of a nine-month-old. It worried me. Other times, she didn't make a peep for a day and a half, and committed herself to calm observation of birds and beetles. She either focused on a task for hours on end, or wasn't able to focus at all.

And then there was the fact that she could read. At twenty-six months, her fingers began following the lines we read to her. Zach tested my theory by "reading" the wrong words to her. Words that weren't printed where her small fingers touched the page. She'd thrown herself on the carpet and hollered for twenty minutes.

Zachary sniffed at Klara's cup. 'The milk has turned.'

Margery took it from him, tasted it, and grunted. 'Hum. Still have a gallon left of that. Should make some nice clabber.' She busied herself dabbing at the puddle on the table-cloth, and checking the contents of the icebox.

Klara had stopped crying and was staring at her hands — two chubby starfishes on white linen. Zach's large hand reached out to cover both of hers, and she leaned down and gave him a slobbery kiss on his wrist.

Margery placed a mug of fresh milk in front of Klara, and then turned to Zachary to discuss a new variety of zinnias she wanted him to grow, and talk about the roof of the annex that needed fixing.

My thoughts drifted away, along railway tracks, over shreds of clothes and skin, and the face of a dead woman I had stared at, trying to find something familiar. Perhaps the coroner would know more.

When Margery stood and brushed crumbs onto her plate, I looked up and asked, 'First patient at nine?'

She nodded.

About an hour and a half, then. That should be time enough to write reports for the police, the coroner, and the post-mortem surgeon. I tweaked Klara's pigtail, kissed her neck, and transferred her to a chair.

'I'll be in my office,' I said, and made to leave.

Catching my brief glance at the sink, Margery pushed out her chin. There were limits to her flexibility, and a mistress who dabbled in the affairs of the housekeeper was far from acceptable. Two years before, she'd thrown a fit when she'd caught me beating eggs, flour, and milk for Yorkshire pudding.

∽

HALFWAY INTO MY REPORT, I was interrupted by a knock on the door. 'Come in.'

Margery stuck her head into my office. 'One Mrs Heathcote is here and asked to see you. She has no appointment, but says you are friends and it's urgent.'

'*Hattie* Heathcote? Has something happened?' I asked, but the woman in question was already peeking over Margery's shoulder.

The door shut. Hattie was beaming.

'No one died, I take it?' I said.

'Quite the opposite.' She sat in the chair across from me and placed her hat on the desk. 'I believe I am with child.'

I pushed my reports aside and grasped her hands. 'Wonderful news! Did you come to tell me, or because you need a physician?'

Blood rose to her cheeks. Hattie was a beautiful woman. She always made me think of Snow White — raven black hair, skin the colour of new milk, her body fine-boned and graceful. What made her stunning were her light blue eyes. And now the blush. She had the intensity of a diamond in the evening sun.

'You know that I wasn't…wasn't able to carry my last two babies to term.'

'I didn't know. I'm sorry.'

She waved me away. 'I'm twenty-five, have two beautiful daughters, and no reason to complain. Robert, my husband, he has been… He wants a son. And so I was hoping that this time…' Her chin began to wobble.

'You are worried you might lose another child.'

'Of course I am!' She dashed a tear away. 'I've had two miscarriages. Who's to know if this one will make it?'

'It's all right, Hattie. Now, tell me about the previous pregnancies, and what your family physician suggested.'

Hattie talked. About the pains that began in the fourth or

fifth month of her pregnancies, the bleeding. About the elderly doctor who wouldn't do much but pat her hand and ask about her diet. She wanted a lady physician, and it had to be me. Her husband didn't approve, but he wanted an heir — as though the Boston elite were royals and there was a throne to be occupied — and so it was decided that I was to prevent a miscarriage at all costs.

What she didn't expect was that my physical examination would extend beyond touching her abdomen through her dress.

I WASHED my hands as Hattie shook down her skirts. She cleared her throat, her gaze following the patterns of the rug.

Clearly, she needed time to compose herself, but I couldn't give her that. I needed answers. 'I can't help but wonder if your husband helped your miscarriages along, Hattie.'

Her head snapped up. 'No! He is ever so gentle when I'm in the family way.'

'He beats you up *only* when you are not pregnant?' My crude choice of words made her flinch. But I found bruises around the genitalia much cruder than words could ever be.

'No. You don't understand. It's… It's just games that we play. He likes it a little rougher. A little…birching, here and there. Am I… Am I not supposed to please my husband?' She was defiant now. Shoulders squared, spine straight.

'You are a grown woman. You know what you want and what you don't want.'

'Precisely.' Suddenly, she deflated a little, then pulled back her chair and sat. 'Don't tell anyone, please.'

'Communication between a doctor and her patient is always confidential. And you are my friend, Hattie.'

'That's the problem. Perhaps it wasn't such a good idea to come here. You might tell Warren.'

'Warren? Your brother? I've never even met him. Honestly, Hattie, I don't ever talk about my patients' issues with anyone but my patients.' I took her hand in mine and squeezed it. 'All right?'

'Oh! I almost forgot! Warren is coming home. And it's about time. You have to meet him, Liz. We'll all be there. It's going to be one of our nights. At six or seven o'clock he'll be back, he said. Oh, please come.'

'Tonight?'

'Didn't I say that?'

'A Freak Consortium night…' I mused, waiting for Hattie to wink with both her eyes — a hilarious thing she would do when she was impatient, or making a joke. It made her look like an owl after too much coffee. When she clapped her lids, I laughed. 'Well, why not.'

She thumped a fist on the desk. 'You will love him!'

'My good friend's seafaring twin brother? I'll probably be jealous and hate his guts.'

3

'And then those hairy *beasts* raced past us, scantily dressed in white linen trousers falling short of the knee, and armless, throatless shirts. Imagine the shock!' Eliza's voice drowned in collective chuckling.

I almost snorted my wine out through my nose.

Hiccuping, Eliza poked Margaret in the ribs. 'And *you* thought they were inmates fleeing some lunatic asylum.'

Margaret raised her eyebrows. 'That's what *you* thought, *I* didn't. I had too much fun watching you blush to tell you about the Hare and Hounds Club runners.'

'*No* hats! And *bare* legs!' Eliza squeaked and collapsed into Margaret's lap.

Margaret lit a cigar, leaned back and puffed it, smug as a cat. She hid her auburn curls under a bowler hat and her long legs in pinstripe trousers. I wondered what she would say if I told her I'd lived disguised as a man for years. She would probably laugh, box my shoulder, and ask me to adopt her.

Margaret touched her fingertips to Eliza's cheek, and Jerome used the moment of distraction to snatch the cigar from her. He stuck it between his teeth and puffed once, twice, and then returned it.

Glowering, Margaret readied her sharp tongue to fling insults at him. She was cut off by a *bang*. The door to the room burst open. A knapsack was thrown in and a dishevelled man followed.

The sharp contrast of blue eyes to black hair — so much like his twin sister — identified him as the prodigal heir of the Amaury family, and the owner of this townhouse that we frequently abused for...well, planning to "overthrow something," as the others called our meetings.

According to Hattie, Warren ran every time his mother tried to arrange a bachelor's ball for him. He'd last disappeared just before his sister dragged me from a rehearsal of the Symphony Orchestra to a drinking hall to meet her friends — the Freak Consortium — which had been roughly three months earlier.

Warren was holding a handkerchief to mouth and nose. Blood soaked the front of his shirt.

Jerome jumped from his armchair. 'What the dickens happened? Who did this to you?' He cracked his knuckles for good measure. Jerome's fists were ready, as always. But for the sake of his father — Judge Fletcher, who had extricated him from several tight spots before...well, before finally threatening disinheritance — Jerome was trying to master the art of self-control.

He didn't like it much.

Broad, dark, and with a violent streak, Jerome was Uriel's antipode. No one really knew why the two were best friends.

'Sit,' Uriel said and tugged at Jerome's waistband, effectively dumping him back onto the chair and snuffing out his wild temper.

Warren mumbled, 'Gobbeb Lubber,' around his handkerchief, and kicked the door shut.

'What?'

'Goh-beb Lubber.'

'He quoted Luther,' Hattie translated.

'Huh-hum.' Warren raised an index finger. '*I bould nob fmell fe foul odour of your name!*'

'Well, at least you didn't use the quote with the farts and the mouth. That's progress.'

A soft cough announced the butler, Owens. 'Will you be needing this, Sir, or may I send the maid to take it away?' He pointed an impeccable white-gloved hand at the knapsack.

Warren mumbled something and waved the bag away. Owens, without ever changing his expression of utter neutrality, curled a pinky around the strap, and carried the knapsack from the room, holding it at arm's length.

Warren followed him with his gaze until he was gone. 'How bib he bo fhat?'

'I hope he sends refreshments,' Hattie said and gently tugged Warren's hand from his face to reveal his injury. The view of his swollen, bloody nose tinged the skin around her eyes green.

'Is it broken?' she asked me.

Warren's gaze followed Hattie's. 'Who'f fhat?'

I emptied my wine, stood, and held out my hand. 'Doctor Elizabeth Arlington, pleased to meet you.'

He eyed me with curiosity, then wiped his palm on his trousers, and took my hand in his. 'B-bwarren,' he said. His gaze fell. His grasp tightened as he turned my wrist. 'Inberefbing.'

He was instantly poked in the gut by his sister.

I extricated myself from his grip.

'You have no manners whatsoever!' Hattie hissed at him. And then to me, 'I'm sorry, Liz. He's horrible. Always had been.'

'Well.' I wiggled the remaining fingers of my right hand. 'It *is* interesting.'

'A dog ate it,' Jerome provided, earning himself a whack on the forehead from Margaret.

'That's what she said, wasn't it?' He rubbed his brow.

I'd lied, of course. The truth lay in the same pit where I'd buried my name and my past.

With a groan, Warren lowered himself into an armchair, snatched the wine bottle from the table and put it to his mouth. He flinched at every swallow, but drained a good portion of it, and then clamped the bottle between his legs. 'Gods, I'll nebber geb used to ib. Gebbing on a ship makes me ill, gebbing obb a ship makes me ill. Perhaps, I shoulb just sebble down.'

Margaret snorted. 'Why not try *not* to get punched in the face?'

'You have to tell us all about your trip. We're running out of material,' Eliza said.

'Doesn't *she* habe enoub queer sb…sb…stories to tell?' he thrust his chin out at me. 'Her tongue smacks of continental life.'

'I've lived quite…sheltered, Mr Amaury. There is no queer story to tell.' An easy lie that was met with a tilt of his eyebrows.

'*Mister* Amaury?' He looked about the room. 'Is she not one of us?'

'She is. Hush now. Liz, check his injury, please. He might have splinters in his brain, the way he talks.'

'All right.' I moved to sit on Warren's armrest. He jerked back.

'I'm a physician, I won't hurt you more than absolutely necessary.'

'And that is supposed to ease my terror?'

'Hold still.' I grabbed his chin and turned his face toward me. His eyes widened.

'How was Chile?' I said by way of distraction.

'Huh?'

Gently, I ran my fingers along the bridge of his nose, feeling for signs of a fracture. 'The tag on your knapsack read "Valparaiso."'

There was a patch of dark stubble at the edge of his jaw. He must have shaved hastily, perhaps without a mirror. His black hair curled at the nape of his neck, partially concealing a deep scratch that was fresh but had stopped bleeding. Bruises were beginning to bloom around his throat. His collar was loose, a button missing. 'But that wasn't a fight with sailors, was it. You must have disembarked in New York, but got roughed up less than half an hour ago.'

'Hrmpf.'

'This might hurt a bit.' I applied gentle pressure to his nasal bone.

His eyes watered as he sank farther down in his chair.

'Could you hear the crunch?' I asked.

'Wish I hadn't.'

'That's the fractured pieces of bone grinding against each other. Put a cold rag on your face, or ice if you have it. And don't quote Luther for three weeks.'

He snorted, bringing forth a gush of fresh blood. Mortified, he clapped the handkerchief to his face and accidentally bumped his nose. He groaned in pain.

'Someone throttled and punched you. Did you pass out? Did you sustain head injuries?' I asked.

He shrugged.

I tapped his cheekbones and ran my fingers across his scalp. 'No fractures as far as I can see.' I placed my palm over one eye, checking the reaction of the other pupil. Then I leaned in and sniffed. 'Cheap gin on your lips. Filthy wood shavings in your hair. Minced meat for a nose. Tsk! Your parents will be scandalised if word of your nightly activities reaches their ears.'

He narrowed his eyes. 'Do you have a problem with me?'

'You salivated into my vintage Bordeaux.' I threw a pointed glance at the wine bottle in his hand. 'A major offence.'

He held the bottle aloft, squinting at the blood-red liquid. 'M'pologies.' Then he put it to his mouth and drank.

'When your sister poked your ribs, you didn't flinch. I assume nothing's broken there?'

He coughed. 'Got kicked, but not bad.'

'Hmm… Lean forward please.' I probed his ribcage, but he didn't seem to feel pain. 'If your kidneys hurt or you find blood in your urine, consult a physician at once.'

'Hrmpf,' he said again and tipped more wine into his mouth.

'Hopeless case. Avoids doctors like the plague,' Hattie said.

I slipped a card from my purse and handed it to him. 'We usually help to avoid the plague.'

'You should see her work with a bone saw,' Jerome said, with a lopsided grin and a flashing incisor. Warren glared at him.

Margaret slid her feet off the table and sat up straight. 'Didn't we want to make a decision tonight?'

Uriel looked up at me.

The Freaks knew I had inherited *a little* money from my late husband, but they had no clue how much it really was. Even Hattie would pale at the amount. Unfortunately, they believed I'd also inherited the wisdom of how to best invest money.

They didn't know I'd grown up in poverty and found discussions of investment strategies more than boring. To grow one's own wealth not by hard work but by shuffling it from one pot to another was disgusting. So I merely said, 'I'm not an investor,' hoping they would leave me alone.

Jerome threw back his shoulders with a derisive laugh. 'Coward.'

'Ah!' cried Warren, waving a fist at Jerome, 'I am tired of the pestilent voice of your sirens!'

'She told you not to quote Luther,' Jerome grumbled.

Warren made a rude gesture with his hand.

Ignoring the two, I turned to Uriel and said, 'The treasury crisis might or might not cause a recession. I have weighed the risks and decided not to act on it. That doesn't mean that *you* can't shuffle *your* money around. Why do we need to decide on anything together anyway?'

'We don't,' Uriel said. 'It's only that no one wishes to be alone in making a stupid decision.'

'So we make stupid decisions together?'

'Er…yes,' Margaret said, snatched the bottle from Warren, rubbed her sleeve over its mouth, and drank.

'I understand that you are worried. Many people are. But it's rarely the wealthy who suffer most from a financial crisis. So if you ask me where I would put my money, my answer is soup kitchens. Give to the destitute. Which is probably not what you wish to hear.'

'Why wouldn't we?' Hattie asked.

'It's the fastest way to make an investment disappear, that's what,' Jerome said.

I sighed and rubbed my brow. 'If you want a magic solution, ask a fairy.'

The others launched into discussions of gold prices, silver coinage, and the economy. I listened only with half an ear as my mind picked through my observations and conclusions on the railway corpse. Part of me wanted to talk to the post-mortem surgeon and ask him about perimortem injuries to the throat and neck. The victim's eyeballs were bloodshot and her tongue swollen. But I hadn't been able to find blood or tissue under her fingernails. One hand had been bunched around a rose petal. Could she have been throttled but not put up a fight? That would be very unusual, if not... impossible.

Had she been smothered?

I looked up, rested my gaze on Uriel simply for the sake of resting it somewhere and calming my mind. His narrow shoulders and fair hair. His silent demeanour. He listened more often than he spoke. A trait only a few men cultivated. His gaze slid to my face. I smiled and he smiled back.

'He's married,' Jerome said.

'To you?' I shot back.

Jerome snorted. Red splotches bloomed around his throat and ears.

For once, Margret didn't use the moment of fluster to poke fun at Jerome. She, Eliza and Warren had just begun arguing about pirates and smugglers.

Warren, on the other hand, struck me as odd — odder than the rest of the Freak Consortium. He had abandoned his handkerchief (never mind my cold rag recommendation to lessen the swelling of his fractured nose) and was now perched on his chair as if to take flight. His backside scooted this way and that, his boots tapped against the rug. And he avoided eye contact. But why?

I turned to Uriel. 'Do you know Constable Lyons from the Boston Police Department?'

'Never heard of the man. Why?'

'I'd like to know if he and his superiors are any good.'

Uriel waited for me to go on. He had a way with silence that could wheedle information out of people who didn't wish to share it.

But I wanted to share. 'I met Lyons at Fall River Railroad. A woman was killed and I was the first to examine her remains. I found evidence that she'd been dead for hours before she was placed on the tracks. But I got the impression that Lyons didn't put too much faith in my assessment. In fact, I don't even know if he forwarded my reports to the coroner and the post-mortem surgeon. I never heard back from either.' I chewed on the inside of my cheek. 'Damn. I should have insisted on seeing the inspector. And I should pay the coroner a visit.'

'Hmm.' Uriel scratched his neck. 'I'm only an insurance lawyer, but I can ask around. Put my ear to the tracks, so to speak.'

'That would be nice.'

'You saw her?' Margaret said. 'The woman on the railroad?'

I turned to her. She looked solemn. 'Yes. I examined her.'

'I heard she was in bits and pieces.'

'She was.' The room fell silent. 'She must have been placed on the tracks as darkness fell. She'd been dead for hours. The train decapitated her and cut off her foot.'

Hattie clapped her hands over her face. Warren passed her the wine bottle. She poured a generous measure into her glass before choking it down. No one said a word.

The grandfather clock by the wall struck eight. I clapped my hands to my knees and announced that I must take my leave because a good book and a young girl were expecting me. I snatched my jacket and hat, and bade them farewell with a bow and a theatrical, 'May our paths cross again very soon, *mes amis*,' hoping they'd forget the grizzly scene I had just painted.

I LEFT HOME EARLY the following morning to pay the coroner a visit before my lectures at the Medical School were to begin. He had his offices on Boston Street in one of the many brownstone row houses. A clerk admitted me, and led me through a hallway to a waiting room. Approaching the hearth, I looked in vain for anything that might catch the water running off my umbrella and the muck dribbling from my gaiters. The fire crackled and popped noisily, and I almost missed the clearing of a throat behind me.

I turned.

The man's clothes were tailored and tight-fitting, but his face was not. His mouth and the skin surrounding it seemed two sizes too large and not attached to his mandible at all. The skin around his eyes sagged, as did his large nose. There was a friendly twinkle in his eyes when he held out his hand. 'Dr Arlington?'

We shook hands briefly. He had a surprisingly firm grasp. 'Yes. Coroner Jacob Rubenstein?'

He bobbed his head.

'Have you received my report?' I asked.

'Only this morning. Is there a problem with it?'

'No, I was just… This morning? Why did the police keep my report for two days?'

'Ah, it's…normal procedure, so to speak. The police and I have our little differences. I'm certain they wanted to make sure all was in order before sending it to me.' His moustache twitched in wry amusement.

'I see. Were you able to identify the victim?'

'The case has been given to Inspector McCurley. She was murdered, you see. And it was he who identified her. A washerwoman by the name of Henrietta Hyde. Worked for several households between Steward and Crescent Street, you see.'

I tried not to say "I see," so I merely nodded. 'May I take a look at the report of the post-mortem surgeon?'

He cocked his head and pushed his spectacles farther up his nose.

'Professional curiosity,' I explained with a smile.

He puffed up his cheeks and bade me follow him.

WHEN I FINISHED MY LECTURE, and all the students were rising to leave the hall, the doors were pushed open. The man who entered was rather short — which is to say, an inch or so taller than I — with a jagged scar that ran from his cheek down his throat. My gaze got stuck there, and I wondered how much blood he had lost and who'd saved his life.

'Mrs Arlington?' he said and took off his hat.

'Dr Arlington.'

'Of course. May I ask you a few questions about the rail-road incident?'

He hadn't lowered his voice. The few students who hadn't yet exited the lecture hall stopped to look at me with a mix of shock and curiosity.

'Off you go,' I said to them and stuffed my folder back into my bag. Then I turned to my guest. 'And you are?'

'Inspector McCurley, Bureau of Criminal Investigation. Shall we sit?' He had the audacity to indicate my desk.

I ignored him.

'Mrs Arlington?'

'Dr Arlington. You wished to ask questions. I'm waiting for you to begin.'

He pulled a small notebook from his jacket and snapped it open. 'Shortly after half past eight on the evening of the fifteenth of May, the remains of Mrs Henrietta Hyde were found on the Fall River Railroad near Savin Hill Avenue. You were one of the first witnesses, and the first to examine the body. What brought you there and when did you arrive?'

'Have you not read my report?'

'I have.' He tapped pencil against notebook.

Slowly, I sucked in air. 'As I've written *in my report*, I was on my way home. If you consult a map, you'll see that the crime scene is directly between this lecture hall and my home on Savin Hill Avenue. I arrived only a few minutes after it had happened.'

'After what happened?'

'The dismemberment of Mrs Hyde's corpse by the train. What else would I refer to?'

'You seem certain about her having been dead for hours when she was hit by the train.'

'I am absolutely certain. Inspector, do you wish me to repeat every statement I made in my report?'

Without looking up from his notes, he said, 'Yes. That's how I take witness statements. You used the term "crime scene." What makes you think a crime was committed?'

I opened my mouth and blinked. 'Given the evidence, it is the only logical explanation.'

'Interesting. PC Lyons' first thought was that of an unfortunate accident. I wonder why you so readily suggest murder.'

'I said crime, not murder. Murder is one of several possibilities. Concealment of death is another. Are there any other questions you might have that can easily be answered by referring to my report?'

'Did you notice anything unusual that night?' he asked.

'You must be jesting.'

'Aside from the dismembered body of Henrietta Hyde.'

'All of my observations are in my report. It's a treasure trove of useful information. I suggest you read it. It's late and I must leave now. If you feel the need for an in-depth repetition of what I've written *in my report*, you will have to arrest me. Good evening, Inspector.' I yanked my bag from the desk and made for the door.

'An excellent idea, Mrs Arlington,' he said by way of farewell.

I thought of all the places one could kick a man to cause a hell of a lot of pain without leaving so much as a faint bruise.

4

*C*andlelight danced across the flowery wallpaper. With a small sigh, Klara's face relaxed. I detached her lips from my breast, and fastened the strings of my nightgown. The tip of her tongue stuck out of her mouth and a smudge of milk glistened on her cheek.

A shiver ran through me, and I tucked the blanket closer around us. Somehow, I doubted the police had caught the man who'd placed Henrietta Hyde's body on the railway. The tramp might have done it, but he seemed too convenient a catch. Wouldn't the murderer — if he'd indeed been among the bystanders — have disappeared as soon as police arrived at the scene?

My breath stopped. Might I have seen him? Had he seen me?

I squeezed my eyes shut, trying to remember faces. But I could not have described the stoker or driver in detail, although I'd spoken to both men. My mind had been on the victim, and I doubted I could pick out a killer from his appearance. Maybe if I saw him again I could…do what? Ask politely if he'd recently committed a heinous crime?

I snorted. Klara twitched in her sleep.

According to the post-mortem surgeon's report, Henrietta Hyde had been strangled, and then her body had lain curled on its side for five to six hours. To cover the deep bruises to her throat, she'd been placed on the tracks, her neck arranged on one of the rails so that the train would cut through the evidence and destroy it.

The evidence, however, had still been there. The internal bleeding stretched from lower mandible to collar bones. It was excessive. Whoever killed her must have done so in a passion.

The post-mortem surgeon hadn't found skin or blood under her fingernails either. I couldn't fathom why she hadn't fought back. If a stranger walked up to me and put his hands around my throat, I would fight with teeth and nails. Had Henrietta been drugged? Had she known her killer? Why had the papers said nothing about her husband? That was indeed odd. Perhaps there was no husband.

I gazed at Klara. Her eyes danced behind her lids. I wondered what she was dreaming. Was she sitting in the garden, watching Zachary? She looked so peaceful that my heart was about to burst.

She mumbled something that sounded like "Dzadza."

When addressing Zach, she sometimes used one "dza," and sometimes a string of two or three. As if wrapping her small tongue around his name was daunting.

I thought of the first time I'd placed my baby in Margery's arms, and the feeling of being torn in two when I left the house to perform an emergency surgery on a neighbour. I'd wept when I came back home and found tiny Klara curled up on Zachary's chest, her mouth closed around his pinky, her face salty with tears. She'd fallen asleep only minutes earlier, and cried again when he returned her to me. She'd only been consoled by my milk and my embrace.

It had surprised me that Zach was the one Klara attached herself to, rather than Margery. But the more I came to know them, the clearer it became why she'd chosen him. Margery kept an arm's length from everyone but Zach. She was kind but rarely warm. I knew she tried with Klara, but it seemed something was holding Margery back. A mistrust or wariness she carried within her. It blew away the instant Zach entered her vision.

Sometimes I wondered about Margery's and Zachary's past, where they'd grown up, how they'd met and fallen in love, and what made her so cautious and him so calm and protective of her.

Klara whined in her sleep. I brushed my lips against her forehead, held her closer to me, and softly sang her bad dream away. She had yet to develop the ability to fall asleep by herself, and she would wake as soon as she sensed she was alone in the bedroom. It was security she sought, and I wished I were able to give it to her. But we weren't safe. Not as long as Moran was alive.

A pang of guilt hit me. Early in my pregnancy, I'd tried to abort her. Twice. Now I lived in constant fear of her abduction and my violent death. And often, I wasn't even there with her. Normal women stayed at home to take care of their children, but I taught classes and took care of strangers. Was I a poor excuse for a mother? Klara didn't speak, didn't even like playing with children her age. Had I caused this?

I inhaled the sweet scent of her hair and thought of my students who abandoned their studies as soon as they found a man. Such a waste of potential!

And there I had it. Wouldn't I be wasting my own potential if all I did was stay at home and hold my daughter's hand while she grew into a young woman? Wouldn't it be a greater loss to watch Klara lead the life society expected of her and not dare pursue her own happiness — because I had lived that very example?

I paused. Would I be able to accept it, if she chose to lead a normal life? To marry, bear children, and not strive for a higher goal?

Yes. Yes, I could, as long as she knew that she had a choice, and the strength to be whatever she wished to be.

And what path would I take? Would I wait two weeks for the toxicologist's report when there was a killer at large? He'd been in the neighbourhood. He might even live close by. Too close to home to do nothing. But launching my own criminal investigation was something I wouldn't do lightly. The last time I hunted a murderer, I'd paid a very high price.

And I had barely survived.

THE FOLLOWING Monday I received a summons from the Boston Police Department to give a witness statement regarding the killing of Henrietta Hyde. I arrived at the Pemberton Square Headquarters on time and was made to wait forty minutes in front of Inspector McCurley's shut door, listening to the high-pitched voice of the boy McCurley was interrogating.

'Me and my chums was near the boat houses, having a good time. Fired off a firecracker or two, and frightened off that chap with the funny hat. Petey, that is.'

Low mumbling interrupted the boy — probably McCurley, asking a question, because the boy said, 'Half past three. He looked frightened enough. No, he just sat there, poking at something between the rocks. The lady? Didn't see no lady.'

There was a pause, then the boy continued, 'My mother keeps a store on Broadway. She's a dressmaker, and also sells the materials for them. My brother and I sell newspapers. He owns a route in the city and I own one in South Boston. But we also sell 'em at the store.'

Another pause.

"Course I know all the faces and names of my customers! No, I never met Mrs Hyde. Read about her, I did. But Mrs Kennison that buys materials at the shop washes for— My papers? I get them at the New England News Company. 'Course, I sweep the store and fix up the windows too and— The chap with the funny hat? Seen him twice before. Spent a night in the shop's basement. Mum didn't want him out in the rain.'

And so it went on. McCurley made the boy jump from one topic to another and made him repeat himself several times. It was annoying but effective, and I told him so when I was finally called into his office.

'So you are an expert in interrogation now,' he drawled.

'Sharp observation and interrogation skills are crucial in my profession. Most patients don't wish to share all the symptoms they experience and even more lie about the severity of them. And some patients are unconscious, so I'm left to interrogate their bodies.' I sat in the offered chair, placed my briefcase on my lap, and pulled out a folder. 'And sometimes I interrogate their remains. Would you like me to walk you through my report?'

He stopped halfway to his chair, then made for the door. 'Brewer! Fetch Boyle for me.' He sat down and steepled his fingers.

When I opened my mouth to speak, he held up his hand, said, 'We wait for Sergeant Boyle.'

It didn't take long. Boyle arrived, scrambled to rip off his hat and introduce himself. As he quietly took a seat, I wondered what role he was to play, for neither did he whip out notebook and pencil, nor did he seem to occupy himself with anything but blinking apologetically.

Inspector McCurley fingered his short moustache. He was freshly barbered — the scar on the side of his face more severe now. Even his eyebrows had been lightly trimmed. 'Now, Mrs Arlington—'

'Dr Arlington.'

'*Doctor* Arlington, on the evening of the fifteenth of May, you examined the body of Mrs Henrietta Hyde. You state in your report that you were on your way home when you found a train blocking the road, and that — according to the time the stoker gave you — you arrived mere minutes after the accident. Is that correct?'

'Yes.'

'You have also stated that Mrs Hyde's body temperature indicated that she had been dead since approximately noon of that day.' He waited, so I gave him a nod.

'Would you care to explain this to me?' he asked.

'It is well known that after death, the temperature of a body decreases by about one and a half degrees Celsius per hour. Her head had been severed and lay several yards from where I found her body. I measured temperatures in the brain and the vagina, and they matched, which confirms the time of death and that the train decapitated the body. Both body parts were at eighty-two degrees Fahrenheit, which tells me that she must have died around noon. I am surprised these facts aren't known to you.'

'They are known to me. What I wish to know is how *you* come to the same conclusion as the post-mortem surgeon.'

I leaned back and crossed my arms over my chest. 'I am a physician and have been performing post-mortems for years.'

'Have you now.'

I was about to open my mouth and tell him that I'd been frequently summoned by Scotland Yard to examine corpses that seemed to have succumbed to a highly contagious disease under suspicious circumstances. Instead, I smiled and lied, 'I was a student of Dr Deffenheim, who was, in turn, a student and good friend of Dr Alexandre Lacassagne. Perhaps you've heard of them? Lacassagne founded the School of Forensic Medicine in Lyon. Unfortunately, I don't speak French and never had the chance to learn from Lacassagne himself.'

'So you are telling me now that you are an expert in forensics?' His voice was dripping with mockery. From the corner of my vision, I saw Boyle shifting in his chair.

'You asked me how I know about post-mortem body temperature, and I have given you the answer.' I produced a small shrug, and — for good measure — a smile.

'I see.' He tapped his fingertips against his desk.

'I would like to speak to the man you arrested.'

He looked up. 'Excuse me?'

'I would like to ask him if he saw anything…interesting.'

'We are not in the habit of allowing the public to entertain themselves with our prisoners. Excepting, of course, should they *insist* on seeing a holding cell from the inside.' There was a twitch at the corner of his mouth.

'Have you spoken to Mrs Hyde's husband?'

He cleared his throat — a neat little noise — and ignored my question entirely. 'Now, Dr Arlington, did you notice anything particular that night? A familiar face among the bystanders? A man behaving strangely?'

'I did not.'

He leaned back and regarded me levelly. 'If you are unwilling to cooperate, you will spend a night in one of our holding cells. And I will make sure yours is far away from our suspect you so wish to talk to.'

'What makes you think I am not cooperating?'

'Your answer came too quickly. A hasty lie, I suppose.'

I snorted. 'I did not observe anything that is not included in my report. I can't help but doubt you caught the right man.

I, too, read the post-mortem surgeon's report. Mrs Hyde was strangled. It appears to have happened in passion, yet she didn't fight back. I see a strong possibility of her having known her murderer. Hence my question as to her husband. The murderer might still be at large, and he's been in my neighbourhood. I have a daughter, and I will protect her at all costs. If you won't find that man, I will.' My voice had grown hard, and only when the last word fell from my lips, did I realise that this was precisely what I must do. I had wasted days pondering the evidence and making half-hearted enquiries about flower growers, and asking a few of my patients if they have known Mrs Hyde. And I hadn't learnt anything of value.

'I see,' McCurley said. He stood and left the room.

I turned to Sergeant Boyle. 'May I leave now?'

'I believe he…just forgot something?'

'Yes. He forgot to dismiss me.' I rose to my feet.

Sergeant Boyle eyed my knickerbockers with interest. 'You came on your bicycle in this weather?'

'It was comparatively dry when I left home. It only started to rain when I arrived here.' A glance out a dusty window told me I would be soaked before I reached the medical school.

'The Inspector has not given you permission to leave,' Boyle said somewhat timidly.

'I have lectures to give, Sergeant.' I slung my briefcase over my shoulder.

'No! Really, you mustn't! He'll be angry and you don't want that. You really don't. And you should tell him what you know. Inspector McCurley can get quite…uncomfortable. And educated ladies like you might regret—'

'Ah, now I know why he called you in. I was supposed to like you very much because you are so much the gentleman — which he obviously is not — that I would tell you all I know. You are to make him look tougher than he professes to be. How very…cute of him.'

That was the moment McCurley chose to step back into the room. 'Thank you for your assistance, Dr Arlington. You are no longer needed.' He said that without looking at me. He simply walked in carrying a stack of papers and dropped them noisily on his desk.

I left with a curt, 'Good day to you too, Inspector. Sergeant.'

On my way out, I wrote on a corner of my lecture notes:
Dressmaker shop at Broadway. Newsboy!
Flower grower with hothouse and yellow roses.
Mrs Hyde's husband, neighbours, friends.

AS I RETURNED HOME EARLY that evening, Margery handed me a package. I opened it and found a bottle of wine. A note read:

VINTAGE BORDEAUX WITHOUT SPITTLE.

Thank you for reattaching my nose. It looks almost like new, although not much prettier.

Warren.

I SMILED and made for the garden, where a deep voice and peals of laughter told of a man trying to convince a small child of the disadvantages of jumping into puddles.

5

*B*ells chimed as I pushed open the door to the dressmaker's shop on Broadway. Bolts of cloth were stacked along a wall and suspended from the ceiling. Cones of yarn in all colours, and jars of buttons, hooks, eyelets, and other unidentifiable paraphernalia populated shelves. A woman sat behind a counter, bent over what looked like a simple, homespun dress for a doll. A lamp illuminated her workspace. As the door fell into its frame, she set her work aside, brushed strands of greying hair back behind her ears, and looked up at me.

I asked her if she knew Mrs Henrietta Hyde, and she said, no, she'd only read about her in the papers. The police had already asked her that, and her boy had been summoned to give a witness statement. Was I with the police or the coroner?

'No, I am with neither. Coroner Rubenstein seems to be a fine man, but Inspector McCurley…' I lifted one shoulder. 'I'm the physician who examined Mrs Hyde's remains, and I can't help wondering about the man the police arrested.'

'A lady doctor?' She huffed. 'Fancy that. Petey wouldn't

hurt a fly. I told the police he didn't do it, but nobody listened. The inspector arrested him anyway. Would you be wanting to buy something?'

'I might need a pair or two of woollen socks. How do you know Petey?'

'Sorry, ma'am, but I don't sell no socks. Petey, he sleeps in our basement sometimes. Nothing inappropriate, mind. Just spends cold and rainy nights down there, when he's around. Cleans up and leaves in the morning to go his own way.'

'How do you know his name, if he doesn't speak?' I asked.

'You've read that in the papers, didn't you? He does speak…slow. Mumbles mostly. But the police don't listen.'

'I know.' I gazed up at the shelves. 'I'm looking for yellow roses. Fresh ones. You wouldn't know someone in the area, would you? Oh! Such beautiful ribbons! May I look at the red ones? And the greens over there?'

She stood and shuffled over to the shelf I'd indicated. 'Don't know any flower seller who has roses this time of the year.' She picked up two spools and placed them on the counter. I unfurled a few inches of embroidered silk. She stared at my right hand, the missing index finger.

'Petey could not of killed her,' she said in a half whisper. 'Everyone knows she's been strangled and dragged about, but Petey can barely hold a bowl of broth without spilling it. He can walk all right, but his fingers and knuckles are…all swollen and red.'

'Your boy saw him that evening, poking at something in the rocks by the shore. Seems Petey can use his hands well enough.'

She shrugged. 'I know what I know. Georgie knows what he knows. Will you buy the ribbons now, or what?'

'Yes, a foot of each, please. And I need to talk to your son. I understand he owns a route here?'

She cut off a length of the red ribbon, rolled it up, and did the same with the green. 'Why would you be wantin' to talk to Georgie?'

'He told the police that Petey was by the boathouses only hours after Mrs Hyde's death. I'd like to ask him what he saw.'

She frowned, chewing on the inside of her cheek. Then she jerked her head to the side. 'He'll be over at Dorchester Heights near the Blind Asylum by now.'

I thanked her, paid for the ribbons, and left.

AFTER DODGING horse carriages and coster's carts, questioning two newsboys who weren't Georgie, and trying hard not to get my bicycle wheels caught in tram tracks, I found Georgie at the corner of Eighth and Mercer leaning against a doorway to hide from the drizzle, hands in his pockets and a cigarette in his mouth. A stack of newspapers was clamped under his arm, rather awkwardly, while he tried to maintain an air of nonchalance. I leaned my bicycle against a fence and sidled up to him.

'Nice weather,' I said, shaking the rain from my hat.

He looked me up and down with what might have been a scowl. Then his eyes grew large. 'You were at the police station!'

'Inspector McCurley is rather charming, isn't he?'

'Don't know 'bout that,' Georgie mumbled, sucked at the last half inch of his smoke, then threw the stump into the gutter.

'You saw Petey, I heard.'

'Sorry, ma'am, but I've work to do.' He pulled the papers from his armpit and made to leave the protection of the doorway.

I pulled a coin from my purse. 'The Lady has a more handsome profile than Queen Victoria, I must confess. Wouldn't you agree?'

Georgie took a measured step back and stared at the nickel on my gloved palm. 'Maybe,' he said, and after a moment of consideration, 'Does she have a sister?'

'Maybe. What did Petey do on the day Mrs Hyde was killed?'

He shifted from one leg to the other, his face drifting from the coin in my hand to a coster's cart rattling past. Once the clatter of wheels had died away, he said, 'Don't know what he done. Saw him by the boathouses and gave him a good scare. Not that he needed it.'

'You threw fireworks at him?'

'Only one.' He looked up, greatly alarmed. 'Don't tell my mum!'

'I don't see a reason why I should. Where was that? Where was Petey, and where were you when you saw him?'

'The boat houses near the Glass Works.'

'Show me where and Miss Liberty will get a sister.'

IT WASN'T FAR, just two blocks down to the murky waters of Dorchester Bay. A short line of huts squatted at the shore, connected to a battered landing. Careful not to slip on the slimy wood, I followed Georgie to the end of the landing. He pointed to a group of barnacled rocks ten yards from where we stood. Water lazily lapped at cracked stone.

'That's where Petey was. And we were right here.'

'What happened when you threw the firecracker at him?'

'Jumped off the rocks and legged it. Screeched like a banshee.' Georgie grinned.

'The sun was out that day. Do you think that's why he sat over there? To enjoy the weather?' Had the man not minded sitting among gull droppings and washed-up rubbish?

The boy shrugged. 'Can never tell with people like him.'

'What do you mean?'

He made a gesture that indicated Petey's mind wasn't all that it should have been.

'He poked at something with a stick, you told the Inspector.'

Another shrug. Perhaps he was finding my funds too limited for detailed responses.

He toed at a slug and pushed it into the water. 'The mud, maybe? Clams? How would I know?'

'You are a newsboy. You see everything, hear everything, and make up your mind about it. I think you are a sharp one, Georgie.'

He blushed a little. 'Well.' He coughed, pushed his fists into his pockets and jutted his chin out.

I handed him the two nickels, and his tongue loosened. 'He might of done it, or might not have. One can never be sure with a man like him.' Again, the twirling of his finger against the side of his head. 'If he was in a passion, why not? He's done queer things before, that's for sure. Like brandishing a plank at me and my chums, shouting gibberish, and then throwing a rotten fish. I'm sure he could of murdered one of us if he put his mind to it. And kept at it long enough. I don't like him sleeping in our shop basement. Always have to clean up after him before mum sees his mess. Doesn't even know how to use a privy.' Georgie spat in the water. The glob of saliva bobbed away merrily until a gull snatched at it.

'You told the Inspector that Petey spent one night at the shop.'

'Said it only because I didn't want to lie outright, and didn't know if mum wanted it known. The neighbours might talk.'

'How tall is he?'

'What, Petey?' The boy squinted at the top of my head and said. 'Maybe a hand or two taller than you, but thin like a bean pole. Not an ounce of fat on his bones.'

'If the police release him, do you think he could help my gardener fix the roof of my annexe?'

Georgie snorted. 'Your gardener better find somebody else. Petey couldn't lift a tile. His hands are strange, knuckles all knobby-like.'

'I thought he brandished a plank and threw a rotten fish at you?'

Georgie looked down at his worn boots. 'Might of been a stick.' He cleared his throat, snorted to collect saliva, then spat again.

'How big was the stick?'

'Like…a twig.'

'I see. Do you happen to know a flower grower in the area? One who would sell me yellow roses by Saturday?'

Georgie's jaw unhinged and he seemed to consider my mental state. Then he pulled himself together, and said, 'No, ma'am, I don't know of anyone. But for another nickel, I'll find one for you.'

And thus, a bargain was struck, and I acquired my first informant.

A FEW DAYS LATER, without any new developments in the case, Klara and I met Hattie at the Boston Music Hall. The others might join us later, Hattie said, as we pushed into the entrance hall. The whole Freak Consortium had season tickets for the public rehearsals, and not a month went by without at least one Friday afternoon spent there, one that extended into the late evening at Warren's house.

The Freaks considered themselves socialists, except for Jerome (who was Uriel's appendage) and me (I seemed to be Hattie's). But our meetings never resulted in any actions taken — to overthrow or organise whatever needed to be overthrown or organised that particular day. They may have been socialists, but they certainly weren't activists. I loved them dearly, and I wouldn't have known what to do if they had taken to the streets and bashed in windows.

Without exception, the Freaks loved art. And so we stood, Hattie and I, shoulder to shoulder in that shabby hall that was bare of all ornaments, letting the music soak our every fibre. Even Klara stopped wriggling in my arms, and leaned her head against my neck, humming with the orchestra.

At some point, Uriel squeezed through the crowd, bent down to kiss Klara's head, and spoke in my ear, 'It's only Warren and me today.'

'Where is he?' I asked.

Uriel turned and stood on tiptoe to point out Warren, who was leaning against a far wall, with a dark expression half hidden by the great number of fashionable hats worn by half the audience who populated the floor.

'What's with him?' I asked.

Uriel leaned closer, batting his eyes at Klara and grinning mischievously. She bashed her palm against his nose and giggled. Uriel snatched her hand, produced a soft growl and pretended to bite off her fingers. Her squeak was cut short by my own hand over her mouth. 'Ssst, little one. Let us listen to the music and ignore the evil uncle.'

Uriel snorted, then whispered, 'Don't worry about Warren. He's always like that.'

'Grumpy?'

'He just wants to be left alone most of the time.'

'You mean the same man who lets us crowd his house?'

'Well, it's—' Uriel began.

'That's nothing compared to the comings and goings at home. Besides… Father has got to him,' Hattie interrupted.

'Oh? So, he'll soon be off again?' Uriel asked.

With a sharp shushing, a woman wielded her umbrella at Uriel, staring him down.

'He's to get married. Father's put his foot down.'

The orchestra began to play a new piece, and our conversation was drowned out by drums and trombones.

THE FOUR OF us took Hattie's carriage to Warren's lodgings. Klara bounced on my lap, squeaking with delight. Warren was still sporting two black eyes that were beginning to fade to a greenish yellow. Disinterested in our conversation, he stared out the window, the light of passing street lamps brushing his face.

'I enquired about Constable Lyons,' Uriel said to me. 'Didn't learn much, though. Only that the Inspector is supposedly a career man, who drives himself and everyone under him pretty hard. He's worked himself all the way up from the gutters.'

'The gutters?'

'He grew up in an Irish gang. That's the rumour. I'm not sure if it's true.'

'If it is, he'll have much better access to informants than any other inspector. Or…might he be corrupt, do you think?'

Uriel lifted his shoulders. 'I don't know. But I can imagine that a man like McCurley has all eyes on him. If he tried something shady, it'd be hard for him to hide it.'

We arrived at Beacon Hill, and transferred our hats and umbrellas to the butler who handed them to one of the maids. With military precision, he instructed the two young women how everything was to be properly brushed off and hung.

'Will you be wanting your supper in the dining room, Sir?'

'Yes, Owens, thank you.'

'Very good, Sir.' The butler lowered his chin a fraction and left.

'You don't like him?' Warren asked me, as he held the door.

'Who do you mean?'

'Owens.'

I must have looked puzzled, because he added, 'My butler.'

'No, I'm just…not very comfortable being waited on.'

'You don't have servants?'

'I have…employees.'

'Where is the difference?'

'No one wants to be a servant. Servants are invisible and have no rights. They can be dismissed without good reason, and without a reference. Does your need for social justice not extend to servants, Warren?'

'That doesn't answer my question. What, in your opinion, is the difference between a servant and an employee?' Warren came to a halt between door and dinner table, creating an obstacle for the others, who had to carefully manoeuvre around us. Klara impatiently tugged at my hand.

'None, perhaps. I should have been more specific: I employ family.'

He frowned, said, 'Hum,' and walked away to load a plate with beans and thin slices of cold beef.

We all sat and ate. Klara stuffed herself with meat, and nothing else, until her face glistened with gravy and stretched with yawns. Words didn't flow easily that night, not until the wine was uncorked and the first sips were taken.

Uriel refilled our glasses, clinked his against mine, and said, 'Are you getting any closer to catching the murderer?'

Hattie choked on her beans. Warren clapped her between the shoulder blades.

'Many murderers are never caught. I would guess about

half will never be apprehended, perhaps a bit less? I'm not a detective.' I shrugged, hoping the topic was closed.

But Uriel only scooted to the edge of his seat, and said, 'You must know *something*. A piece of evidence, a trail you are following. Anything? Come now, at least distract Warren from his…misery. I'm sorry, my friend,' he added with a glance at Warren.

Warren wiped his mouth with a napkin and turned to me with an expectant look.

'Oh, well. In that case, let me see… There's a suspect, but I'm guessing the evidence that links him to the case is weak. He was arrested at the scene and might have been merely a bystander. But then I'm not privy to the Inspector's information. There were no witnesses to the crime, as far as I know, but there's a body that speaks volumes. She was with child, was throttled, and didn't fight back. A toxicologist is analysing samples of blood and organs to see if she'd been drugged. It's possible she knew her killer and couldn't believe that he or she meant to murder her. I'm greatly surprised that neither the papers nor the police have mentioned Mrs Hyde's husband. I'll have to find his address and speak to him. And I'm so far unsuccessful in trying to find a flower grower who sells yellow roses in May. It's of interest because she had the fresh petal of a yellow rose in her hand when she died. But the flower could have been imported, so…that piece of evidence might be altogether useless. Finally, none of my patients, neighbours or acquaintances had knowledge of a man who grows them in Boston, which means, it must have come from farther away. Probably south of here.'

Klara slipped from my lap and walked up to one of the bookshelves. Hastily, I followed and wiped her greasy hands before she could touch anything.

'You should have asked the aristocracy,' Warren said with

a sideways glance at Klara, who had begun to draw out one book after another, and place them on the floor.

'Mr Stone is not a commercial grower,' Hattie said.

'He tells everyone his roses are only a hobby. But don't believe a word of it, sister. Not only is he highly particular about who he sells to, but his prices are steep. To put it mildly.'

'Does he grow yellow roses?' I asked.

'You can get every colour from him, as far as I know.' Warren shrugged and picked up a pad of paper and some small pieces of charcoal from a box on the bookshelf that Klara was raiding.

'And how do you know? If I may ask?'

'The benefit of having a mother who repeatedly tries to force a bachelor's ball on me,' he said and began scratching charcoal across paper.

'Bloody dammit, but I'm a bucket! I should have asked Georgie.' I slapped my forehead and Klara squeaked in delight.

'Who's Georgie?' Uriel asked.

'A newsboy. He probably knows where the victim lived.'

'And the…bucket? Dare I even ask?'

'A bucket is… Well, it means *empty vessel*.' I tapped my temple.

Uriel snorted. 'You are doing pretty well for a fledgling detective, Liz.'

I opened my mouth to point out that this wasn't my first time solving a crime, but then shut it and nodded.

Uriel turned to Warren and tapped his knuckles on the table. 'Get it out of your system, brother.'

Warren looked up. 'And what precisely am I supposed to get out?'

'You could rail at us now, and…you know, *feel* better.'

Warren sighed. 'I appreciate your offer, but screaming won't solve my problem.'

'So your father gets what he wants. Again.'

Warren froze. A muscle feathered in his jaw. 'It appears so.' He shuffled his papers into a pile and left the room. A few moments later, piano music wafted from a room down the corridor.

Uriel looked at Hattie. 'I think he's going to leave in a day or two. Don't you?'

She dropped her gaze. 'Not this time.'

'Where's Klara?' I asked. 'She was sitting right here only a minute ago.'

'She followed Warren. She's fine.' Uriel held the wine bottle over my glass. Upon my nod, he refilled it. 'Do you need me to do some more detecting for you?'

'Have you done any detecting yet?' I asked with a grin. 'Can you find out who Petey's attorney is? If he even has one yet. Petey is the tramp the police arrested.'

'Was the bill of indictment accepted?'

'I…don't know.'

'Hum… I'll try to find someone who's close to this and might be willing to share information with you. But I can't make promises.'

None of us touched on Warren's looming wedding for the remainder of the evening. When the clock chimed eight, I rose and followed the music to see if I needed to relieve him of Klara's presence. The door to the room was half open. He sat hunched at a piano, long fingers trailing across the keys. By his feet, Klara lay on a pile of pillows. She didn't move.

'Hello, Klara,' I said softly.

Warren threw me an irritated glance.

I walked up to my daughter and found that she was fast asleep, a fist pressed to her mouth, a woollen blanket tangled around her legs.

Dumbfounded, I sat back on my haunches. 'She's sleeping.'

Warren kept playing.

Was that Chopin? I looked up and asked him.

He shook his head.

I noticed that he played without music sheets. 'It's beautiful.'

'Don't speak now,' he murmured. And after a moment, 'Please.' Eyes shut, head tilted, he stroked the keys with utter focus.

And that was when I understood. 'You composed this.' Still, he wouldn't reply or react in any way. 'It is perfect.'

He slowed his play. 'Have you ever felt…utterly and completely cornered?

Cold washed over me. 'Yes.'

There was a flicker in his eyes. It quickly vanished. 'And what did you do, if I may ask? Did you run? Did you allow yourself to be trapped?'

'I do not wish to talk about it.'

He dipped his head, as though in agreement, but then he said, 'So you are trapped.'

I saw it for what it was — a challenge. And it made anger roil up my throat. 'I allowed myself to be trapped for one reason only.'

He kept his gaze on me as he changed the tune to something slower, sadder.

'I waited for the right moment,' I continued. 'And then I made sure I would never find myself in that situation again.'

A faint smile played around his lips. 'Something makes me doubt yours would be the right tactic to solve my little problem.'

'Why not.' It slipped out of my mouth, although I wasn't interested at all. In fact, I wanted him to stop talking. I didn't want him to share information, only to ask me to share mine.

'I have caused enough damage.'

'Says who?'

'My parents.'

Ah. So that's what this was about. 'Do you love her? Does she love you?'

He twitched a shoulder. 'I have seen her once. We exchanged pleasantries.'

I let him play another piece, and yet another, before I answered, 'So you wish to limit the damage you might be causing. But a loveless marriage could be…toxic.'

'I doubt others see it that way.'

'Do *you* not see it that way? Or your bride? What about your children?'

Abruptly, he stopped. The silence startled Klara and she woke with a soft cry. I picked her up and she nestled her face against the crook of my neck.

He glanced at her, and then at me. Narrowed his eyes. 'Are you happy?'

Startled by his directness, I blurted, 'I need to bring my daughter home.' With a huff, I pushed myself up from the floor, Klara in my arms, her fingers curled tightly around a lock of my hair.

Warren accompanied us back to the sitting room. When I made to sort the books back onto the shelves, he stopped me with a wave of his hand. 'Don't worry about it. I'll do it later.'

I nodded my thanks and asked Hattie for Mr Stone's address. She took Klara while I picked up a pen and one of the papers Warren had used earlier.

My breath froze in my lungs. There were Uriel's and Klara's portraits on one page, and on the other, my own. The likeness was stunning. Perfect. I felt the blood drain from my face. I couldn't slip the drawing into my pocket without the others noticing. And I shouldn't, because Warren could draw me as often as he liked. I had to put a stop to it at once.

Turning to him, I ripped Klara's and my portrait to tiny bits.

Warren gaped. 'You destroyed them!'

'I find it utterly unsuitable of a man to keep my likeness and that of my daughter in his breast pocket,' I said coldly.

'You are…mad.' He bobbed his head once, then shook it and looked at Hattie. 'And this …this…harpy is your friend?'

Uriel choked down a nervous laugh. Briefly, I wondered if he were more shocked by my behaviour, or by Warren's.

Hattie stood, jammed a fist in her hip, pointed the other hand at Warren, and spat, 'Don't be a dolt, Warren! It is inappropriate to draw or photograph a lady without her consent!'

Warren blinked, genuinely confused. 'It is?' He looked first at me, then at the shreds of paper.

Klara chose the moment to start whining.

'It's time for bed,' I said and picked her up. My farewell was brief, making Hattie's forehead crinkle with concern.

Sometimes, I wished I could tell them the truth: No one, not even a friend, could be allowed to have a picture of me. I was too afraid of it reaching Moran and his cronies, no matter how unlikely that was.

THE SECOND VICTIM

6

*O*ne sunny morning, Georgie showed up on my doorstep and proudly handed me a small piece of paper. 'The bloke's address. Er…Mr Stone's address, I mean.'

I didn't tell him that I knew it already. Instead, I asked if he knew where Henrietta Hyde had lived. He looked at me as if I were the only person unaware of Mrs Hyde's every secret.

'Number 3 Newman Street,' he said, pocketing his nickel. 'Be needin' anything else?'

'Not today.' I slipped the note into my pocket and watched Georgie dash off. He nearly ran over Mr Cratchitt, who was delivering the morning mail.

'Good day, Dr Arlington!'

'Good day, Mr Cratchitt. How is your wife?'

'Round like a dumpling.' He flashed a toothy grin. 'I have a letter for you.'

'She has only two weeks left. I'd better keep my shoes on when I go to bed.'

He shook his head and adjusted the shoulder strap of his bag. 'I bet she's too fast for you. Last time it only took ten minutes. *I* didn't even manage to leave the bedroom.'

'I could give you a lesson or two in midwifery.'

He threw up his hands. 'Hell, no! She's a beast when the pains are on her. I'm sure she'd kill me outright if I tried to help.' As he threw back his head and laughed, the sun bounced off his spectacles.

'Well, in that case, I send her my best wishes.'

He winked, walked back to his bicycle, and began pushing it down the road. A small bell fastened to the handlebar clinked softly as he went.

I leaned back against the doorframe and thought of Petey. *Number 3 Newman Street. Damn.* The tramp had been seen at the railway ogling Mrs Hyde's corpse, and only hours earlier, he'd sat on a rock a mere hundred yards from her home. Perhaps it was time to admit that I was wrong, and Inspector McCurley's instincts weren't all that bad.

I shut my eyes and listened to our blackbird singing its heart out of its chest. Klara had declared the birds *ours* after she discovered a nest with two blue eggs in the ivy by the annexe.

The air was balmy, with scents of—

Shocked, I realised that summer was nearly there, and by the end of it, Klara would turn three.

I ground my teeth and opened the letter.

Dear Liz,

I learned a few things about your Inspector McCurley, and I don't like the half of it.

McCurley is the youngest inspector on the detective squad (he's only 30), and among shady individuals and newspapermen he's called Quinn "the Pit Bull" McCurley. Rumour has it that he got the nickname when he broke away from his gang. That ended in a bloody battle, in which he bit the gang leader (I laughed so hard at this), and earned himself a knife wound to the face. But I doubt there is more than a speck of truth in all this nonsense.

When McCurley was working as a patrolman, he solved the murder of Congressman Ned Leroy, and was immediately promoted to detective. Need I tell you that this is unheard of?! Only three years later, he caught the leader of the Great Silk Robbery Gang (they stole $10,000 worth of mulberry silk bolts), and that promptly earned him a position at the Bureau of Criminal Investigation.

Newspapermen loved McCurley up until last winter when McCurley's wife died under suspicious circumstances. The widely-accepted version of what occurred is, that when McCurley left to talk to an informant in the dead of night, his wife placed their infant daughter on the bedroom floor, opened the window and jumped down three stories. There were no witnesses. McCurley found the two of them about an hour later. His wife and daughter were transferred to City Hospital. The child nearly perished from hypothermia, and her mother died the following day from her injuries.

The unofficial story is that McCurley was at home when it happened — this because he refused to name the informant. And there are whispers that he pushed his wife.

Since that night, the mood in the detective squad has shifted. The Chief Inspector has hinted at retiring McCurley. But doing it so soon after this personal tragedy and without a trace of proof would shine a bad light on the squad. Still, it seems McCurley has only months left at Headquarters. Unless he solves his next great case.

Don't you think the timing of Mrs Hyde's spectacular death is rather strange?

I hope you'll take my advice. Now I'm almost laughing again because I know that you are not one to take good advice. Make an exception just this once, will you?

Stay away from this man and this investigation, Liz!

An acquaintance of mine works at Headquarters. He's not overly eager to divulge information. But a few beers usually help loosen his tongue, and so I acted the drunk bastard for my lady doctor friend. Ha!

Let's talk on Friday. Will you come?

Yours,
Uriel.

PS: Stay away from McCurley!

PPS: As to your question about the tramp's attorney: the bill of indictment was accepted the day before yesterday, and an attorney is to be assigned to his case by the end of this week.

BEHIND ME, Margery cleared her throat. I almost jumped out of my skin.

'Mrs Hughes is waiting,' she said.

'Thank you.' With trembling fingers, I pushed the letter into its envelope and made for my office.

AFTER LUNCH, Klara and I followed Zachary into the garden and watched him weed the flowerbeds. My mind was bouncing from one problem to the next, unable to approach a solution. My hand kept straying to the crumpled note in my pocket. 'Zach?'

'Hm?'

'I need to leave for a short while. Will you keep Klara company?'

'I was already wondering where my assistant had got to,' he said and winked at Klara who came bounding across the lawn.

. . .

NEWMAN STREET SMELLED of coal tar, smoke, and sun-warmed muck. Number 3 was at the corner of Mercer Street, just across from the Glass Works, which was vomiting a great amount of soot into the sky.

It took several attempts to find a neighbour willing to share information about Mrs Hyde, but eventually, a chimney sweep set down his brushes, stretched his back, thumped his help — a boy no older than six — on the head, and gestured for him to hold a coil of rope.

'Mrs Hyde's husband was a rat, that's what he was. Left her two or three years ago. Following the gold, he said. Went somewhere down south, I believe.'

'California!' squeaked the boy.

The chimney sweep raised his eyebrows. 'And what do you know, nappy-pooper?'

'Heard Mr Marlowe say it.' The boy started drilling an index finger deep into his nostril.

Snorting, the chimney sweep said, 'Marlowe doesn't know his own arse.' He coughed. 'Sorry, ma'am.'

'And her husband hasn't been seen since?'

'No. Mrs Hyde was sharing a room with Miss Munro. But now that Mrs Hyde is gone, Miss Munro found another place to stay.' He shrugged sadly.

'Where can I find Miss Munro?'

He stuck his pinky into his mouth, dug the nail through gaps in his teeth, and sucked in air with a hiss. 'Up at Dexter. Right at the Bay.'

'Do you know the man who…courted Mrs Hyde?'

At that, the chimneysweep brayed like a donkey. '*Courted* Mrs Hyde? I don't know anyone what *courted* her.' He rubbed tears from his eyes.

'So she earned money offering…other services?'

'That you can say.'

'Hmm. I see. Well, I thank you for the information.'

He put two fingers to his hat and wrenched the coil of rope from the boy's grip.

FINDING MISS MUNRO was surprisingly easy. I hadn't expected that she would be home, even less that she would be abed in the middle of the afternoon. She looked me up and down, tugged the lapels of an ugly, brown robe tighter around her curves, and asked me what I wanted.

As I introduced myself and told her my business, her shoulders sagged. 'Are you with the police?'

'I'm a woman. How could I possibly be with the police?'

'What would I know? Seems like women take all kinds of occupations these days.' She spat it out like a foul bite of meat.

'May I come in?'

She jerked her chin sideways and stepped back. Her room was small. A pallet stood at the far end. A single, naked window looked out at the smokestacks of the Glass Works. Crumpled clothes were piled on a chair, on the window sill, and below that on the floor.

'I was about to clean up,' she muttered.

'Mrs Hyde was in the family way,' I said, watching Miss Munro for a reaction.

She huffed. 'She had a bun in the oven all right.' Then her face fell. 'She didn't deserve this.'

'Very few people do.'

'Etta is the kindest creature I know. Was, that is. Too trusting. I guess… I guess that's what did her in.'

'Quite unusual in her profession.'

Miss Munro frowned. 'What do you mean?'

'I heard she worked not only as a washerwoman but also as a prostitute. To be so trusting is—'

'Nonsense! *I'm* the whore. *She's* the decent one. Was…the decent one of the two of us. All them hollow-brained mules out there,' she made a sweeping gesture toward the window, 'think her guilty by association.'

'But someone must be the father.'

Miss Munro pulled in a breath. 'She didn't talk about him. Which was odd. We told each other everything. Even… We even talked about my clients.'

'And you don't have the slightest idea who the man might be? Or when Mrs Hyde first met him?'

Miss Munro's brow furrowed. She shook her head. 'Damned if I know.'

'Did she ever mention a Mr Stone?'

There was no flicker of recognition at the mention of the name. But she said, 'Maybe she did. It's a fairly common name.'

'He's a flower grower who lives near Franklin Park.'

She pushed her hands into the pockets of her robe. 'No. I don't think I ever heard her talk about a flower grower.' A muscle worked in her jaw.

I waited, but when she didn't continue, I said, 'I found a yellow rose petal in her hand. Unusual this time of year.'

Her gaze sharpened. 'You are the doctor who examined her. The papers wrote about you.'

As far as I knew, they mentioned briefly that a woman physician had provided the first insights. My name hadn't been mentioned, and I was glad of it.

'Is it true?' she whispered.

'What do you mean?'

'That she was…' Miss Munro flung out an arm. *Scattered.*

'Yes.'

She touched a trembling hand to her throat.

'Did anyone hate Mrs Hyde?'

A shake of her head, eyes downcast. 'I don't know. It seems...that I don't know anything. I mean, Etta and I lived together, talked about everything. Or so I thought. But I don't have the faintest idea who could have killed her.' She looked up at me. 'That makes me a piss-poor friend, don't it?'

'No one would ever need the police for a murder if good friends always knew in advance who was plotting it.'

She smoothed her rumpled hair and nodded, almost smiling.

I handed her my card. 'If something comes to mind, or if you hear anything, please do let me know. Or if you need help.'

She glanced at the card, the address, and flipped it around. 'Help?'

'I'm a physician.' It was like a punch to my gut when I realised that I hadn't offered medical treatment to the poor for a very long time. In fact, not once since I'd moved to Boston. All my patients could afford to see me. They paid well, although I didn't need a penny of their money. In London, I had lived in a slum, treating prostitutes, vagrants, criminals and... *Oh gods, Garret. I don't even know if you are still alive.*

'What is it?' Miss Munro asked.

I shook my head. 'I just realised that I'll be late for an appointment.'

CASE NOTES, JUNE 7, 1893

**Notes on the body of Mrs E. Hughes, Wednesday, June 7, 1893
(body found between elevator of Boston Wharf Co. and New
York and New England Railroad)
Quinn McCurley, Bureau of Criminal Investigation**

*B*ruising to throat and neck consistent with
strangulation. Faint bruising to forearms. Fingernails
broken and bloody, with thick layers of dirt under them. Outer
clothes in disarray. Stains and tears on back of jacket and skirts,
most pronounced on both elbows (photograph 9). Deep scuff marks
on boot heels (photograph 12). No signs of struggle on the ground
where body was found or in vicinity thereof (photographs 13 to 18).

AWAITING POST-MORTEM SURGEON'S REPORT.

. . .

ITEMS FOUND ON BODY: a cotton handkerchief; a small purse containing 6 one-cent coins, 1 twenty-five cent coin, 1 fifty-cent coin; a small chain with two keys and a buttonhook; a small likeness of a child.

Tucked into her corset was a photograph of what appears to be a pencil drawing of Dr Elizabeth Arlington's face. Both drawing and photograph are of professional quality. No identifying markings on either. <u>Information to be kept within Bureau!</u>

Assigned Detectives Burke & Collins to tail Arlington for next 72 hours.

CONNECTION BETWEEN HUGHES AND HYDE? Coincidence?

Both victims heavier and taller than Arlington. <u>Accomplice?</u>

7

*T*he sun was drying dew off the grass and spiderwebs in our backyard. I hadn't spent my early mornings on the porch for…had it been a full week already? A week of rushing from one lecture to the next, from one emergency to another. I'd had no time to go to the music hall and meet the Freaks, and only with difficulty had I managed to carve out time for my daughter.

But this day held no such obligations.

Margery emerged with a basket of food and said that she and Klara were ready. A few moments later, we left the house.

Klara made nose prints on the window of the cab and invited me to draw faces into the clouds of condensation she was leaving on the glass. Margery was absorbed in a romance novel about a governess and a lord. Occasionally, she cleared her throat, dashed a glance at me, and then quickly back to her book.

I pinched my lips together, trying not to laugh.

We arrived at Franklin Park. Klara used our blanket as a cape or wings, I wasn't sure which. And she wasn't either, because at times she hopped and ran, making bird-like noises, while other times she stalked this lady or that, tipping a non-existing hat in the most chivalrous fashion.

We found a spot by a pond and spread out our things. Klara and I skipped stones (well, I skipped and she plopped), while Margery stuck like a barnacle to her book. As the sun climbed higher, people began to flock to the park. Bicyclists wove through pedestrians, ladies twirled their parasols in the breeze, gentlemen began taking off their hats and fanning their faces, and soon the first children were noisily demanding to be taken to Crescent Beach.

When Klara had pulled off her shoes and stockings, and was wading knee-deep in the pond, I told Margery that I needed to see someone, and I would be back in half an hour, or so.

She moved down to the water's edge with her book and stuffed a candy into her mouth (and had to sacrifice a second one to Klara, whose attention had been pricked at the candy wrapper noise).

'Did he kiss her already?' I asked.

Margery opened her mouth, shut it, and waved me away.

As I approached the Forest Hill Cemetery, I noticed a man following me at some distance. Earlier, he'd been sitting by the pond across from us, reading a newspaper. I stopped walking and pretended to tie my shoelaces. He strode past me.

Perhaps I was being oversensitive.

A flash of light pierced my eyes. The hothouse at Weldon Street glinted in the sun. I walked up to a fenced-in garden and waved at a man who was bent over a row of lavender. 'Excuse me? I'm looking for Mr Stone.'

The man straightened, pressed a hand to his back, the

other shielding his eyes from the sun. He was at least a head taller than I, and massive in the shoulders. 'And you are?'

'Mrs Chloe Newby is my name. I heard Mr Stone grows the best roses in all of Boston.'

His answer was a derisive snort.

'Are you Mr Stone?' I kept my voice light and on the edge of naiveté.

He grunted in the affirmative.

'I'd like to purchase two dozen yellow roses for a dear friend.'

'Short- or long-stemmed?'

I should have brought Zach with me. I could only guess, so I said, 'As long as they are yellow.' I knew it was the wrong answer as soon as the words had left my mouth.

'I'm not interested.' He turned back to the lavender and recommenced snipping off dried stems.

'It is rather urgent. You see, I need them by Sunday morning, but can't find anyone who sells yellow roses.'

'I'm not interested,' he said again, louder this time.

'Please, have a heart, Mr Stone.' I disliked the whine in my voice, but it showed effect. He straightened up again.

I added, 'She loved them so.'

His nostrils flared. He had noticed the past tense. 'Get away from my fence,' he snarled and pointed a pair of clippers at me.

I lifted my hands from the garden gate. 'Mr Stone, I—'

'I'm not selling my roses to be dumped on a pile of *dirt*.'

'Not even for Henrietta Hyde's grave?'

All blood fled from his face. He hardened his jaw, turned away and disappeared into his house.

≈

As I entered Inspector McCurley's office the following day, he choked on what looked and smelled like scorched beans. He was less groomed than the last time I'd seen him. Stubble nearly hid the prominent scar on the side of his face.

He swallowed, wiped his mouth, and seemed rather shocked to see me. 'And what brings *you* here, Dr Arlington?'

As I told him about Mr Stone, McCurley only scratched his chin, a mocking scowl tilting his mouth. 'So you found the *real* murderer. Congratulations.'

'I did not say that. All I said was that there might be another suspect. But, really, Inspector, I have no wish to keep you from your luncheon.' I nodded at the plate of burnt beans in front of him.

'And you think I haven't already looked into it?'

'You have?'

'What do you think I'm here for?' He placed the fork aside. 'There aren't many flower growers in the Boston area, even fewer who grow roses in hothouses.'

'Does Mr Stone have an alibi?'

McCurley leaned back. 'And what makes you think I'm in the mood to share information with you?'

'Because you want to get rid of me?' I suggested.

'He has a *very* good alibi.' He forked more beans into his mouth, chewed as though they were sand, and said casually, 'Do you know a Mrs Elizabeth Hughes?'

'She's my patient.'

At that, he paused for the smallest of moments. 'When did you last see her?'

My skin began to prickle. 'What has happened to her?'

'When did you last see her?' he repeated, slow and insisting.

'A week ago. In fact, it was the first time I saw her. She is a new patient.'

'What did she want from you?' His mouth worked like a

revolver, firing questions at me before I even finished talking.

'Without a warrant, I will not divulge patient information. What has happened to Mrs Hughes?'

'I will arrange for a warrant.' McCurley pushed his half-eaten food aside, lit a cigarette, and leaned back in his chair. 'Her body was found two days ago.'

I clapped a hand to my mouth, stumbled to a chair, and sat down.

McCurley was watching me. Smoke curled around his mouth and up to the ceiling. He flicked ash toward an ashtray and missed it by half an inch. Then he said, 'She was strangled.'

'No,' was all I managed. A clump formed in my throat. I fought to swallow it. 'Was it the same man who killed Mrs Hyde?'

A shrug, as though it didn't concern him in the least.

'What did the post-mortem surgeon say?'

McCurley produced something between a cough and a laugh, and asked, 'Where were you yesterday and the day before?'

'You are jesting.'

He picked up a pencil, opened a drawer and retrieved a notepad. 'Details, if you please.'

I blinked, shook my head, and said, 'The day before yesterday, I spent nearly the entire day giving lectures at the medical school, and attending to patients.'

'Time?'

'Patients from nine to eleven, lectures from one to five o'clock.'

'When and where did you take lunch?'

I detailed my day to him, waited until he finished taking notes, then I continued, 'If you need information about a patient of mine, you'll have to show me a warrant first.

Yesterday, I spent a few hours at Franklin Park together with my daughter and housekeeper. I left them around noon to see Mr Stone and returned about half an hour later. I spent the afternoon in my garden and the public library. The head librarian will remember me because I was searching for newspaper articles on murders similar to the one of Mrs Hyde.'

With a huff, McCurley leaned back in his chair. 'Do you know what irritates me the most? People playing detective.'

'Oh, I'm sure you know plenty of those.' I made a sweeping gesture encompassing Headquarters.

'Mrs Arlington—' he growled.

'Very well, let's put aside pleasantries for a moment, *McCurley*. You wished to know where I was, what I did, and the names of all the people who can corroborate my account. I have given you this information. Now, I would be much obliged if you could make me a list of—'

He threw his head back and laughed. 'You want *me* to give *you* information? That is the most hilarious thing I've heard today. And believe me, I hear hilarious things every day. Every single day. Things that make me doubt mankind has any brains whatsoever.'

'I do know the feeling, McCurley. And I see that my time here is wasted.' I stood. 'When will you release Petey?'

He snorted.

'Why did the newspapers not report on Mrs Hughes's death?'

'They will report it tomorrow morning.'

'So you withheld it—'

'I have other matters to attend to now.' He gestured toward the door. 'You can expect me shortly with a warrant.'

'Where was she found?' I insisted.

McCurley narrowed his eyes and worked his jaw. The scar on the side of his face rippled.

'You shouldn't eat that, you know. It's unhealthy.' I pointed to the burnt beans.

He jerked his pencil toward the door, a cold stare fixed on my face.

'Good day to you, too, Inspector,' I said and left.

8

The Boston Post, Saturday, June 10, 1893
ANOTHER RAILROAD MURDER!

On Wednesday, the body of Mrs Elizabeth Hughes was found near the New York and New England Railroad. About three o`clock in the afternoon attention was drawn to a pair of boots sticking out from beneath the elevator of the Boston Wharf Company. Several workers alerted the Boston Police Department, which secured all evidence and sent the body to the morgue to be examined. Mr Hughes is being held in custody for questioning.

~

hen Margery barged into my office, her curls askew and the skin stretched tight over her usually soft face, I knew without her needing to tell me that the police had arrived.

'I'll be with them in a moment,' I said and turned back to my patient. 'Mr MacArthur, I really cannot recommend ear candling. If you would allow me to extract—'

'That won't do, Miss.' He shook his head fiercely, a mop of white hair flopping with the movement. 'My father and my grandfather have done it with great success, and my ears are no different.'

'Honestly, a great mass of earwax is clogging your ear canals. Your hearing is impaired and soon you'll suffer from ear infections. It would take me less than ten seconds to extract—'

'I *cannot* allow you to stick that fearful metal thing into my brain, Missus.' He was still wagging his head.

I sighed. It always ended this way with Mr MacArthur. I recommended a treatment, and he told me that he knew better. 'How is your chest feeling these days?'

'Splendid!' As if on cue, he produced a horrifyingly deep and rattling cough.

'You probably don't want me to recommend fresh air yet again,' I mumbled, wondering why he even bothered seeing a doctor if he never listened to an expert's advice. He wasn't even lonely. Several of my elderly patients came simply to have someone to talk to, but MacArthur had what? Fifteen or sixteen grandchildren crowding his house?

Maybe that's why he insisted on keeping his ears plugged: less ruckus to listen to.

A knock sounded, and McCurley pushed the door open.

Irritated, I massaged my temples. 'Inspector McCurley, if you have the audacity to arrive unannounced, at least show the courtesy to wait until my patient has left the room. You could have walked in on a woman in a state of undress.'

'I was told the patient was male.'

I smacked the desk. The stethoscope rolled off and bounced on the floor. 'Well, in that case, count yourself lucky you didn't barge in on an enema! I would have thrown the clyster at your head!'

If possible, McCurley's expression darkened even further. But he dipped his head and left.

Mr MacArthur cleared his throat until he had my attention. 'Miss, your language leaves a lot to be desired.'

I picked up my stethoscope, and bit out, 'Is there anything else I can *not* help you with?'

Mr MacArthur frowned, cupped an ear, and said, 'Excuse me?'

Gods, how I wished to be back in a slum! I inhaled a deep breath, stood, and said loudly, 'The next patient is expecting me.'

'Oh, yes, of course.'

I helped him stand and shuffle from my office. Three men were waiting in the corridor. I recognised Sergeant Boyle, who ripped off his hat with one hand, and held out the other. I shook it.

The third policeman was introduced as the stenographer, Mr Halverton, who mumbled, 'Ma'am,' by way of greeting, and nothing more.

I called to Margery to bring tea and led the men into my office.

'The warrant,' McCurley said, handing me a slip of paper.

I unfolded it, and read. 'You want to see *all* my files?'

'Yes. If you please.'

I crossed the room to a chest, pulled out the top drawer, and stepped back.

McCurley motioned to Sergeant Boyle, who heaved out a stack of files, placed them atop the chest, and began rifling through them while muttering to the stenographer, who scribbled away on a notepad.

'I need to see your appointment book.'

I snapped it open, turned it around and pushed it across the desk. We sat down on opposite sides. Slowly, methodically, McCurley leafed through my book and paused. 'Hattie

Heathcote. Amaury family. Interesting.' Then he continued scanning patient names, occasionally making notes.

I watched Sergeant Boyle dig through the drawer and the stenographer write down all that Boyle pointed out to him.

'Am I a suspect?' I asked the inspector.

'Should you be?'

I couldn't help but laugh. 'McCurley, why is it that you never give a straight answer?'

He leaned back. 'Tell me about yourself.'

'Are you flirting with me?'

Boyle dropped a file to the floor.

McCurley tugged at his collar. 'Where did you study medicine?'

'At the Zürich University.'

'Is that how it's pronounced?'

'Yes. The Germans invented the Umlaut to make the language *umständlich* for foreigners.' I smiled.

'And what precisely is *umsh...andlick?*'

'German for *cumbersome*.'

He didn't even blink. No one ever understands German humour.

'Why do you have a British name but a German accent?'

My neck prickled. I kept smiling. 'My father was a British merchant, my mother German. I was born in Germany and spent most of my childhood there. My nanny was German. My father was very busy. Hence my first language happens to be German, not English.' It went against my strongest values to tell lies about my mother, who'd died only days after I was born, and my father who had done everything for me. And who'd been murdered because of me.

'When did you move to Switzerland?'

'Around the time I was thirteen or fourteen.'

'*Around* the time? You don't know that precisely?'

'No. I find birthday celebrations a waste of time.'

'Where did you go after you graduated from university?'

'Here and there.' I didn't take my eyes off McCurley. Untrained liars avoided eye contact. Their gaze will drift as though ideas are to be found in the air around them. 'Back to Germany, then to Britain, and now Boston.'

'Where in Germany and Britain?'

'Berlin and London.'

He tapped the pencil against his notepad. 'The other day you told me that you don't speak French. But you lived in Switzerland.'

'There's no need to learn French when one lives in Zürich.'

'Don't the Swiss speak both languages?'

'Some do. Although I doubt they'd be pleased should you insinuate they speak German. Swiss German sounds very different from…German German.'

'Interesting.' He didn't sound at all interested. If anything, he seemed bored. I knew it was a charade. 'Are you widowed or divorced?' he asked.

The prickling grew worse. 'Widowed.'

'Tell me about your husband.'

'I prefer not to.'

His eyes narrowed a fraction. 'Why not?'

'Tell me about your dead wife.'

Boyle and Halverton stopped muttering, scratching, moving. They seemed to cease to exist. Or to be waiting for an explosion.

McCurley's facade did not slip in the least. It didn't even twitch. In a voice so calm it drove gooseflesh down my arms, he said, 'You seem to be confusing a few things here, *Dr* Arlington. Allow me to clarify for you. I am the inspector, you are the witness. I ask questions, and you answer them.'

I watched how his hand curled around the notebook in

his lap. Before his knuckles could whiten with tension, he relaxed his fingers.

'You seem to be confusing a few things here, *Inspector* McCurley. But I will gladly clarify them for you. This is my practice, not a court. I'm sitting in a chair, not a witness box. You are a police officer, not an attorney. You may ask questions directly related to this case, and no more. And I may choose to answer. Or not.'

He smiled, as though he'd got all he wanted or expected to get. 'The second victim was your patient. Why did she come to see you?'

'She complained of pain in her lower abdomen.'

'Only that?'

'It was debilitating pain.'

'Hmm. Did she speak of her husband? Her children?'

'As I've already said, I saw her only once.' I cut a glance at the other two men in the room and crossed my arms over my chest. 'She mentioned private matters.'

'Go on.'

'She was…experiencing pain during intercourse.'

The stenographer didn't twitch a muscle. Boyle, though, blushed violently, and dropped his head as though he wished to hide in my chest of drawers. *Hide in my drawers.* I nearly burst out laughing.

'Did she say anything that would cause you to suspect her husband had had a hand in her death?'

'No. If I had suspected her husband was about to murder her, wouldn't I have come to you before she died?'

'What did she say about her husband?'

With every question he asked, with every inch he wouldn't budge, I grew from being irritated, to angry, to furious. I had to hold my voice under tight control so as not to snarl at him. 'She said they had been married for nearly ten years, and that recently she had been experiencing pain. She and her husband talked about it. He was saddened by it, tried to help in any way he could. That doesn't sound like someone intent on killing her.'

'You would be surprised.'

'No, I wouldn't. Did you talk to Petey?'

McCurley slowly sucked in a breath, and I added, 'Did you find someone who understands him?'

'Are you trying to distract from something? Your patient, perhaps?'

I rolled my eyes. That seemed to annoy him. 'If your main suspect — or main witness — can't make himself understood, he can't possibly tell you what he saw on the day Mrs Hyde died. By the by, did you notice that both women have a name that begins with the letter H?'

His shoulders sagged. He looked like he believed I was an idiot.

'Ask Georgie's mother,' I said. 'She understands Petey's mumbling.'

'Georgie? The newsboy? How would you know his mother understands Petey?'

'When I'm bored, I like to play detective.' I winked at him.

He jerked in his chair. After a moment of consideration, a grin spread on his face, rippling the scar on his cheek and throat. 'You seem to believe your powerful friends can protect you.'

'What?'

'One of your patients is Hattie Heathcote. I doubt she comes all the way simply to see a doctor. Is she a friend?'

'She is. But I began *playing* detective long before I met her.' That, I definitely should not have said. I wanted to slap myself. The twitch around the corner of McCurley's mouth indicated satisfaction.

So *that* was his tactic: abrasion until the wall gave way. And then I did snarl. Not so much because I was angry with him — although I was — but mostly because I was *furious* with myself. 'You have no talent for interrogation whatsoever. How the deuce did you end up in the detective branch?'

Boyle sounded like he was choking on something. The stenographer scribbled on undisturbed.

'You are aware, of course, that you are the only connection between the two victims.'

'Yes. Me, the railroad, and the letter H. Why do you think that is?'

He pointed his pencil at me. 'You tell me.'

Groaning, I buried my face in my hands. 'Not only do you *never* give straight answers, you avoid asking straight questions. No, I did not kill either of the women.'

'That wasn't what I was thinking, but thank you for clarifying. I was more wondering whether you had an accomplice.'

'What for?'

'Both victims were taller and heavier than you,' he said.

'I assume they might even be heavier than *you*. But I'm quite sure you could have strangled them. And so could I.'

His pupils constricted. Before he could reply, I said, 'By the gods, McCurley, I did not kill them. I merely wish to broaden your horizon. Your killer doesn't have to be a great brute to strangle two women. He could be my size. It's a question of where to strike. Oh!' I sat up straight.

'Yes?' It sounded like a purr.

I opened my mouth and snapped it shut. Then I touched the tender spot just below my breastbone. 'Have you ever struck a man right here, below the sternum?'

McCurley pulled up an eyebrow.

'Did the toxicologist find poison in Mrs Hyde's organ samples?'

'No.'

I smiled. 'Strangulation is a rather slow death. Depending

on how practised your killer is, it might take fifteen seconds to…hum…perhaps two minutes to lose consciousness. Don't you agree?'

'It might.'

'And yet, Mrs Hyde had neither blood nor skin under her fingernails. There were no signs on her body that indicated she fought back. Fifteen seconds is a very long time to die and do nothing about it. But if you've ever been struck right here,' I pointed again, 'you would know that a person is unable to move for at least fifteen seconds. Unable to breathe, either. Probably even lose consciousness.'

'If it occurred as you say, the post-mortem surgeon would have found bruising.'

'Ah, no. Not necessarily. You see, the diaphragm sits just behind this spot. And there are many nerves right here. The minimum force necessary to cause the diaphragm to spasm is so low that it would not bruise the surrounding tissue. At least not noticeably. Mrs Hyde's body was mangled by a train, and I think that very faint marks of perimortem bruising could have been — in this particular case — discounted by most post-mortem surgeons. What I mean to convey is that it's not in the body mass but in the technique. Your murderer could well be a woman.'

His gaze drifted to my hands that were grasping my elbows. 'Boyle, Halverton. Give us a moment.'

Boyle grabbed the stack of files he'd been rifling through. Halverton picked up his notepad and pencil, and both men hurried from my office.

McCurley bent forward. 'How did this happen?' He jerked his chin toward my hands. I dropped them to my lap. 'The scars on your middle finger are from a knife. Did someone *cut* off your index finger? Your husband, perhaps? Have you been snapping at his heels, too?'

I gasped. 'You are asking me what *I did* to warrant such

treatment? Do you believe these two women *did* something to cause their own deaths? That they provoked a man into killing them? Go to hell, McCurley!'

Again, he would not answer. But his expression... It turned the blood in my veins to ice. Unspeaking, he slipped a hand into his jacket and pulled out a photograph of a drawing. Pushed it across the desk for me to see. And stopped my heart.

'Where did you find this?' I breathed.

'Does it look familiar to you?'

'Yes. I see that face every time I look in a mirror.'

'Who drew this portrait?'

I shook my head. A lie. Another lie. I was drowning in lies. 'I don't know. Where did you find it?'

'On the body of Mrs Hughes.'

9

argery was in the kitchen, preparing lunch. 'Are they gone?' she asked without turning away from the range.

I pressed a fist to my heart. Tried to breathe. 'Yes. They are. Would you please send a note to the medical school to inform them that I won't be giving lectures today?' My own voice was a stranger to me.

She turned. The spoon in her hand clattered against a pot. 'Are they arresting you?'

'No, of course not.' I tried to look normal. And failed miserably. At that moment, I couldn't have even defined "normal."

Klara's laughter trickled through the house. 'Where is she?'

Margery flinched. 'What's wrong? What did the police want?'

I turned and rushed from the kitchen. 'Klara? Klara!'

Her giggles came from the front yard. And a deep voice I did not recognise. With my heart in my mouth, I raced to the door and yanked it open. McCurley and Boyle turned in unison, eyebrows raised. Halverton smiled at Klara as she plucked a candy from his palm, unwrapped it, and stuffed it into her mouth.

I strode up to them and took my daughter's hand. She squeaked. I loosened my grip at once. Doe-eyed, she blinked up at me, her chin trembling. I picked her up and buried my nose in the crook of her neck. 'I'm so sorry, my dear,' I whispered. 'I thought you were a big, strong bear, and I gripped your paw too hard.'

She sniffed but immediately recovered from the small shock. I carried her into the house, not turning to answer McCurley's sharp gaze.

'Have you seen Zachary?' I asked Klara.

'Dsadsah!' she cried, pointing toward the garden behind the house.

'Would you like to cook lunch with Margery?'

She wriggled from my arms, dropped to the floor, and dashed off. Not toward the kitchen, of course, but to the garden.

We found Zach scraping dirt off a spade near the toolshed.

'We need to talk,' I said to him.

He straightened to look at me. His face fell. 'What did the police say?'

'It appears…' I gazed at Klara who must have sensed that something was wrong, and was clinging to Zach's leg like a kitten to a tree trunk. 'I need to work on…things. There is a…hidden room in the wall by my bed.'

Zach slowly set down the spade.

'Just below the candleholder is a sliding panel the size of your hand. When you touch your fingers to the wall below the candle holder, you'll find a notch in the wood. Push it aside, and you'll find a handle. Use it to open a hidden door.'

'W…whatever for?'

'To get away should…you need to. There is an old tunnel that was used for smuggling. It leads to a hatch in the floor of a boathouse near the shore. Be careful, the tunnel will be wet. You can unlock the hatch and the door of the boathouse with a key you'll find in a bag with medical supplies.'

Zach opened his mouth, but I held up my hand to stop him. 'You'll find a revolver and ammunition in the antechamber. Make sure to pack some water and a little food. There are bandages, disinfectant, and a tourniquet in a small bag just behind the door. Some of my tools, needles, and thread.'

Klara rushed over to me, unsure what this all meant, and scared by the hollow tone of my voice. I picked her up and held her against me. 'Everything is all right,' I whispered into her ear. Then to Zachary, 'I will show you a photograph of a man. If you see him on the premises or in the house, do not talk to him, do not ask him what he wants. Make sure Margery and Klara are on their way through the tunnel. And then…' *Kill him,* I mouthed. 'Do you understand?'

Zach shook his head.

'His name is Moran. He will not hesitate, so you mustn't either. He has one target.' I tipped my head toward Klara. She didn't notice the gesture. Zach's eyes grew large. His shoulders quivered.

'The tunnel is the reason I bought this house,' I added.

'I thought you rented it.' Zach seemed utterly lost. 'You said you…' He shook his head again, frowning.

'I've said a lot of things that aren't true. And I'm very sorry I had to.'

His hand compressed around the spade handle. A brief nod. Spine straight, chin set. 'I'll keep her safe.'

With a trembling voice, I continued, 'It might not… Moran might not be here. But there are signs that tell me he…might be close. Two months ago, he was spotted near Paris. And I know that he is…searching.' It was so hard to convey all relevant information without using words that would scare Klara witless. How much did she understand of my insinuations?

'I know now where I have to…look to find out where he is. I'll go tonight.'

Zach's gaze was glued to my daughter. I saw resolution, and a fierce protectiveness that bordered on rage. There were moments when I wished he weren't married.

And then there were moments I was happy he had Margery. This was one of them.

'Zach?' I said softly. His eyes found mine. 'I am glad you are here. I am happy my daughter has you both. Please know that your future is taken care of. You will never need to worry about money. In case…' The sun dabbed small rainbows into my vision. I blinked them away. 'Promise me that you will not let her out of your sight. Not for a moment. That you will carry the gun at all times. Tonight, Margery and Klara will sleep in my bed, and the secret door will be left ajar. Should you need it. Guard them. When I return tonight…' I put emphasis on the last word, to let him know I would return. That I wouldn't risk my life foolishly. 'I will not walk, but skip along the hallway so that you know it's me. Anyone walking quietly, sneaking in… You know how to use a revolver. It's the same make I have. *Do not hesitate.* The man is a hunter.'

'I promise,' he whispered.

'Mama?'

My chin dropped. Zach made a strangled noise.

Klara hid her face in my chest.

I kissed the top of her head. 'Can you say it again?'

She bumped her mouth against my throat, again and again, producing a *bababababa* noise. Then, she lifted her head and declared, 'Mamamamamamammamamammaaaaaaa!'

Joy exploded from my chest, and I laughed until my vision swam.

Klara clapped both hands to my cheeks and pressed a slobbery kiss to my mouth.

QUIETLY, I shut the door and crossed the room, the thick carpet muffling my footfalls. The softness of my approach felt absurd. I wanted to rage, not be silent. Tear down the house, and not be soft. A step from the bed, I held the bullseye lantern aloft. A light blue glint sent my heart into my throat and my feet staggering back.

Warren's eyes were half open.

But he did not move. Did not even blink. The flame caught his irises. He looked straight at me, unseeing. His chest rose and fell as soft hisses escaped his nostrils.

I scanned the room, the clutter on the nightstand, the pile of books beneath the bed, the pair of slippers, but I found no weapon within his reach. Calming myself with deep breaths, I retreated to a chair, sat on the armrest, and placed the lantern on a table next to me. Then I shifted the beam to his face.

Grunting, he turned away and threw an arm over his eyes. A moment later, he snored.

I opened the lantern's hatch to spread more light in the room. 'Warren Amaury.'

He took a deep breath and mumbled into his sleeve.

'Wake up.'

No reaction.

'Warren! Wake up,' I bit out.

Nothing.

I pulled back the hammer of my revolver. The metallic

snick produced an instant effect. Warren's body snapped to attention. *How interesting.*

He jerked upright, blinked at the gun in my lap, then up at my face. His Adam's apple bobbed. 'I should have kn-kn-kn…' With a furious growl, he threw the back of his head against the headboard. '…known the man would have no s-s-scruples.'

I felt a cold smile spreading on my face as my heart dropped to my toes. I'd been right. But Warren? Why *him*?

'Where is he?'

'How would I know? N-n-n…' Again, he slammed his head against the wood. 'New York was where I last saw him. B-b-but that he'd go *that* far.' He thrust his chin toward me and my gun.

'What are you talking about?'

'Well, obv-v-v…' Warren sucked in air, and let it out with a growl. His hand came up to his face. 'I hate it. Obviously he w-w-wants…' He dropped his hand and in a flash, it shot forward. A small object hurtled at me. Hit me. A world of pain opened its maws and poured a nauseating mix of darkness and flickering lights into my brain.

My head hit the floor. A weight fell onto my stomach. I batted at it — him — but he caught my wrists and clamped them under his shins.

'Well, well. Never in my wildest dreams did I imagine you worked for McConaughey.' His stutter was gone.

I'd never imagined him being such a friend-betraying pig of a bastard. 'Who?' I pressed out.

'Come, now. I know what you want. And what McConaughey wants. The question is, *why* would you agree to it?'

'Who is McConaughey?' I tried to move my arms, but they were firmly pinned under his shins. His knees were pressing into my upper arms. 'You are hurting me.'

He laughed. Then he leaned close to my face, effectively increasing the pain in my arms. 'I don't care.'

I smashed my forehead against his nose. The pain in my head nearly drowned out the satisfying *crunch* of his nasal bone.

'Ohmygodnotagain,' he groaned, tipped backward and... freed my arms.

Two quick punches to his chin sent him sprawling to the floor. I pounced on his ribcage and pinned him the same way he'd trapped me earlier. I found my gun on the floor next to his shoulder. And grabbed it.

'Where is Moran?'

Warren blinked. 'Who?'

'We won't get anywhere like this. Let me explain the situation to you: Moran has sworn to kill me and abduct my daughter. Maybe to kill her, maybe to send her to strangers to do whatever they wish to her.'

I set the mouth of the revolver against his throat. His eyes widened. 'You will be *very* dead, Warren Amaury, if you don't tell me where Moran is. I don't care why you work for him, so don't you even get started on excuses or explanations. All I want to know is where he is. You have two seconds.' I applied more pressure to his Adam's apple.

He opened his mouth, but nothing came out. He tried again. His eyes began to water. 'I-I-I...' He shut his eyes, and then...he began to sing. 'I have no idea what you are talking about, and this is so embarrassing. I can't even string two words together without sounding like a jackhammer or a castrated hound.'

'Are you joking?'

He set his jaw and shook his head.

'I don't believe you,' I said.

He managed a one-shouldered shrug.

'You drew portraits of me and gave them to someone. Who?'

Warren looked stunned. Genuinely stunned. His gaze shifted to the door. And then I heard it, too.

Footfalls.

A knock sounded, followed by the voice of Owens. 'Mr Amaury, Sir, I heard strange noises. Is everything all right?'

I nodded at the gun.

Warren had the audacity to roll his eyes. 'I am in the company of a lady,' he sang out. And then with a sure voice, 'She is a pretty wild thing, Owens.'

There was a pause before a sour reply came, 'Bragging is unnecessary, Mr Amaury.'

'Well, stopper your ears, will you!'

'Good night, Mr Amaury, Sir. Try not to break the furniture.'

Warren looked up at me, all fear gone despite being held at gunpoint. 'Let's begin anew, shall we? I am Warren Amaury. Sometimes I sing. I doubt McConaughey sent you, and I swear on all that is holy that I have no idea who Moran is.'

I pushed the gun harder against his flesh. His face reddened. 'Let's begin anew, shall we? Let's begin with you being honest for once.' I leaned closer. His eyes flared. Yes, there was fear, perhaps even panic. I whispered, 'Have you ever read about men who come between a mother bear and her cub? All that's left of them is bloody ribbons. Do you truly want to put yourself between me and my child, Warren?'

'I s-s-swear…' He swallowed, his eyes darting about the room. A tear escaped from the corner of his eye. As he looked back at me, I found resolution in his face. 'Whoever used that portrait against you, it wasn't me. I have no idea who did it, but I can help you find him.' He cleared his throat.

'Now, would you be so f-f-forthcoming and get off me. It's r-rather uncomf-f-fortable.'

'I see no reason to be forthcom—'

He bucked and threw me off, pinned me with his arm across my throat. I retaliated with a sharp right hook. His jaw rattled.

'Bloody hell!' he hollered, shoved me away, and sat back. 'Who taught you that?'

'My gardener!' I hissed and jumped for the gun that lay between us.

But Warren was faster.

He snatched it, snapped open the cylinder, and tipped the bullets onto his palm. Then he tossed the gun in my lap. 'So. Time to talk. Let's call it *a trade of information*. An answer for an answer. Why did your gardener teach you boxing?'

I scooted far out of Warren's reach, and leaned against an armchair. This wasn't going the way I'd planned. But talking would give me enough time — and perhaps enough informa-tion — to decide on my next move. 'Who said he *taught* me? I needed a sparring partner, so I asked my gardener. Now it's my turn to—'

'Not so fast. You did not explain why your gardener is your…pug. You barely even answered the question.' Warren huffed a laugh. 'The *gardener*, for Christ's sake!'

'Don't you dare mock him!' I jabbed a finger at Warren. He held up his hands. I continued. 'As I said, a man wants my daughter, and I am protecting her.'

'And that includes shooting?' He dipped his gaze to my gun.

'It's not your turn, it's mine. To whom did you give my portrait?'

He pressed his mouth to a slash. 'I have not given it to anyone. I'm not in the habit of giving away my scribbles.

Especially not when they depict a woman.' Even in the faint light, I could see him blush. He turned his gaze away.

'How, then, do you explain the fact that a drawing that's undeniably yours was found on the body of a murder victim?'

He gaped. 'What?'

'You heard me.'

'How do you know it's mine?'

'I've seen your portraits. And it's… It's clear from the way you draw the eyes.' I explained.

'Is it?'

'They are alive. I've never seen that before.'

His gaze drifted to the nightstand.

'You keep drawings of me in your nightstand?' I was aghast.

'I keep whatever I'm currently working on in my nightstand.' He stood and rummaged in the drawer, then strode past me and left the room. I followed him to another room with a cluttered desk, and shelves upon shelves of books. He worked his way through stacks of papers and folders, drawers, and even the dustbin.

'I can't find it,' he finally said.

'Find what?'

'My sketchbook. The one I was using last.'

'How convenient.'

'Be quiet for a moment,' he barked, sat in a chair behind the desk, and propped his chin on his hand. The other hand drummed on the polished oak surface.

I walked back to the bedroom, picked the bullets off the rug, and slid them into the cylinder. When I returned to Warren's office, he looked wary.

'I'm currently not planning to shoot you,' I said.

'I tend to disagree.'

'Really?'

'After what I tell you, you may wish to put a bullet in my stomach. Makes for a painful and drawn-out death.'

'We shall see.'

He rubbed his brow, and said, 'You weren't here last Friday.'

'I had...things to do.'

'Everyone was here but you. We drank. We had fun. And later that evening, Hattie caught me drawing you.'

I couldn't believe it! 'You drew my portrait? *From memory?*'

He shrugged. 'I have a photographic memory. It's mostly annoying. Anyway, Hattie took the sketchbook away and threw it on the shelf. But it's not there anymore. The servants don't touch these things, so...'

The thought sickened me. Warren betraying me was... well, I could stomach *that*. But Hattie? She was a friend. She'd...befriended me and dragged me with her. Had insisted I get to know the Freak Consortium. Why?

He saw my grip on the gun tighten. 'If you put that gun anywhere near my sister, I will have you killed.'

'I need to talk to her.'

'I am aware of that. That's why I'll accompany you when you visit her *tomorrow*.'

Yes. It would draw too much attention if I showed up at her house, woke up her husband and children, and pointed a gun at her. But one whole night to wait? So much could happen in a night. 'Who was in your house last Friday?'

He paused, scratching his neck. 'As I said. All the Freaks but you. Hattie would never do anything against your wishes. She's protective of you. She knew you didn't want me to draw you, so she took the portrait from me. She gave me hell.' He grinned. 'Whoever gave it to the...murderer, it wasn't Hattie.'

'You knew I didn't want you to draw me, but you did it anyway. Why?'

He shrugged. 'Because I could.'

'To hell with you, Warren Amaury!'

He held up his hands. 'I swear, I would have burned it that same night! Or maybe in the morning.'

'Hattie probably took it, so you wouldn't take it to bed with you,' I shot at him. His violent blush told me I had hit the mark. 'Really? Gods, Warren, for that alone you've earned yourself a good kick in the ballsack!'

'You don't understand,' he mumbled.

'And what precisely do I not understand?' I hissed.

'It is not…what you think. When I draw, I…enjoy what's behind the…the m-mask. I d-d-draw…' He rose and walked once again to the shelf, pulled out a sketchbook, and gave it to me.

I flipped it open, held it closer to the light, and found… 'Scantily-clad women? *This* is your defence? Sketches of prostitutes?'

10

*T*he street lamp where I'd left my bicycle was… naked. Blast it! I kicked at it, only to end up hurting my toe. 'Cockchafers!'

I looked up at a lit window in Warren's townhouse. He had a telephone, perhaps he could… No. I didn't want his help.

But I *had* to get home. Fast. To make sure Klara was safe. And Zach and Margery.

There was no cab around, so I started off at a run, the bump on my forehead throbbing with every step.

The drawings Warren had shown me… To describe them as *unusual* wouldn't do them justice. The man had the ability to put pain and beauty on paper with just a few pencil strokes. And without the slightest trace of self-consciousness, he'd talked about brothels and prostitutes, knowing where each of the women he'd drawn lived. Their past. Their clients. The things the women loved and hated.

And as he had listened to them with wide-open senses, he'd brought their very souls to paper.

I'd told him that if he ever again drew me, I'd burn down

his house. He assured me that being woken up with a gun in his visage had been quite enough of a warning.

I was passing the Common and still had not spotted a cab. It was maddening!

I thought of Zach and Margery. I would tell them tonight. All they needed to know. Despite my head swimming and my eye aching as if a small hammer and anvil were embedded behind it.

I walked down Washington Street into a seedier area of Boston, and passed a narrow alley near the asylum. Noises reached my ear. Those of a man running. An instant later, someone shot past me followed by…a ghost? No, a man in his nightshirt. His hair and moustache were on end.

McCurley?

The *slap slap* of his naked feet on the cobbles echoed off the walls. As he rushed past me, he bit out, 'Hide!'

Then he screeched to a halt. That's when I noticed the loud footfalls of the other man had stopped.

Silence hollered in my ears.

Time slowed to a crawl.

I felt for the warm, smooth leather of my holster, the butt of my revolver — coarser, rougher. A little colder.

In the corner of my vision, a dark silhouette stood perfectly still.

I turned. The figure was raising his arm. A gun in his hand.

Smoke curled from the mouth of the man's gun. The muzzle gaped at me. I hadn't heard the shot. Or had I? Was I hit?

I blinked.

Only then did three sharp *cracks* cut to my ears. And ring in my head.

I stared at my outstretched hand, my gun. There, too, was a wisp of smoke.

Time snapped back into place. And a breadth of impressions slammed into me. The small twinge of pain in my right wrist. The rustle of clothes as the man sank to his knees. The grunt from his mouth. The dribbling of dark liquid from his lips. He coughed, and a spray of blood hit the pavement. Heated discussions behind windows. Lights flickering on all along the alley. Heads bobbing in and out of view. Terrified mutterings, whisperings.

And then McCurley moved. I jumped in shock. I had totally forgotten about him.

He circled the dark figure that was beginning to tip aside.

I did not move.

The man was now flat on his back. His legs were twitching. McCurley kicked his gun aside, knelt, and put his hand to the man's throat for a moment. My feet stepped forward of their own accord.

McCurley whirled around. His gaze slid from my shoes, to my knickerbockers, to the gun in my hand. And up to my face. He looked as though he were seeing me for the first time.

'*You?*'

'Were you expecting someone else?' I was surprised that my voice was so calm. 'Who is this man?'

'Pale-eyed Joey. Convicted of triple murder. He escaped a month ago, and thought he should take revenge on the officer who arrested him.' McCurley rose to his feet. 'Why do you have a gun?'

'Why wouldn't I?'

'I aimed for his leg,' he said. 'To stop him. You shot him in the heart. Why? It wasn't necessary.'

'He pointed a gun in my direction. It was either the heart or the head. I thought you might need to identify him, so I refrained from blasting off his face.' In fact, I had thought none of those things. All I'd seen was the muzzle of a gun staring straight at me. And I'd simply reacted.

McCurley looked incredulous. 'Well, there's nothing we can do about it now.' He shifted his weight somewhat awkwardly. His nightshirt reached only to his knees and…

'Your foot is bleeding.' I slipped my revolver back into the holster and buttoned my jacket over it.

McCurley looked down at his foot. A small puddle had formed. Skin was badly torn off the outer side, and the small toe had swollen to nearly the size of a pigeon egg.

He winced when he moved.

'You bleed, you feel pain. Why, you almost have me convinced you are human.'

'Says the Banshee.'

I looked across to the dark, huddled form. 'I killed a man.' My mind registered the words I was speaking but seemed unable to process the information.

'What happened to your face?' McCurley asked.

'It met a handsome young fellow.'

He didn't even react to that. He merely emptied the cylinder of his gun and whacked the butt against a lamppost. Five times.

'No police box nearby?'

'No.' And he whacked the lamppost some more.

'How long until they come?'

He shrugged. 'A few minutes. I'll wait here. You may go home, but expect a summons tomorrow or the day after.'

'Hurrah! And thank you for stopping a murderer and saving my life, Dr Arlington,' I muttered and made to leave. But stopped. 'I heard three shots. Are you hit?'

He looked again at his toes, then at the place where he'd been standing when the shots were fired, and back at the front of his nightshirt. There were no bloodstains. 'Doesn't look like it.'

'I would appreciate if you didn't mention my name to the newspapermen.'

He narrowed his eyes at me. Then dipped his head in what I hoped was assent.

Seeing that bullets had stopped flying, people opened their windows and craned their necks.

'This is Inspector McCurley, Boston Police Department. If anyone has a telephone, please summon my colleagues.'

There was very little hope anyone had a telephone installed in their home. But it served the purpose of calming the populace.

'Look, Mom, he's in his nightshirt!' a youngster crowed. Someone giggled.

McCurley turned to gaze up along the alley. I felt, rather than saw, him stiffen as his eyes caught on an open window at the far end of the alley. A woman bent out, looked toward us, waved, and cried, 'Mr McCurley, are you all right?'

In a heartbeat, he was moving. I followed, not sure I even should. But his look of panic had struck a chord in me.

'Step back from the window, Miss Hacker!' he shouted from afar.

'But…'

'For heaven's sake, woman! Step back from the window. I'm coming.'

The high-pitched cry of an infant rang through the night just as McCurley reached the door to the house. Third-floor window, I recalled.

'Is that your daughter?' Immediately, I realised it was the wrong thing to ask. I told myself to not look at the pavement where a body must have crashed down.

He froze, his face ashen.

'I will go up and see what she needs. You do your job.' I motioned toward the corpse.

His mask of icy detachment did not waver. If he considered my suggestion, he didn't show it.

'Do you want *me* to guard the man? So you can later accuse me of manipulating the evidence?'

Hesitating, he looked up at Ms Hacker who didn't seem sure what to do next, then back at me. Without a word, he turned and marched off as briskly as his injured foot allowed.

I huffed, then called up to the third floor, 'Ms Hacker, would you please open the door for me? I am with Inspector McCurley.'

After several long moments, she unlocked the house and beckoned me in, the screeching child in her arms.

We ascended the stairs, and all the while the little girl was hollering her heart out.

'Is she ill?'

'Leedin is all right. She's just hungry, is all. It's just that…I don't have enough milk.' She turned her head to hide her scowl.

'Are you the wet nurse?'

A stiff nod.

'Is that her name, Leedin?'

'It's Líadáin.' She spelt it for me as we crossed the second landing. 'It is Gaelic and means grief.'

We entered the apartment. It was darkness and chaos. Everything whispered the small girl's name: *Grief*.

The few pictures on the wall were hung with black cloth. A bouquet of wilting marguerites stood in a vase next to a photograph of a woman. She, too, was framed in black. But no cross, no rosary hung nearby or anywhere else in the room. Plates with bits of leftover food stood on a table. Dirty clothes clung to the backrests of all three chairs in view.

The air was sweltering with odours of soiled nappies.

'May I open the window again?' I asked.

'Go ahead if you want him to bite off your head.' She

tugged on the laces of her nightgown as she sat down. 'If you don't mind?'

'Please, take your time.' I sat a little away from her to give her space, but close enough to observe. 'Where is your own child?'

She thrust her chin toward a door.

'Your chamber? I see. A son or daughter?'

'My son Billy.'

I guessed that she wasn't married, and the child was illegitimate. She must have counted herself lucky to have been given this post. Or was there more to it?

'Is Billy your first child?'

'Yes.' She flinched as Líadáin latched on.

'McCurley is the father?'

'What! No! Did he say that?'

'I'm sorry. No, he said no such thing. He says rather little.' Quietly, I watched her breastfeed McCurley's daughter. A soft breeze played with the curtains. 'How old is Billy?'

'Three months.'

So McCurley must have employed a different wet nurse before he'd found Ms Hacker. Had the first wet nurse abandoned her post? I wiped the concern away and wondered how to best help Ms Hacker feed the two children. I thought about iceboxes to store cow's milk now that the days were getting warmer but discarded the idea. Large dairies notoriously produced milk of questionable quality. And few mothers would know how to properly sterilise it before feeding it to their infants. 'Is there a housekeeper?'

'Mrs Beamish.'

'Does she cook for you?'

Ms Hacker snorted.

'A maid?'

Both eyebrows shot up her forehead. 'Are these lodgings too dirty for Your Highness?'

Ah, so she knows how to fight back. Despite her youth. Good for her. 'I'm sorry. I don't mean to criticise you. I think you do too much and sleep too little. Maybe even eat too little.'

She didn't answer.

'I'm a physician,' I said softly. 'May I recommend a more comfortable position for breastfeeding?'

She was holding herself so stiffly, her back and arms must be sore.

'Are you in pain?' I asked.

'It's normal.'

'Believe me, it's not.'

MCCURLEY APPEARED ABOUT HALF an hour later. He looked around the flat and at the open window, an expression of utter alarm sliding into place. 'What happened?'

'They are sleeping.' I motioned to a chair. 'Sit. I need to talk to you and check your foot.'

He limped over to Ms Hacker's door, ripped it open, froze midway, and stepped back to close it softly. '*What* happened?'

'Sit down, and I will tell you.'

Pain flashed across his features as he sank into a chair. I doubted it was from his injury. With a wet flannel and a towel Ms Hacker had given me earlier, I got to work. Once the crust of blood and dirt was gone, it was obvious that McCurley's foot had looked worse than it really was.

'You stubbed it rather well. The small toe is fractured. And you'll lose this bit of skin here. It makes no sense to stitch it back on now that it's dried around the edges. You can cut it off with a pair of scissors in a day or two. But for now, wash the wound with soap before you go to bed. Wrap it in gauze. Keep it clean, and it will heal quickly.'

My gaze slid to the hem of his nightshirt. 'Bloody hell! Have you checked between your legs?'

He snatched at the hem and knocked his knees together as though I'd kicked him in the groin. Then he looked down. And found the frayed bullet hole I'd referred to.

'You were extraordinarily lucky. Two inches farther left or right, and he'd have hit your thigh.' I rolled back on my haunches to give McCurley more space. 'Now I'm glad that I shot him in the chest. A hole in his leg wouldn't have stopped that man from getting what he wanted.'

All blood drained from McCurley's cheeks. Cold sweat beaded on his temples. He clapped a hand over his face and groaned.

'You aren't bleeding. Chances are that everything is still attached.'

His eyes snapped open. For the first time, I noticed they were dark blue. He almost smiled then. Almost.

'I must ask you a question.' I stood and placed towel and flanell on the table. Then I turned to face him, arms akimbo. 'Are you taking advantage of Ms Hacker's predicament?'

He blinked. 'Excuse me?'

'You understood my question perfectly well.'

He clenched and unclenched his jaw. Swallowed. 'I understand your concern. What you are insinuating is disgustingly common, I know that much. And I commend you for your courage to ask. And no, I do not take advantage of Ms Hacker.'

I nodded once. 'I'm sure she's grateful for this post. But she is about to collapse. She cannot possibly cook and clean for you, breastfeed two small children, and stay awake constantly to care for you all. She's already lost two teeth from malnutrition. She can barely produce enough milk for the two babes. She looks frail, underfed, and she's not getting enough sleep. If you want to keep her, you'd do well to listen now.'

He leaned back, his expression open for once.

'Your housekeeper will provide warm meals three times a day. If Miss Hacker is sleeping, the housekeeper will let her sleep, and keep the food warm for her. And your housekeeper will find someone to do the washing. Have you any idea how much work the nappies alone are? No? I thought not. And your daughter is to sleep in Ms Hacker's room.'

'No.'

'Why ever not?'

McCurley swallowed, inhaled, and said hoarsely, 'It is the only time I have her.'

A clump formed in my throat. 'I…see. Does your daughter wake up often at night?'

'She's hungry. She needs to grow.' A defensive statement. It made me like him a little bit.

'How old is she?'

'Six months.'

So her mother must have killed herself only a few days after birth. I frowned. 'The girl looks small for her age. Has she always been smaller than other babies?' Upon his bristling, I added, 'I'm a physician and a mother. I know what I'm talking about. I'm trying to help, McCurley.'

He tilted his head a fraction, considering. 'She has always been small. But she should be…chubbier. I know that. I don't know what else to feed her. One doctor says babies should eat condensed milk with sugar, another says they should only be fed cow's milk with barley flour. It seems they can't even agree on such a small thing.'

'And they'll never agree on it, because they've never raised a child. And most likely never will. You are doing the right thing by employing a wet nurse.'

He huffed. 'But I can't afford two of them. Although…I could perhaps ask my bank for—'

'There's no need for a second wet nurse. A healthy woman can produce enough milk for two children. But she needs rest and good food to be able to do that. Can you afford to pay your housekeeper for the meals and the cleaning?'

'Yes. Of course, I can.'

'Good. Do that. And insist on her helping Ms Hacker. She's young, nearly a girl herself. And she's overwhelmed. I would be, too.'

'But I won't allow my daughter to sleep in her room. Not the whole night.'

'A compromise, then. When she's been fed, your daughter begins her nights in your room. Once she's hungry, you convey her to Ms Hacker's room. I don't care what the neighbours might think. Or the housekeeper. As long as Ms Hacker is comfortable with the arrangement, you bring your daughter to her, help her settle the child. Whether you then take her back to your own room, or leave her with Ms Hacker, is up to you and Ms Hacker. See that your girl gains enough weight.'

I held his gaze, watching his reaction, and added, 'You might wish to consider allowing your daughter to sleep with you in your bed. She will rest better, and your warmth will help her gain weight. Especially for colder nights.'

He nodded once. 'She's been sleeping there since…winter.'

I didn't know what to say to that. There was probably nothing useful I could have said anyway. To fill the void I asked, 'How do you pronounce her name?'

'Líadáin.' *Leothine*. The softness with which he spoke sent a pang through my chest. He looked down at his hands, and whispered, '*Beloved is the little voice which I hear, I do not dare to be happy about it. But what I say is merely: This little voice is beloved.*' He cleared his throat. Once. Twice. 'You probably don't know the verse.'

I didn't dare move. 'Who wrote it?'

Abruptly, he stood. 'Líadáin Uí Chorca Dhuibhne. Twelfth-century Irish poet. You will want to return to your home now. I thank you for your help. You'll find a police carriage in the street waiting to convey you.'

He limped to the door, opened it, and we said our goodbyes.

The truce was over.

11

*I*t hit me as soon as the police carriage had clattered away. Trembling, I grasped the gate and vomited into Margery's favourite rosebush.

I killed a man!

My vision was swimming. It mattered little that he'd been a convicted murderer. I had taken a life and violated all my values and beliefs. What made it worse was that there had been no hesitation. Not even a trace of it.

I'd had my gun out faster than I could think. And shot the man in the heart before… Was that before or after I realised he had his gun pointed at me?

It must have been after that, or was it? How could I ever be sure? It all happened so fast. Had I shot a man before being absolutely sure he was a threat? *Why* had I been so ready to take his life? How could I have been so coldblooded?

A new wave of revulsion and nausea hit. I spat and retched until I heard a faint creak from our front door.

My hand went to my side, feeling for the holster. A silhouette appeared in the shadows. And a familiar voice. 'What happened to you?'

'I killed a man.' The words were out before I could snap my mouth shut.

Zach stumbled to a halt on the walkway. 'The one you were looking for?'

I wiped my mouth and...cackled. I was going mad! I certainly was. And then I wept. Haltingly at first, but when Zach's arms came around me, the floodgates opened.

He patted my back, muttering, 'There, there,' and when I sat back to run my sleeve over my face he said, 'Let's have a drink,' and manoeuvred me toward the kitchen.

'Klara?' I managed to gulp out.

'Sleeping next to Margery. They are safe. We are safe.'

I nearly cackled again.

He sat me down on a chair, plopped two mugs on the table, and a bottle of rum.

'Any word from the cable office?' I asked.

'No.'

Disheartened, I sighed and moved to the sink to wash out my mouth.

I had dispatched an encrypted wire earlier that day. Even with the time difference between London and Boston, an answer should have arrived. 'When did you last check on Klara and Margery?'

'You asked that only two minutes ago,' he said softly and motioned me to sit with him again. 'I left them when I heard you retching.'

He lit a candle, placed it on the table, sat down, and folded his hands. Then he discovered the bruise on my face. 'What...'

And that was when we heard Klara wake up with a muffled cry. I jumped up, but Zach pressed me back on the chair, and said, 'I'll get her.'

A moment later, he returned with Klara wrapped in her

favourite wool blanket. Her face was nestled against the crook of his neck. She'd fallen back asleep in his arms.

I pulled back his chair and he lowered himself into it.

'I think she feels my fear. She grows up feeling unsafe.'

Zach scanned my face. 'I don't think so. She's brave, courageous. But there is so much going on in her head. Much more than in most adults. I think…' He paused and traced his index finger over the bridge of her nose. The gesture made my knees soft, and I was glad that I was already sitting. He smiled down at Klara and said, 'I'm afraid she'll be too much for this world.'

'What do you mean?'

'She'll probably want to sail across the ocean all by herself when she's twelve. And she'll know exactly how to do it. She'll have read all the books on the topic, talked to sailors, inspected ships, learned about navigation and the weather. And everyone will tell her she is foolish, that she doesn't have the skills to do it.'

I gulped. 'You are probably correct.'

My gaze was trapped by my daughter's fist wrapped around Zach's index finger. I couldn't stop my hand from reaching out and cupping his. 'There's so much beauty here. The contrast between your large hand and her small one. One soft and one calloused, one young and one…not so young,' I said and pulled away.

'One black and one white,' he added.

'Yes, that too is beautiful.' Why had I got the feeling I needed to defend myself? I rubbed my tired eyes, then tipped rum down my throat.

Zach huffed. 'Yes, some of you white people…' Abruptly, he broke off and shook his head. 'No, this has nothing to do with you. I'm sorry I said that.'

'What has nothing to do with me?'

He shook his head again. 'A memory. Dark one. Came back when you said you killed a man. What happened?'

My gaze trailed over the items on the table in front of him. A small bowl with bits of porridge — probably Klara's. A jug of cider with a saucer serving as a lid. A teapot. A crust of bread on a small plate. Klara must have had one of her midnight meals. She was growing so fast.

Zach picked up his mug and downed the rum. And with determination, he repeated his question, 'What happened to you?'

'I had an argument with a young man. He threw a baseball at me and…hit me on the head.'

'An argument.' Zachary's voice crackled with sarcasm.

'In a way.' I fell silent. Zachary began fidgeting with a seam of the tablecloth.

'Why don't you and Margery have children?' I asked. 'You would be a wonderful father.'

He looked up sharply, and I added, 'What I mean to say is that if the cause is physical I might be able to help. She's still of childbearing years.'

He grunted. I wasn't sure if a small laugh had not hidden in the gruff noise. He must have known that I needed time, that I couldn't talk about what happened so soon after. That I craved distraction.

But his expression grew severe, his jaw worked, and his eyes lost their warmth. I wasn't so sure anymore that I wanted the distraction he was about to offer.

He washed a hand over his face and the coldness dissipated. He even smiled a little. I drew in a breath I didn't know I was holding.

'When I was a boy,' he began, 'I believed the world was white. That everybody was white. *Everybody*. All the men of importance, men in power, men with money. All white. The master and the mistress. White. Only mother was…mother.

The colour of her skin was that of warmth, shelter, of an embrace when somebody hurt me. But one day... One day I saw my own reflection. Truly saw it. I saw myself in the mirror the way the white world saw me, how the men in power, the master and the mistress, and even their neighbours saw me.'

His voice was that of a storyteller, with the same softness that he used when he read to Klara. As though he spoke of someone who had lived hundreds of years ago in a far-away kingdom.

'The blackness wouldn't come off, no matter how hard I scrubbed. And then I looked at the men in power, the men with money and influence, and I knew that there was no place in that white world for me. That I would never amount to anything. A few years later I learned that we will always be slaves. *Always*. A girl from the neighbourhood turned thirteen, and a white man began pursuing her. Threatening her and her dad. The man was wealthy, had friends in high places. He sold pretty black girls to them. She begged me to take her away, to protect her. I swore I would.'

His gaze dropped to Klara. Her lids were soft with dreams. 'We didn't get far. The police caught us, locked us up. Didn't explain for what. When the sheriff let *that* man in, I knew I had failed her. It took me nearly two years to find Margery and steal her away. They'd taken out her uterus, so they wouldn't get her with child. Babies were a bother to them. Margery and I went from farm to farm, picking blueberries, oranges, strawberries. Lent a hand to whoever needed cheap workers. She asked me to promise her to never let a man touch her again. And so I kept protecting her in the only way I knew.' He looked up, and added softly, 'At first, our marriage was a ruse. But over the years, we learned to love each other. Our wedding was small, only four people.'

I rubbed the moisture off my cheeks, placed my hand on his shoulder, and croaked, 'I'm sorry.'

'It is her secret as much as it is mine.' There was a warning in his tone.

'Why are you trusting me with this now?'

'Because it is time for Margery to trust someone. Someone who isn't me. She and I talked about it, and she asked me to tell you. She said she wouldn't be able to…not without crying. And she doesn't want to cry. Not in front of anyone.'

He chewed on his words for a moment before he continued, 'You are keeping a lot of secrets and…I've suspected for a long time that you are running away from something. And that this something or someone has been frightening you very much in these past weeks. I'm afraid that Margery and I will lose what we have come to consider our…niece.' He dipped his chin toward Klara.

Somehow, I had the impression he'd wanted to say 'daughter.' I managed a small nod.

'We are hoping that you'll tell us before this *something* comes to our home, and that you won't run away without us.'

I was lost for words. My jaw felt loose on its hinges. My throat was as heavy as a rock.

'You wonder how I know.'

'It scares me. How could I have been so careless, so… obvious.'

'Margery and I have spent much of our lives on the run, but she didn't suspect anything until I told her you wanted me to spar with you.'

'There's a boxing club for women in London,' I blurted out. Klara twitched in her sleep.

'That might well be, but how many gardeners are asked by their mistress to punch her in the face twice a week?' He poured more rum into our mugs. 'How many gardeners are asked by their mistress to refurbish the basement so that the neighbours aren't disturbed by her target practice?'

I clapped my hands over my face. Nervous laughter bubbled up my throat.

'You might wish to reconsider the photographs, though.'

I looked up. 'What photographs?'

'There are none, and that is the problem. One would expect you to keep a likeness of your husband, at the very least. Of your parents and siblings. But there is not *one* photograph in this house.'

Dumbstruck, I sat back. 'You are...observant.'

'Staying alert protects Margery.'

'But you don't have to protect her anymore.'

'I believe I do.' His arms tightened a little around Klara. She stirred and pressed a fist to her mouth. 'Will you tell me what happened tonight?'

Softly, I brushed a lock of hair from my daughter's face. 'Yes.' And I told him everything. About Warren, McCurley, and pale-eyed Joey. And when I began to talk about Moran...

Zach held up a hand. 'Tell both of us tomorrow. This is too important to be done only half-conscious. You are about to drop off that chair, Liz.'

'I'll...sleep on the couch. My bed is occupied,' I said.

'Margery woke up when Klara did. She'll be back in her own bed now.'

Zach carried Klara into my bedroom. I was so wrung out, that I fell asleep the moment my arm curled around my daughter.

SUNRISE FOUND us in the kitchen. Cups of steaming tea, pancakes, bacon, and maple syrup were laid out. Zach and I were bleary-eyed, Margery was gruff and her hair dishevelled, and Klara was drawing faces into powdered sugar on her plate. We shared glances and heavy silence.

The doorbell nearly tipped me from my chair. I was at the door before Margery could even move. With the telegram, a New Testament, and a pencil and piece of paper in my hands I returned to the kitchen and sat back down.

Zach eyed the book. 'I didn't know you read that.'

'It's the key to a cypher.' For a book cypher to work, each party had to use the exact same edition. The one I was using was Rheims' New Testament, Pocket Edition, published by Burns and Oates in 1888.

It took only a few minutes to decipher the first line:

S tracked M to Perpignan two days ago.

My spine melted. I put my face in my hand as water began pooling in my eyes.

Zach patted my arm. 'Bad news?'

I shook my head. 'No, this is good news. Very good news.' I filled my lungs, and continued decrypting the message:

Tracking A.K. from continent to America impossible. But weakness in our plan now realised: E.A. has no past. Arrangements with British Consulate forthcoming.

'What?' I dashed the wetness from my cheeks, and accidentally brushed the tender and swollen spot over my eye. I flinched.

Margery stood and fetched ice from the icebox.

'It's not what I feared. But we should…' I looked at Klara who was still occupied with her sugar drawing. I didn't want her to hear what I needed to say. 'We should sit in the garden. The blackbird chicks must have hatched by now.' This caught her attention. 'But first, we eat and clean up. Then we watch birds.'

WHILE KLARA WAS intent on pretending to be a shrub to better watch the blackbird parents fly in and out of their nest, I quietly spoke to Zach and Margery, and told them everything. Well, nearly half of everything. Perhaps a quarter. 'Please understand that I trust you. But I'm aware that I might be terribly wrong in that assessment.'

Zach was about to protest.

'Let me finish, please. The problem is that people change. Situations change. I have to weigh that possibility — the very real danger to my daughter's life — against the advantage of having you both on my side. On her side.'

Zach's nostrils flared, 'We would never do anything to harm her!'

Briefly, I placed my hand on his. 'I know. But how many of your friends would you trust with your life? Or with the life of your wife?'

'No one.'

Odd, how hard and ready the answer fell from his lips.

'You see my dilemma. But...' I touched the goose egg on my forehead. 'I told someone last night. A very small, but essential bit that might be enough for him to...find out who I really am.' I watched them. How their gazes flattened, their shoulders stiffened. How mistrust slowly crept in. 'Very little of what you know about me is true. My name, my past, everything is a lie. I'm not a merchant's daughter. I was born in a small village in Germany. My mother died just after she gave birth to me. My father was a carpenter. He raised me alone. There were times when he didn't know what to feed me.'

Zachary's lids slid to half-mast, cautious, wary. Margery

went back to staring at the treetops. I had the feeling that she saw her own memories in the foliage.

'My father's best friend financed my stay at university. I studied medicine. That was back in Germany. Women are *still* not allowed to...' I twitched a shoulder. 'Anyway. I pretended I was a man.'

Margery turned, mouth agape.

Zachary blinked. 'And then?'

'I graduated, of course. And then Harvard Medical School awarded me a scholarship.'

They clapped their hands to their mouths. Margery didn't produce a peep. Zach chortled until he could hardly breathe. 'Harvard! You fooled those arrogant pricks!'

I grinned. 'They never guessed.'

'Look at her.' Zach nodded in Klara's direction. She stood on the lawn, holding up several leafy twigs to hide her face and chest. She took a very slow step toward the nest. 'She's been at it since we sat down here. One step forward every time one of the birds is in the nest.'

'She's nearly there.'

'Don't take her away,' he whispered with an urgency that wrenched at my heart.

'I don't want to. But there might come a time when I don't have a choice.'

'Promise that you'll talk to us.'

Klara took another step forward. Mother blackbird paused, cocked her head, and flew off without a warning cry.

'I promise.'

He squeezed my wrist. 'Thank you. Go on with your story now.'

And so I did. 'There were moments when the wish to tell the truth was...overpowering. Logic told me that it was ridiculous to believe the female of any species is worth less than the male. But I had to remind myself that I couldn't fight the beliefs of old men. That I can't eradicate stupidity with a snap of my fingers.' My gaze met Margery's. 'This must be so much worse for you.'

She turned away again, her chin set.

Zach reached out and touched her arm. 'What came after Harvard?'

'Ah, yes.' My gaze drifted over the grass to a faraway place. 'I went to London. Worked as a bacteriologist and was…good at it. The police consulted me from time to time. And one day, I…was pulled into a crime that… No, I can't say I was pulled into it. I pulled myself into it. I could have ignored the subtle signs, could have reported all my findings to the police. But I knew they wouldn't investigate it further. I met a man — a detective. From the moment he laid eyes on me, he knew I was a woman. It *terrified* me. We investigated the death of a man who appeared to have died of cholera, and yet…more. We found that a group of physicians had tested pathogenic germs on him and on many others. I infiltrated the group. Eventually, I met the man who controlled them, who financed their experiments. Or rather…I was abducted by him. He held me prisoner for half a year. Until I poisoned him.'

My hands were shaking. I curled them to fists in my lap. Cleared my throat, and braced myself. 'Klara is his daughter.'

Zachary sucked in a breath. Margery leaned against him, still staring ahead, unseeing. She appeared so…hollowed out. What was she seeing as she listened to my story?

'The detective and I learned that this man's plan was to use dangerous germs as weapons. We destroyed everything he had built, got all his men arrested. Except one of them: Colonel Sebastian Moran. The one on the photograph.'

Zach opened his mouth, but I held up my right hand. 'He did this. He cut off my finger, and…' I told my lungs to stop pumping so fast. One breath in. One breath out.

There. 'And on the day Klara was born, he almost killed us both.'

I touched a hand to my shoulder. 'Clean shot. Merely half an inch from a major blood vessel, and close to Klara's head.' Just thinking of it made my stomach roil and my fists curl. *Talking* about it was…unbearable.

Stoically, Zachary nodded and caressed Margery's arm.

'The detective I told you about is hot on Moran's heels. He spotted him only two days ago in France.'

'Does he have a name? This detective?'

'I can't give you his name. It's not my secret to share and of no importance. What you need to know is the name and the face of Moran, and that he used a silent air rifle when he was hunting me. And that…' I cleared my throat. 'He swore to find us when Klara turns three.'

Margery jerked away from Zach and looked straight at me. 'That is very soon.'

'Yes.'

'What is your real name?' Zach asked.

'It is of no importance.' My voice came with a honed edge.

He dipped his chin. 'I understand, but I'd like to know it anyway.'

I touched my lips. It hadn't spoken my own name for a very long time. I wondered how it would feel… 'Anna.'

Briefly, Zach smiled. 'Thank you.'

I nodded.

'Do you think he can find you? And why did you think it's him who threatened you? Or…whatever you discovered that terrified you.'

'A man of the…British government wrote that Moran can't find us. I believe him. Our plan was intricate, carefully laid out. But someone else — the man I confronted tonight — did a foolish thing. He drew my portrait, and it got into the hands of a murderer. I keep thinking that he has a connection to Moran. It's unlikely, but this feels so much like what Moran would do. This show of power.'

Zach looked puzzled.

I added, 'The police found a photograph of that portrait — my portrait — on the body of Mrs Hughes.'

'The new patient?' Margery asked with a squeak in her voice.

'Yes. It was in the papers yesterday. My portrait on her body is…' I shook my head. 'I was so certain that it *must* have been him. Moran. He revels in the terror of his prey.'

'He's not the only one.'

Shocked, I looked up. The words had come from Margery's mouth but hadn't sounded like her at all. Never before had I heard her speak with so much hate.

THE THIRD VICTIM

CASE NOTES, JUNE 30, 1893

Notes on Dr Elizabeth Arlington, Friday, June 30, 1893
Quinn McCurley, Bureau of Criminal Investigation

*R*egistered as Elizabeth Arlington, nee Bowles, of 21 Savin Hill Avenue. Born September 1862. Claims to have moved to Zurich at age of 13 or 14 (1875/76), and studied medicine there (until 1884/86?).

WIRED overseas to confirm Arlington's statement. Replies as follows:

Zurich University: No alumni (medical or otherwise) registered under E. Bowles.

Zurich Police Headquarters: One Elizabeth Edwards, nee Bowles registered, born 1843 in Wales, lived in Zurich between 1861 until her death in 1870.

12

*H*attie spilt tea onto her fine morning dress. She placed the cup back onto the saucer, and flicked at the droplets with nervous fingers. 'I don't understand. How is this even possible? Are you sure the portrait was one of Warren's?' Again, she scanned my bruised eye. And again, she frowned at it.

'In the portrait found on the body, my face was drawn in great detail. Warren put effort into my eyes and mouth. My hair was mere outlines, a few shadows here and there. One ear was only hinted at, the other hidden by my face. I looked directly at the viewer.' I threw a glance at Warren, who had the courtesy to drop his gaze. 'I looked as though I wanted to start an argument. Or throw things around.'

Hattie muffled a cry. Warren coughed into his elbow bend.

'That night...' Hattie began, wringing her hands. 'When Warren wasn't looking, I slipped it in my purse. But I didn't give it to anyone! I swear, Liz. I would never—'

'You *stole* my sketchbook?' her brother asked. 'Why would you do that?'

'I didn't want to destroy the portraits with everyone around.'

'So you took the sketchbook home with you.' I forced calmness into my voice. She'd said *portraits*. Plural.

She bobbed her head, stood, and rang the bell.

A maid arrived and dipped her knees.

'Angie, would you fetch my purse, please.'

We waited in strained silence. Hattie sipping her tea and eyeing her brother. I sat picking my nails under the table. Warren stared at the curtains.

The maid arrived a few moments later, delivered the requested item, and was sent away again.

Hattie pulled a brownish booklet from her purse and placed it in front of her. 'See. It's here. It couldn't have been any of Warren's portraits.'

My heart skipped a beat. I made to grab the sketchbook, but Warren was faster. He leafed through it and declared, 'They are gone.'

Hattie dropped her teacup. It tumbled off the edge of the table and clonked onto the thick carpet. 'I think I'm going to be sick.'

I searched first her face and then Warren's, trying to figure out who was lying. But both seemed equally stricken. 'Tell me precisely what occurred that night. I need to know every detail. No matter how unimportant you think it is.'

And so they talked. Warren began, and Hattie supplemented. Most of the details of that night I knew already. It had been one of the casual meetings of the Freaks. The group met at the rehearsal, then ate and drank at Warren's townhouse. When Warren needed the lavatory some time later that night and the others were deeply immersed in talk about investment options, Hattie had slipped the sketchbook into her purse.

No one had seen what she did.

They had left Warren's around eleven o'clock that night, and…

'You went home directly?' I asked her.

'Yes. No! I…briefly went over to our parents to pick up something.'

'What did you pick up?'

'A list. A guest list for the ball.'

Warren groaned. I told him to shut up, and turned back to Hattie, 'Did you have your purse with you at *all* times?'

'Well…' Her gaze drifted out of focus. She squinted and centred herself with a deep breath. 'I had it in my hand when the butler admitted me.'

'You didn't have your key?' Warren asked.

'I forgot it. And then…' Her eyebrows bunched together. 'I left the purse in the hall and went to see Mother, who had retired early. We talked for a few minutes. Then she gave me the guest list, and I left.'

'With your purse,' I supplied.

'Of course.' She cocked her head. Something seemed to dawn on her. 'Oh, actually…'

'What?' Warren shot at her.

'Shut up, Warren. Let her think.' I punched his arm, lightly, but enough to remind him that I could do more harm if necessary. He cut me a sideways glance and huffed.

'I forgot my purse,' Hattie said, eyes large. 'I left it in the hall and only noticed that I'd forgotten it when I got home. There was nothing I'd need right away, and nothing valuable in it, so I didn't go back. I asked one of the footmen to fetch it for me the next morning — I mean, today — and then I went to bed.' She looked up sharply. 'But he wouldn't have ripped out the pages. None of our footmen would ever dig through my things and…and *steal* from me!'

'So you—'

I held up my hand. 'Warren, if you keep interrupting, I will kick you out.'

'This is my house,' Hattie protested. And then to her brother, 'If anyone kicks you out, it'll be *me*. And I *will* if you don't keep your mouth shut.'

He held up his hands in mute surrender.

'So you noticed your purse was missing when you arrived home last night, and you immediately told a footman to fetch it for you the next morning?'

'Yes. The footmen are all up early. Four or five in the morning. He would have gone to my parents and told one the maids that he'd been sent to fetch my purse.' Nervously, Hattie was rolling the hem of the tablecloth into a long sausage.

'Who would have had the opportunity to take pages out of the sketchbook?' I asked Hattie.

'I don't believe any of the servants—'

'I'm not asking who *might* have taken them. I want to know who was in your home or your parents' house that night. Your father and your mother. All the servants. Guests?'

Hattie's eyes grew larger. She flicked a glance at Warren, who for once was helpful enough to nod encouragement at her.

'I think…' she said tentatively, 'I'd better write them all down for you.'

'I will.' Warren pulled out another sketchbook and sat at attention.

'How many portraits?' I asked to start.

Warren cleared his throat and mumbled, 'Two.'

'Only of me, or of me and my daughter?'

'Only you.'

At least I had that. 'The list, Hattie,' I reminded her.

And so Hattie began. 'Mother and Father, and all of their servants. And the guests. Father entertained the Lords

Wray.' She waited until Warren had written down all the names. Eighteen servants at the Amaury mansion. The master, the mistress, and the three Wray brothers. Then, Hattie, her husband, their children, and another twelve servants.

'Oh!' Hattie squeaked and touched her lips. 'Mother said deliveries were to be sorted out early the next morning. That would be…nearly a dozen men who must have been in the scullery or the kitchens receiving instructions on what was needed for the ball. I'll have to ask the names.'

Overwhelmed, I sank against the backrest of my chair. 'This is…much more than I expected.' How could I ever find out who, of all those people, had taken my portraits?

'I'll interrogate every single one of them!' Hattie slapped the edge of the table, her chin set, and eyes brimming with resolution. The roll of tablecloth she'd bunched together unfurled and dropped down onto her knees.

I shook my head. 'You won't say a word.'

'What?'

'I will question them,' I said.

'Impossible,' Warren interrupted. 'This is the aristocracy you're dealing with. You can't walk into our homes and ask questions. Not even the police would dare such a thing. Not on mere suspicion. The rules are different where we are concerned.'

We fell silent and stared at our teacups until Hattie said, 'I have an idea.'

Beaming, she looked from Warren to me. 'You are my physician, Liz. You walk in and out of my house whenever I want you to. And you will attend the ball, so you can talk to the Wray brothers. Officially, you are keeping an eye on me. And…' She tapped on the list in front of me. 'The deliveries will be made the evening before the ball. So, this is when you come to "examine" me, to make sure I'm fit for dancing the next day. I will show you around. That's what friends do, isn't it?' She winked with both her eyes.

'Isn't that a bit too late?' Warren said.

'What?'

'The ball is in a month. Do you want to wait a month to catch a killer?'

'Of course not. I'll talk to the servants and collect information when I *examine* Hattie. I'd planned on doing that frequently now anyway.'

'Father won't be happy about you attending the ball.' Warren looked from me to his sister, his brows knitted together. 'This will all take some convincing. Difficult, but it should be possible.'

'I'll talk to Father,' Hattie said to Warren. 'He can't but agree to my precautions.' And then to me, 'It would help if you could show a pedigree.'

I clapped my hand to my mouth and wheezed a laugh. Hattie joined in. Only Warren looked forlorn.

'And when would our first appointment be, Dr Arlington?'

'This afternoon or tomorrow morning.'

She chewed on her lip, then nodded. 'All right. Let's do it tomorrow morning. I'll send my coach to pick you up. Or do you want a new bicycle?'

CASE NOTES, JULY 5, 1893

**Notes on Dr Elizabeth Arlington, Wednesday, July 5, 1893
Quinn McCurley, Bureau of Criminal Investigation**

*W*ired overseas to find traces of Arlington for the years 1880 to the present. Replies as follows:

Berlin Police Headquarters: No person registered under either name as Berlin resident in the indicated time period.

Berlin University: Women are not permitted to study or practice medicine.

Scotland Yard, London: No person by the name of Elizabeth Arlington or Elizabeth Bowles, born September 1862, was registered as a resident of London or the surrounding area in the specified period of time.

Who ~~the bloody hell~~ is this woman?

13

*A*fter breakfast I took Zach aside. 'Find an apartment at the other end.' I nodded in the general direction of the shore, where our tunnel ended under a boathouse. 'I would like for us to spend the nights in a safe place. Just in case.'

Zachary didn't even look surprised. He slowly nodded, his mouth compressed. 'Makes for a sounder sleep if we don't have to worry about you being strangled and dumped on some railroad tracks.'

My shoulders sagged. 'I'm so sorry this is happening.'

'It's not your fault.'

'Will you see to it, while I visit Hattie?'

'Yes, of course, I will. How big or small do you want it? The apartment?'

'It's just for the nights. It only needs to fit the four of us comfortably.'

He nodded. A deep frown carved his forehead as if already considering the size and number of rooms we'd need.

'And Zach?'

'Hmm?'

'It doesn't matter if the rent is outrageous. Don't worry about money. Just make it happen.'

'Does this feel uncomfortable?' I observed Hattie's face as I palpated her lower abdomen.

'No. Should it?'

I smiled and shook my head. 'You'll be my eyes and ears from now on.'

'You mean I'm to help you catch a killer?'

'No, for this. For your baby.' I nodded at her belly. 'Your uterus feels soft now. But I want you to examine yourself every day. Give me your hands now.'

I showed her the location of her uterus, and how to gently examine it. 'When it contracts it gets round and smooth, and hard, like a polished rock. Should you feel your uterus contracting more often than every half hour, or if you feel pain, or start bleeding, I'd like you to call for me immediately.'

'Is it dangerous? Will I lose my baby again?'

'No. Nothing points to an unusual pregnancy.' I pulled down her chemise and patted her hand. 'Sit up. I'll help you dress.'

Hattie was silent as I buttoned the back of her morning dress. Then she turned and looked at me with a profound sadness. 'Do you think I did something wrong? That I made myself have miscarriages?'

'What? No! Who would suggest such a horrid thing?'

She picked at the frills of her sleeve. 'It's just what I think sometimes.'

I thought back to the women I had tended, back when I'd lived in St Giles. Women who gave birth in filthy, over-crowded rooms. In stairwells or in the streets. Miscarriages were considered an everyday occurrence, a solution to a problem, even.

'Hattie,' I said softly. 'Nature has a way of knowing if a child cannot survive outside the womb. If the embryo or foetus is not perfect, your body will reject it.'

'Do you think it's Robert's fault?'

'I don't think it's anybody's fault. Miscarriages are common. But healthy babies are much more common.'

The corners of her mouth twitched. I took her hand in mine. 'Is he kind to you?'

Her expression hardened. 'Robert? Of course he is.'

'You can always come to me. If you need anything. You and your daughters.'

She jerked back as though I'd punched her. 'He is my husband, not a monster!'

I nodded once. 'Why don't you collect data for me? Write down what you have eaten, how you've slept, your physical activities — including intercourse — and compare that to the instances you felt your uterus harden.'

'Inter…intercourse? You want me to…' Her cheeks acquired an intense shade of strawberry red.

'You will notice that your uterus hardens tremendously when you climax.'

'Elizabeth Arlington!' She boxed my shoulder, and then all humour fled from her face. 'You mean to say that…relations with my husband are bad for the child?'

'No. They aren't. On the contrary. They are good preparation for a smooth birth.' I winked, and she tut-tutted me.

'And no tight lacing,' I reminded her.

Hattie rolled her eyes.

WE WENT DOWN to the kitchens and I made a point of enquiring about Hattie's diet, her eating habits, and remarked how food might affect her health. We were a picture of concerned mother hens. We chattered away as we picked through the contents of the biggest icebox I'd ever seen, and — as planned — Hattie steered the topic to the purse she'd forgotten at her parents'. And that her diary had been in it. And how stupid it was of her to have kept it in her purse, and not in her nightstand.

I nodded solemnly, and blurted, 'Why don't you ask them if the footman who fetched your purse for you... What was his name? Towers? Why don't you ask them if he talked about reading it?' My arm motioned at all the servants in the kitchen.

Hattie screeched, scolded me for my horrible working class mouth — one not befitting a friend of an Amaury or a Heathcote — then tossed her head and stomped from the kitchens.

I put on a mask of pain and surprise. After much huffing and puffing, I asked the servants if my suggestion had really been so horrible. They all agreed with Hattie. Throwing around accusations was not kind at all, and in this household, it was definitely *not* tolerated.

I apologised profusely and explained that all I'd wanted was to help Hattie. Because she was terrified of yet another miscarriage. Her anxiety about someone having read her diary was just making everything worse. And her worries weren't entirely unfounded because two pages of the diary were missing.

In a heartbeat, the servants went from affronted to concerned. The scullery maid muttered to the kitchen maid. The cooks added their opinions to the matter, but none had any clue who might have stolen two pages from the Mistress's diary. The footman was trustworthy, everyone said. He had been in employ for years and never done anything uncouth. He hadn't even raised his voice toward the clumsy boot-boy. Not once.

But they would find the culprit, surely they would!

I had to tamper down their enthusiasm, pointing out that wild rumours would only weaken Hattie's delicate constitution. But perhaps they could be very…discreet?

I LEFT the kitchens to find Hattie in the breakfast room. She was sitting on a chaise longue, sipping tea. I gave her a small nod. She stood and said loudly, 'I'm glad you are done chatting with the servants. You must have *entirely* forgotten that you wanted me to show you the stables.'

The maid who was placing a silver bowl with biscuits on the table paused and frowned at me.

Hattie had no acting skills whatsoever.

'I can't allow you to go horseback riding until your child is born,' I said.

'Silly thing! These horses pull carriages. We don't keep our riding horses here.' She strode up to me, grabbed my arm, and pulled me along. 'And?' she pressed through the side of her mouth.

I muffled a snort. 'We have acquired a gaggle of amateur detectives. They will talk to the rest of your servants, and to your parents' servants. They'll make a list of everyone who was in the Amaury mansion while your purse was there. And they have promised to be discreet.'

We reached the stables and climbed the stairs to the footmen's quarters. Mr Towers was sitting at a small table, drinking ale with another man. They looked embarrassed when we found them idle. They jumped from their stools, unsure where to put their hands, their hats, or what to say in their defence.

Hattie sent the other man away and came straight to the

point. 'Mr Towers, you kindly fetched my purse yesterday morning… Oh, I am sorry. My manners! This is Dr Arlington, she is my friend and personal physician.'

Towers held out his hand to me, and said, 'Ma'am—'

'Anyway,' Hattie chattered on. 'There was a small notebook in my purse and it's missing a few pages. Do you, by any chance, know who might have taken them?'

Towers seemed hit by a sudden bout of exhaustion.

'I am not insinuating that you took them,' she continued before he could even open his mouth. 'But there were an awful lot of people at my parents' house that morning and perhaps someone…'

I cleared my throat. 'Hattie, would you give me a minute with Mr Towers?'

Her spine snapped straight, she muttered, 'Of course,' and turned on her heel.

Mr Towers's eyes followed her until the door shut.

'My apologies. She's very worried,' I said.

He sank back on the stool. 'I didn't do it.'

'I believe you,' I lied to put him at ease. 'But we have to find the person who did it. And you can help me.'

He sat erect. 'I can?'

'At what time did you pick up the purse?'

As he scratched his chin, his gaze flitted from my face to the door and back again. 'Half past seven.'

'That was the time you left the house?'

'Yes. And I went directly to the Amaury mansion.'

'Who admitted you?'

Towers's Adam's apple bobbed. He avoided my gaze. 'The maid.'

'Which maid?'

'The kitchen maid, Miss Brophy. They…know me there because I often run errands for Mr and Mrs Heathcote.'

'You entered through the gates, I assume.'

He nodded.

'Who did you see on the way to the…' I waved my hand for him to continue.

'Kitchens. I entered the kitchens through the back of the house. The servants' entrance. Said hello to Peck and Howe… the coachmen, then knocked at the door and went in.'

'So you first went up into the coachmen's quarters?'

'No! They were standing outside, watching the boys muck the stables.' Mr Towers picked nervously on a hangnail.

'Who else was there?'

'Just Peck, Howe, and the boys. Uhm…Billo and Alfie. I said hello, then knocked at the backdoor, and went in.'

'It was Miss Brophy who admitted you?'

'Yes, ma'am.' He bobbed his head, suddenly eager to please. Too eager to distract from the slight blush that stained his ears.

'What else did Miss Brophy do?' My words had the effect of a cocked revolver.

'Nothing! She admitted me and went on with her…work.'

I said nothing and waited.

'I swear! It was nothing. Only a peck on the cheek.'

I nodded once, pulled the list of names Hattie and Warren had given me from my pocket, and flattened it face down on my lap. 'I need the names and location of every person you saw that morning.'

Towers's gaze dropped to the piece of paper. Curiosity on what might be written on the other side seemed to burn under his skin. He cleared his throat. 'Peck, Howe, Billo and Alfie by the stables. Miss Brophy in the kitchens, together with Miss Trattles and Miss Sowerby.'

'The cooks?'

'No, kitchen maids. The cooks were talking to delivery men. About meat, vegetables, fruits…' He shrugged.

'The names, please.'

'Don't know the cooks' names. Never asked. They are new. But O'Toole was there. He delivers meat to the Amauries and the Heathcotes, and...' Towers scratched his chin and narrowed his eyes. 'McCaffrey is his name, yes. He delivers vegetables and French potatoes and the like to the Amauries. And the man with the oranges and pineapples was...' Towers eyes got stuck at the ceiling beams for a few moments, then he said sheepishly, 'I can never remember if his name is Cow or Crow.' He shrugged again.

'Who else was in the kitchen?'

He rattled down a handful of names of scullery maids and delivery men, then went on to describe how he went to see the butler, Mr Grimshaw, to enquire after Hattie's purse. 'I had to wait for half an hour.' Towers puffed up his cheeks.

'Mr Grimshaw was busy?'

'He was giving instructions on bouquets and garlands to the flower grower.'

I felt a prickling rush down my back. 'What was the man's name?'

'Why, Mr Stone, of course.'

14

The possibility that Hattie or Warren — or perhaps both — were lying to me, that they'd had a hand in the murders, horrified me. Towers's statement about Mr Stone having been in the house when the portraits went missing came as a relief. A face I knew. A friendship I did not need.

But I knew these emotions for what they were: a dangerous, foolish bias. I allowed myself the luxury of wallowing in the false feeling of safety until Hattie's coach turned into Savin Hill Avenue. And when I alighted and shut the door to the carriage, I shut away that bias.

Because everything was possible.

Warren could be the killer.

And so could Hattie.

As soon as I rumbled into the kitchen, Margery pointed a knife at two messages on the table.

I'M PLANNING to ask a private detective to help you solve the case. I'll call on you later this afternoon to tell you more about the man.

Warren.

WHAT A STUPID IDEA. But perhaps he could tell me more about McCurley? Whether the Inspector desperately needed to solve the next great murder to keep his post at the Bureau of Criminal Investigation. And if he might be a man who manipulated evidence.

Or would go even further than that.

'Speaking of the devil,' I muttered as I read the second message.

Ms Hacker is feverish and in pain. She is unable to breastfeed the children and insists that your recommendations as to her eating and sleeping habits are to blame. Please come as soon as you can.

Quinn McCurley

'SHE IS IN HER ROOM,' McCurley said and stepped away from the door. His daughter was bawling in his arms.

'Your note read that she blames me for her illness. I'm puzzled, to say the least.' I set down my bag, pulled off my dribbling Mackintosh, and looked for a hook to hang it.

More wailing cut through the thin walls. Ms Hacker's boy was as unhappy as was Líadáin.

'You'll have to ask her. Give me your raincoat. I'll hang it for you.'

I picked up my bag, and he walked me over to Ms Hacker's chamber, knocked, and opened the door without waiting for her response.

I entered, and the screaming intensified. McCurley retreated and shut the door. Rain hammered against the window of the small room. Ms Hacker was abed, a blanket wrapped tightly around her. In a crib next to her, her boy was waving his tiny fists, hollering himself blue in the face.

'Ms Hacker?'

She clapped her eyes open and focused on me. 'It's all your fault.'

I sat on the edge of the bed. 'What is my fault?'

'Well…this!' She pulled down the blanket. Her engorged breasts were straining against the fabric of the nightgown, blue veins crisscrossing her pale skin.

I rubbed my hands together to warm them up, then touched her forehead. I pulled a thermometer from my bag and stuck it into her mouth. 'When did the fever start?'

'Yesterday,' she spoke around the instrument. 'We did everything you told us. Mrs Beamish cooks for us. A woman does the washing. I'm eating and sleeping more, and the babes were happy because I had more milk. And then…it wouldn't *stop*. It just got to be more and more. I was *leaking* for Heaven's sake. But then…nothing. No milk. Not a drop. But my breasts…got like *this*.'

The screaming in the sitting room paused briefly. I heard McCurley speaking to his daughter in a calm, low voice.

'All right. Open your nightgown, please.' I clamped my hands under my armpits to further warm them before examining her. Her breasts were rock hard. Her temperature was one hundred and three degrees. Too high already. 'I'll be back in a moment.'

I entered the sitting room where McCurley was walking in circles, rocking his daughter who went from hiccupping to hollering the moment she saw me. 'Where can I get hot water and a towel?'

He stopped. 'You need to perform a surgery? Here?'

'Of course not. I need to get the milk flowing. Keep Líadáin ready. I'll also need several pillows.' He pointed me to his bedroom where I fetched the pillows, and then to a corner by the door where I found a sink and a small cooktop. Tea was steeping in a pot. 'That'll do.'

I brought the pillows to Ms Hacker, and then returned for towel, teapot, and a bowl.

I helped her sit up and pull the nightgown down to her hips. I cushioned her back with a pillow and arranged two more under her arms, another on her lap, while the towel soaked in the hot tea. I wrung it out and made sure it wouldn't burn Ms Hacker's skin. Then I placed it over her breasts. Every minute or so, I would dip the towel into the hot tea, and place it back onto her breasts. 'Can you feel it already?'

She grunted. 'I think I'll pop.' She peeked under the warm towel, where milk was trickling from her nipples.

'Excellent.' I picked up her screeching son and tucked him under her left arm, his legs curled up against her side. 'Put your hand on the back of his head and hold him like a…'

'Football?'

'Yes.'

We shared a laugh.

When I went to the sitting room to fetch Líadáin, McCurley seemed reluctant to hand her over. I had no time for that foolishness but left the door to Ms Hacker's room open for him. I didn't know what arrangement the two had, but I wouldn't lock him out as long as Ms Hacker did not insist upon it.

I positioned Líadáin opposite Billy. The girl had screamed herself into such a fit that she refused to suckle. I grabbed a nipple, squirted milk into her mouth, and quickly squished her face against Ms Hacker's breast. One last protest, and she began to suckle greedily.

Ms Hacker hissed in pain, but then she relaxed. 'I feel like a sow.'

'Is it all right to come in?' McCurley asked.

I looked enquiringly at Ms Hacker. She only shrugged.

'One moment,' I said, warmed up the towel once more and placed it back over her breasts, more or less covering everything the two babies weren't hiding from view.

McCurley stopped near the door. 'Do you need anything else?'

'No,' I said. 'You'll want to be in your office.'

'I have a day off.' He neither retreated nor moved farther into the room.

Trapped by social conventions, he couldn't even see his own daughter, because she was attached to the breast of a woman he wasn't married to. In a way, I understood that other people found such notions necessary, but I had no patience for it.

'May he come closer?' I whispered to Ms Hacker. Again, she only shrugged.

I waved him to a chair nearby. He sat, then stood back up, and moved the chair to the other side of the bed so he could look at Líadáin without staring at too much of Ms Hacker's exposed flesh. His gaze was soft. It nearly shocked me into silence.

'It was a good thing you called for me,' I said, briefly wondering if I should tell them that this could have developed into mastitis had they waited but a few hours longer.

But I decided against it. 'What occurred is that the mammary glands learned to produce a greater amount of milk. But too much pressure built up, preventing the milk from coming down. The breasts engorged and got feverish.'

I kept my eyes on Ms Hacker, watching for signs of embarrassment. But she answered each of my statements with a small nod. So I continued, 'It is all perfectly normal.

Every time one of the children has a growth spurt, it will need more milk and suckle more vigorously. The mammary glands will react by producing the extra milk, and then it might happen again that the milk won't come down and you'll get feverish.'

She frowned.

I brushed her hand that rested on her son's head. 'Don't worry. You know what to do now.'

'Tea and towels?'

'Hot water is enough. I only used the tea because it was already hot. As soon as you feel that your breasts are too full, try to get one or both children to drink. They don't need to empty your breasts. Relieving the pressure is what's important.'

She nodded, and smiled at the small pile of nursing babies. 'This is comfortable.'

'Any position that's comfortable for all three of you is good. You can be half asleep feeding them, they won't care. The more relaxed you are, the better. My daughter and I fall asleep that way. Breastfeeding.'

'How old is she?'

'In September she'll turn…three.' I croaked the last word, and only then did I recall McCurley's silent presence. He had his eyes on Líadáin, but something told me he hadn't missed a word. Or how it had been spoken.

'I will leave you now. Call for me should you need me.' I snapped my bag shut and stood.

'A word, if you please,' McCurley said.

Once in the sitting room, he closed the door to Ms Hacker's room, and pushed his hands in his pockets. He looked at me, waiting for…what precisely?

'Yes?'

'Your fee.'

'Oh. She paid me already.'

He regarded me from head to toe, nodded once, and said. 'You are lying.'

It was a slap to the face. All the pent-up frustration of the past days boiled up. 'You arrogant ass. I didn't come for *you*. I came for her and the children. Seeing Ms Hacker and the babies happy is all the payment I need today.'

'I wasn't referring to your fees,' he said softly. There was no coldness, no professional mask in place. At least, I couldn't see one. I found this new version of him terrifying.

'I don't have time for your games.' I made for my Mackintosh.

'You lied about your name. And about countless other things.'

I froze.

'The problem is... I can't do anything about it. Why would the Chief Superintendent march into my office, *lock* it from the inside, and order me to stop investigating your past?'

'I couldn't imagine,' I croaked.

'I did not mention to anyone that I was searching for you. Or rather, for traces you might have left in Zurich, Berlin, and London. The Chief Superintendent would not tell me why he wanted me to stop digging, but he hinted at diplomatic relations with the Crown. Would you care to explain this to me?'

The Crown? Mycroft must have outdone himself. Or whatever forger he'd employed. And that was twice now. Twice he'd saved my sorry behind. And one day he would demand I pay him back.

Foreboding clogged my throat. I swallowed. 'Even if I wanted to explain this to you, I simply cannot.'

'You understand I have a murderer to catch. So far, I see only two possibilities. One, you know the perpetrator and are protecting him. Two, you know him but you have no idea that he is the killer. Either way, you have the information I need. The Chief Superintendent said nothing about *not* pursuing you for a crime you may have committed on American soil. And I greatly doubt he would dare insinuate such a thing.'

'I have not committed a crime.' It sounded lame coming from my mouth. Of course, I'd committed a crime! Several, even. Back in London.

'In fact, you have.'

'Excuse me?'

McCurley smiled. 'In England, it might be normal procedure to allow any and all village physicians to perform a post-mortem examination whenever they stumble across a body by the roadside. But here, things are handled differently. Post-mortem surgeons are important officers, appointed to make all the medico-legal examinations for the city of Boston. They are medical witnesses for the state. In conducting a post-mortem examination of Mrs Hyde's body without authorisation and qualification, you violated the law.'

'I am qualified.'

He shook his head. 'No one appointed you.'

'So? I didn't even perform a *full* post-mortem! And why are you telling me this now? Why did no one arrest me after I committed this…' I threw out an arm. 'This *trifle?*'

'Because only the appointed postmortem surgeon and the detective leading the case are permitted to file a complaint. Professor Goodman was pleased enough that you measured the temperature of head and torso more than an hour before Mrs Hyde's body was transferred to him. Thanks to you, the time of death was more accurately determined than the professor could have hoped for. He, however, is only *one* of the two men who could get you behind bars.'

We stared at one another, neither willing to budge.

'Who are you, Dr Arlington?'

'Go to hell, McCurley.'

'I'm sure I will. But not just yet. I analysed all the information at hand and came to the conclusion that you do indeed possess considerable medical knowledge. I don't know where or even *if* you studied medicine. But you do wish to help. You *care*. Or seem to. It's what collides so substantially with what I know about people who plot and execute a murder. People who do it not to protect themselves or others, but because they crave power over another's life.'

I said nothing.

'However, knowing that you had no problem shooting a perfect stranger in the heart — having seen your cold-bloodedness with my own eyes — I can't help but wonder how many layers of pretence you are wearing. How many lies you've spun.'

Countless and many more. 'You don't know me at all.'

He narrowed his eyes. 'Enlighten me, then.'

'Sod off.' I turned and pulled my Macintosh off the peg by the door.

Before I could turn the doorknob, he said, 'I know that something terrifies you. I saw it when you snatched your daughter away the day we collected evidence at your practice. I heard it just now as you mentioned her. I promise I won't put her in danger. If you wish, I can offer protection. My instincts tell me that you want to catch the murderer as much as I do. But my instincts also tell me that something is *very* wrong. If you answer my questions truthfully…'

I shook my head and pulled open the door.

'…I will share my case notes with you.'

15

I was still seething when I pushed open the gate to our front yard. But when Klara came bounding down the walkway, holding out a wilted dandelion, the anger peeled off me.

'Is that for me?'

Mischief glinted in her eyes. She nodded once, grinned, then shook her head and stuffed the flower into her mouth. Giggling, she ran back into the house.

I followed her inside but then stopped to check the time. Nearly noon. Only two hours left to prepare my lecture on the epidemiology of typhus. I found a chair and put my face in my hands, wondering if I should quit my post at the medical school for women. The effort seemed futile. So many of my students gave up their studies. Most of them were disciplined, talented, and intelligent enough to become physicians. But as soon as some Billy or Tommy asked for their hand, they threw it all away.

I was wasting my time.

WHEN I RETURNED from medical school late that afternoon, Margery informed me that that a gentleman was waiting for me in the sitting room. 'Name is Amaury. Handsome young man. Brought flowers.' She said it as if bouquets were routinely used to bludgeon people to death.

'Where's Klara?'

Margery pointed under the kitchen table, before retreating and bumping her hip against the doorframe in the process.

I bent down and lifted the tablecloth. Klara was surrounded by paper and pens. She had completed a drawing of Zachary's straw hat atop his broadly smiling face, and was working on another with herself and me sitting under a tree and reading a book. She looked up at me and pointed at her newest creation.

'Good idea,' I said. 'But I must say hello to Warren first. Would you like to come?'

Her dark curls slid over her eyes as she went back to drawing.

'All right then. I'll be back soon.'

As I left the kitchen, I heard her scramble from her hiding spot and follow in my wake.

Warren sat by the bay window. His long legs were crossed and his hands were lazily twirling a bouquet of wild flowers. The afternoon sun bounced off marguerite petals.

As I entered, his eyes slid from the garden to my face, and then down to where Klara was hiding behind my skirts.

He jumped up. 'Oh, hello, young lady!' Theatrically, he sank to his knees and scooted up to Klara. 'May I offer you these flowers, Milady?'

I looked down at my daughter, who still clung to my skirts, her face half-hidden in the folds. 'Would you like to put them in a vase? Margery can help you find one.'

She stared at Warren, puzzling over his unusual behaviour.

'I see that you keep foregoing verbal communication,' Warren said with cheer.

I threw him a sharp glance.

'I have a habit of doing the same,' he whispered and winked at her.

A heartbeat later, a small hand reached out…and bopped his nose.

'Oh, your mother loves doing that, too. Only, she's much less charming about it.' Very gently, he bopped her back. Klara squeaked, jumped at him, and wrung his neck with her arms.

'*Uhmpf*. Careful. I need my windpipe uncrushed.' He glanced up at me, mouthing, 'Help!'

I laughed. 'Just pick her up. She doesn't bite. At least… most of the time.'

We fetched a vase for the flowers, and a book for Klara, and then sat on the porch with the coffee, milk, and biscuits Margery had swiftly prepared and delivered.

'This is a beautiful place,' Warren said after a long pause.

'It is. I love it here. When the winds are high, you can hear the sea beat against the shore. It's like listening to Nature's heart.'

'I think I know now what you meant when you said you employ family.'

Somewhere in the depths of the house, Margery scolded Zach. 'Do you think me the Queen of the Bleeding Fairies? I just polished that!' Zach responded with apologetic mumblings. Something about "just making a couple of pancakes" and "a starving hole in my stomach."

'She hates it when he touches the range,' I said under my breath. 'It's spotless. One has to approach it with utmost caution.'

'Terrifying!' Warren made big eyes, barely able to conceal a grin.

I poured us a second cup of coffee and said, 'I don't need your private detective. In fact, I don't want him. Too many cooks spoil the porridge.'

'Really? Is that why the police putter about aimlessly? Too many detectives?'

'One leading investigator per crime,' I pointed out. 'Not two. Your private detective is a man. He won't let me lead my own investigation. I'm better off alone.'

He looked hurt, so I hastened to add, 'Besides, I have you and Hattie. I don't need anyone else.'

Turning his attention back to the garden, he said, 'Well, I might ask him to find the two missing pages of my *sister's diary*.'

'All you will accomplish is giving the murderer ample warning that he's hunted not only by the police but by a private detective and several amateur detectives also. Which might actually delight him, because all those people would be tripping over each other, blocking each other's view.'

He studied me then. 'And you know that how?'

I smiled and lifted an eyebrow.

Huffing, he turned away. After a long moment, he cut a glance at my daughter who was deeply immersed in a book about songbirds. 'Have you found out anything useful yet?'

'I'm not sure. Do you know the names of the new cooks your parents employ?'

'No. But I can ask.'

'Good. And I need to know who had access to Hattie's purse.'

He dipped a biscuit into his coffee. 'Careful. Insinuating that someone took something from Hattie's purse that night is the same as pointing a finger at Grimshaw. That something was taken the following morning, that's…a little different.

Several strangers were in the house for whom the butler had no responsibility. But suggesting it happened on Grimshaw's watch…' Warren shook his head. 'Accusing the Lords Wray would be even worse. Father would make sure your reputation was ruined and that no one would ever offer you a post. You'd have problems up to the hilt.'

'So you want me to keep my mouth shut. Leave my daughter and myself unprotected?' I nodded in Klara's direction.

'That's not what I'm saying. I'm just saying you need to be careful. Let me do the asking.'

'You are not a detective.'

'And *you* are?' He set the empty cup down a little too hard. Klara looked up at him, tilted her head, and then continued reading.

'Have you read the morning papers?' Warren asked.

His tone raised all the tiny hairs on my neck. 'No. Why?'

'Another body was found. Two days ago in Back Bay Park near the Boston and Albany railroad line.'

'Did they give a name?'

'Millicent Dowling.'

Relief washed over me. I bent over Klara and kissed her hair. I didn't really listen to Warren blathering on about how short the article was, that no details were given on where she had lived, and that the police were keeping the news reporters on a tight leash.

All that mattered to me right then was that I didn't know this woman. I could let myself believe that the connection between the first two victims and me was only a coincidence.

16

I was still clutching his note when the door to McCurley's apartment creaked open.

'Good evening, Dr Arlington. Thank you for coming.' He stepped aside and offered to take my jacket.

I snarled at him. 'Am I to assume we are to keep playing this charade of doctor and patient? Are you aware that what you are doing is illegal?'

'Tea?' he asked.

I threw the crumpled note in his face, hung my jacket, walked over to a chair, and sat. 'Where are your case notes?'

He picked up a teapot and two cups, set them on the table, and pulled a thick folder from a leather briefcase that was worn beyond its years. The folder landed on the table with a thud. 'You are welcome.'

I narrowed my eyes at him. He remained standing, hands in trouser pockets. Hadn't he planned to interrogate me first? Well, I was certainly not going to remind him.

I pulled the folder toward me and snapped it open, quickly rifled through post-mortem reports, notes, sketches, and photographs to make sure everything I expected to see was there. And then I found notes from his search for me in Europe. I stared at them for a moment. Then crumpled them.

McCurley drew a sharp breath. I slipped the balled-up notes into my pocket, snapped the folder shut and looked up at him. 'You asked why your Chief Superintendent hinted at a diplomatic incident between England and America. I was surprised to hear that my...friend had gone that far. However, after thinking it over, I believe the measures he took aren't entirely misplaced.'

McCurley pulled back a chair and sat across from me, the thick file, teapot and cups between us. An almost casual encounter.

'I witnessed a crime that threatened the very...' I cut a glance at the door to Ms Hacker's room.

'They are sleeping,' he said, as he poured tea.

I shrugged. 'It doesn't matter. I cannot divulge sensitive information. The British government has a vested interest in keeping me safe, including all the information I have relating to the crime I witnessed.'

'All right.' He sipped at his cup, never taking his eyes off me.

All right? I placed a hand on the case folder and pushed it toward him. 'Walk me through it.'

'Just one question.'

My hackles rose.

'You mentioned the other day that you started — I quote — *playing detective* long before you met your friend, Hattie Heathcote. Did you witness that crime, or were you investigating it?'

'I helped investigate it.'

'You have to give me a bit more than that.'

'Do I? Has it ever occurred to you that forced cooperation is nothing but parasitism? Or that I can simply disappear and start a new life far away from you and the murderer?'

'There is nothing simple about starting a new life. You have to be willing to pay a high price. To never see or talk to your friends again. To get accustomed to a new name, to teach yourself to look up when that name is spoken. You'd have to make your daughter forget her friends, her home, her name, her past. Can you do that?'

I ground my teeth. 'What makes you believe the man who killed Mrs Hyde also killed Mrs Hughes?'

Here, McCurley dropped his gaze. He fingered his moustache, then leafed through the case notes. There was a letter, handwritten in black ink.

'I know because he told me himself.'

THE THIRD THROAT was not as tender as the first, but how I soared after I killed her! You should try it. All the tensions, all the hatred vanish once the bitch's heart stops beating. Not for long, though.

You still have not figured it you, have you, little policeman?

'THE THIRD THROAT. Millicent Dowling. The papers reported about her yesterday,' I said.

'Yes. She was found three days ago in Back Bay Park near the Boston and Albany railroad.'

I nodded. Warren had told me as much.

'Do you know her?' McCurley asked.

'No. I never heard the name. Do you have a photograph?'

This, too, he pulled from the folder and placed it in front of me. I'd seen it briefly as I was flipping through the notes. Now I looked closer. A woman of about thirty-five years was lying on her back, her eyes staring straight up at me. Her jacket, blouse, and skirts were in disarray. Her throat was marked with bruises. Something about her…

I held the photograph I little farther away, squinted, and then shut my eyes.

And remembered the pretty nurse who'd stolen a kiss.

Bile rose up my throat.

'What is it?' McCurley asked.

I held up my hand, then clapped it over my face. *Why? Why? Why?* Millie Dumont had been her name. She'd been a nurse at Harvard Medical School and must have married after I left Boston. That's why I hadn't recognised her name. Because she'd changed it.

'Dr Arlington?'

I shook my head. Gulped a few breaths, and looked back at McCurley's notes.

Mechanically, I picked up the letter from the murderer and held it up against the light. 'He wrote it with his left hand, but he's right-handed. There's a smudge at the upper corner where his right hand must have held the paper. The text is free of errors. I wonder if he wrote it down, corrected it, and then copied it with his left hand.'

I placed it down in front of me and ran my fingers around the edges. 'The paper doesn't seem unusual. Have you analysed it?'

'Twenty cents a pound writing paper. You can get it anywhere. The same goes for the envelope.' He cleared his throat. An almost tortured sound. 'There's something else. We found the photographer who copied your portrait. He said the client insisted that only one copy be made, and on taking the negative with him. The other copy the client wanted made was of *this*.'

He picked a photograph from among the case notes. The picture was half the size of his palm. He pushed it toward me.

At the bottom of the photograph a line read:

Harvard Medical School. Bacteriology Class, Summer 1883

'HE LEFT the negative with the photographer. As well as the original. He wanted us to find it.' His gaze held mine as he asked, 'What does the bacteriology class of the summer of 1883 mean to you?'

I leaned back in my chair and lied outright. 'It means nothing to me.'

McCurley nodded slowly. 'I can't help but get the impression that you are protecting a murderer.'

'I am doing no such thing. Did the photographer describe the client?'

Eyeing me wearily, he copied my defiant posture. 'Why would I share information with you when you give me nothing in return? You didn't even look closely at the files. Three minutes, at the most, and then you closed the folder as though it didn't interest you at all.'

Anger set my teeth on edge.

McCurley continued undisturbed, 'As you are unwilling to cooperate, I will arrest you for unauthorised conduction of a post-mortem examination, and on the suspicion that you wished to manipulate evidence to your own advantage.' He stood, and pressed the knuckles of one hand against the table, holding the other out to me. 'Dr Arlington, if you would follow me to Headquarters now.'

Time slowed to a crawl as I pictured myself punching his solar plexus. But he'd grown up in the streets, in a gang of ruffians and criminals. He would know how to fight with his fists. He would be much faster than I.

I threw a brief glance at his chest that was so enticingly close, and I balled my fists and pushed myself up. I unfurled my hands and shook the tension from them. He caught the gesture and changed his stance. Ready to fight.

I huffed a small laugh, bitterly amused with myself and my naivety. The trap I had stumbled into. 'Another man before you did the same. He forced me to cooperate with him. He abducted me. He kept my father prisoner and had him murdered. This...' I held up my right hand, '...was hacked off by one of his henchmen. And my daughter is...'

I shook my head, set my chin, and stuck my face close to his. 'Be ashamed of yourself, McCurley! You are abusing your position of power to force me to submit to what you so prettily call *cooperation*. And if I don't do your bidding, you will go so far as locking me up, forcing me to leave my daughter unprotected. You are a cold-blooded *bastard*. Your arrogance will get people killed.'

With great effort, I stepped back from him. 'All right, then. Have at it. You have my *cooperation*. But once this is over and you have caught your killer, I want you out of my life. I don't want to see hide nor hair of your ugly visage.'

As I spoke, his shoulders began to sag. He coughed and pressed a hand to his stomach. His face darkened with an emotion I could not decipher.

Abruptly, he pushed the folder across the table. 'Take it. Read it. Copy what you need. I will pick it up at your home tomorrow morning. You don't need to answer my questions. Not one. I didn't mean to threaten you, I... Well, yes, I guess I did. I made a mistake. Please accept my apology.'

I had no idea who this man was that stood before me. But I would have been a fool not to take the opportunity to learn more about the murderer.

So I grabbed the folder and left without a word.

17

The moon hid behind a thin blanket of clouds. A perfect night for an ambush. I heard soft footfalls on the steps to our porch. A plank creaked just by the backdoor. I cocked my revolver. The doorknob turned. McCurley's silhouette appeared in the frame.

'Shut the door,' I said.

He paused, then did as I'd asked. 'Why is it dark here? Where *are* you?'

'I'm sitting on the floor to your right. Walk three steps into the hall and sit down. Please.'

'In the pitch dark?'

'Yes.'

'What are you planning?' He was still standing, hadn't moved an inch. His eyes must have adjusted to the dark because he sought my outlines and seemed to have found them. He'd slightly turned, facing me fully.

'I plan to tell you about the killer.'

Unspeaking, he folded his legs and sat on the floor.

I scooted closer to him so that my shoulder was touching his. 'Place your right hand next to you. Palm up.

'What?'

'You heard me. Place your hand on the floor, palm up. I will measure your pulse.'

'My...pulse? What the deuce is this?' He began to move away from me.

'You accepted my invitation, so I assume you wish to hear what I have to say. Unfortunately, you are able to control your facial expressions all too well. The skill of an expert liar, don't you agree?'

After a moment, he answered, 'Probably.'

'You need information from me, but I can't give it to you without knowing the effect it has on you. So, if you please, move back to my side and lay your right hand on the floor next to me so that I have the opportunity to gauge your reaction by measuring your pulse, and we can proceed.'

Haltingly, he scooted back until his shoulder touched mine. I felt his arm move as he placed his hand where I wanted it.

'So you'll know when my heart beats faster. Will that tell you if I lie?'

'It will let me know when or if you feel strongly about something I tell you.' At least that's what I hoped for.

He twitched as I placed my hand on his arm. I curled my fingers around his wrist. 'The moment you take your hand away, this meeting is over. Should I get the impression that you lie, this meeting is over. You may choose not to answer my questions, but I strongly advise you to tell the truth. Do you understand?'

'Yes.'

I pushed up his sleeve and placed my index finger on his pulse. 'And now we wait.'

'What for?'

'For your heart to calm down. You have the physique of an athlete, so I am guessing your resting pulse to be between forty and sixty beats per minute.' I didn't know if his heart rate would tell me anything about him, but it was better than trying to decipher his impenetrable mask. A liar might be able to control his facial expression, but breathing and pulse were much harder to influence by sheer will.

McCurley stretched his neck and rolled his shoulders. I listened into the silence, trying to gauge whether the quiet made him nervous, or whether he felt comfortable with it.

'The house is empty,' he whispered. His pulse hitched.

I didn't answer. There was no need to tell him that he was correct, that Margery, Zach, and Klara were safely tucked away. He must have wondered what it meant — this empty house. Whether I was a threat to him. Or whether I was pulling a prank on him, or wished to look important.

I thought back to earlier that morning when I handed him back the folder with his case notes. I hadn't said a word, and he had hidden his disappointment, nodded and left. He must've thought me unwilling to share my insights. Or perhaps he believed I had nothing important to say.

'When did you find my note?'

'When I arrived at my office and opened the folder,' he answered.

'And did you decide right away to follow my invitation?'

'Yes. Why wouldn't I? It's what I hoped for.'

'Did you bring a colleague?' I asked.

His heart kept beating in a calm and steady rhythm. 'I thought about it, but then decided to come alone.'

I believed him. And then I made an educated guess. 'Are you holding a gun in your left hand?'

His pulse stumbled. 'No. Yes,' he said cautiously.

'As expected.'

He cleared his throat.

'Put it on the floor to your left.'

I heard the clonk of his revolver against the floorboards.

'Will you tell your daughter how her mother died?'

His wrist jerked in my hand, but he pulled himself together and relaxed into my grip. His pulse thrummed a staccato. 'That has nothing to do with this case.'

'I will ask you several personal questions tonight. I haven't the time to get to know you, Inspector. But I need to decide quickly whether I can trust you with sensitive information or not.'

'You trust me enough to allow me into your house in the middle of the night,' he pointed out.

'I trust myself.' I dropped my middle finger to the trigger guard of my revolver.

It took him a few moments to process my statement. Before he spoke, I could feel his pulse pick up.

'You have a gun pointed at me.' A simple statement, not a question.

'Yes.'

'But if you shoot me, you will be arrested.'

'You think so? A stranger broke into my house in the dead of night. I feared for the life of my daughter. So I shot him.'

His hiccupping heart gradually slowed. And then he said with a dead voice, 'I see.'

'Would you answer my question, please?'

He filled his lungs, once, twice. 'I don't know yet. I am not sure if I will ever find the strength to tell her the truth. Will you? Will *you* tell your daughter about her father?'

'Yes.'

'Who was he?'

'A cold, scheming bastard. A criminal mastermind. Because of him, I know how to find your murderer. I have one more question for you. If you are still willing.'

I felt McCurley move, heard the scrape of his palm across his jaw.

'All right,' he said.

'What happened to your wife?'

His hand contracted so fast, I nearly lost my grip on his wrist. All the muscles in his arm coiled.

'McCurley,' I said softly, 'My aim is not to torture you. The information I'm about to give you can jeopardise *everything* that I have. My daughter's safety. My freedom. Believe me when I say that I have plenty of reasons to walk away from you, and only very few reasons to tell you what I know.'

A growl erupted from his chest.

I clamped down on his wrist. 'You treat your Ms Hacker with surprisingly little respect, your Sergeant Boyle like a doormat, and me like a cockroach you found in your meal. You might have a murderer to catch, but that is not enough incentive for me to lay myself bare for a man who shows nothing but unkindness and arrogance whenever I see him.'

'This conversation is over.' He yanked his hand free and stood. 'May I pick up my gun and leave without getting shot?'

I sighed. 'If you really want to leave, then go. I don't need you to find this man. He will come to me. He plans for me to be his grand finale. But to explain to you how I came to this conclusion, to tell you everything I know about the killer, I would have to trust you with my life. So you see my dilemma. I need to know that I'm talking to a human being, and not an empty shell. I need you to trust me a little before I can trust you with my life and that of my daughter.'

I watched his barely discernible silhouette in the pitch dark. The outlines of his shoulders, his compressed fists.

His breath was heavy. Perhaps undecided, perhaps bracing himself. At last, he emptied his lungs and sat back down

I curled my hand around his wrist and placed my finger on his pulse.

'Thank you,' I said.

'You might regret this.'

'And so might you.'

I waited in silence for him to begin.

With measured breaths, he calmed his heart. 'I keep Ms Hacker at a cool distance, else she might believe I would marry her one day. She's young and naive.'

'I can see that.'

'Boyle agrees to be treated like a doormat whenever it helps to interrogate witnesses and suspects. Most people believe that men in uniform have authority. A hierarchy is immediately accepted. Even in plainclothes, as the detective leading the investigation, I am above everyone else. Most witnesses treat me with respect. Most suspects feel at least a trace of fear of me. Very few people resist all authority. You are one of them. In such cases, I make sure to call in Boyle.'

'You wanted me to spill my guts to the kind man, while you made a show of being the tough inspector?'

'No. I use Boyle to gauge character. Most of the people who abhor authority do so only because they want to be the top dog. They want to feel superior. The moment the biggest bully — which would be me — leaves the office, they turn on Boyle. He's a kind and shy man. So naturally, they believe him to be at the very bottom of the hierarchy.'

His heartbeat was calm and regular.

'And what does that tell you? That people can be pricks?'

He chuckled. 'Yes. That and bullies. It's often criminals who abuse Boyle. Verbally, mostly. The ones who try to assault him are in for a surprise.'

I took my clammy hand off his wrist and rubbed it against my trousers. Then I placed my finger back on his pulse. 'And what did you learn about me?'

'That you don't give a damn about hierarchy, and that you seem to find all policemen equally useless.'

'I would have told you that, had you asked.'

'But you are not a bully. It's an important bit of information when one is looking for a murderer.'

'Why have you treated me with so much contempt since the very moment you walked into my lecture hall?'

'That's how I work. Highly educated people often believe they know better than the police. I've heard that some of them even *play detective*. I did not treat you with contempt. I needled you where it would annoy you the most, hoping to make you tell me things you wished not to.'

'It worked.'

'What makes you think the murderer wants you?'

'There is one more question you need to answer,' I reminded him.

'You said in the beginning that I don't need to answer all of your questions. That I may choose to remain silent.'

'And so may I.'

McCurley moved a fraction. He cocked his head, and I could almost make out the faintest glint of his eyes.

'Why are we sitting in the dark? And why is the house empty?'

'You are sitting here because you agreed to listen to me. And I am sitting here because…I am waiting for a killer.'

His spine snapped straight. 'You know him.'

'No. I do not. Or rather, I hope I don't.'

'But you believe he will come tonight?'

I shrugged. 'Evidence and experience tell me that he wants to scare me senseless before he strikes. He might come and take a look in the next few days. Perhaps he already has. I don't know.'

'But why you?'

'I can't tell you that yet. Not before you've answered my question.' I leaned my head back against the wall and shut my eyes. I had all night. It was McCurley's decision whether he wished to talk or not.

I listened to the rough song of the crickets, the crescendo of the nightingale that lived in one of the neighbours' gardens. And to McCurley, fighting a battle with himself. His heart was racing.

'We lost our first child. Our son was born prematurely and lived only a few minutes. Ailis...my wife, she...hurt herself. Nearly killed herself. The hospital staff committed her to an asylum. She spent half a year there.

'When she was released, she seemed better, but she... She never talked about what happened there. She seemed normal. Doing fine. Strangely so. We didn't dare have another child, but then it...just happened. And while the child grew inside her, her composure cracked.

'I realised then that all this time, she'd been...faking. She'd professed to be well because she was terrified of being sent back to the asylum. I was blind to it. I didn't want to see her suffering. When our baby was born healthy, Ailis was happy. Again I let myself believe all was well. Until...'

His wrist was vibrating under my palm. His skin was ice cold and sweaty. I forced myself to keep my hand where it was, to keep my finger on his pulse, because of the price Klara and I would have to pay if McCurley was a liar and a cheat. And so I kept torturing him.

'Until I found her sitting in the open window, her legs thrust out into the cold night, and in her arms...Líadáin. She wanted to kill my daughter. The madness in her eyes was... I've never seen anything like it, and I pray I'll never see it again. I jumped and grabbed for Líadáin. It was her leg that I managed to snatch. I broke it when I tore her away from her mother. And Ailis...fell. The only noise she made was that... when her body...' He groaned and knocked his head against the wall behind him. 'The thought of pulling *her* back in didn't even touch my mind until after the funeral.'

It was similar enough to what Uriel had told me. But I

found his account more believable than the rumour my friend had heard in a pub.

I took my hand off McCurley's wrist. 'The click you will hear in a moment is me releasing the hammer of my gun.'

I placed my revolver onto the floorboards and waited for McCurley's breath to return to normal. I wasn't proud of what I was doing. But I kept telling myself that it was necessary. 'I've noticed a small asymmetry in how Líadáin kicks her legs. If you allow, I'd like to examine her hips to see if—'

'I'm not letting you near her again.'

'I understand.'

He snorted. 'Your turn.'

'Did you bring the photograph of the bacteriology class?'

'Yes.'

'Good.' I struck a match and lit the candle I had placed on the floor before McCurley was to arrive. 'I've laid it all out on the kitchen table. Follow me.' I didn't look at him. Mostly because I wanted to give him space. I'd violated his privacy and was trying to make up for it. A little, at least.

'If you are afraid he's watching, won't he see us now?'

'The curtains are drawn,' I explained. 'My daughter usually has a midnight snack in the kitchen. To anyone outside, the house appears perfectly normal. But don't get too close to any of the windows.'

We entered the kitchen. I lit the gas range and heated water for tea. McCurley dipped his fingers against my notes, carefully, as though afraid to touch them.

'*What* is this?' he asked.

'A glimpse into the mind of the Railway Strangler.'

18

*M*cCurley ran a hand over his face, muttering, 'So that name spread.'

'People have a need to put a monstrous name to a monster.'

He frowned at me. 'Why are you wearing men's clothing?'

'Trousers come in handy if I have to fight off an assailant. Sometimes I think women are made to wear gowns so that they can't defend themselves. Considering that the vast majority of assailants are men, the notion that women are supposed to feel safe in the company of a man is ludicrous. Tea?'

He huffed a laugh, and nodded at the cup in front of him. He placed the small photograph I'd asked him to bring on the table and tapped his index finger on the faces of twenty-four young men. 'Is he among them?'

'Do you believe the killer sends you a photograph of himself? No. This picture connects all your dots. But that's the end of our story and must come later. The beginning is important. I will walk you through my conclusions, and you tell me if they line up with yours. Or not.'

A nod. No impatience or anger. Good.

'We have three victims,' I began. 'All strangled. All dumped by a railway. All women aged between twenty-eight and thirty-six. All healthy and of reproductive age. Yet none was violated.' I moved the sheet of paper that contained those major points in front of us, and placed my mug on a corner.

McCurley nodded. 'I was wondering whether the victims being women might, in fact, be unimportant to the killer.'

'Exactly! Have you checked for similar deaths among men and children?'

'Boyle's dug back through ten years of homicide records. We found several cases that might or might not have been committed by the Railway Strangler. The most recent death by strangulation that looks similar to our three dead women was a boy, aged eight. Happened three months ago. The father is in custody and swears he didn't do it. Evidence says he did. And he has no alibi.' McCurley turned his attention from the files to me. 'That's not in the case notes I gave you, because I'd dismissed it as irrelevant. And the killer wrote about three victims.'

'He could be lying.'

'I know.'

I tapped on my notes. 'Let's take one step at a time. On May 15, Henrietta Hyde was found on the Fall River Railroad near Savin Hill Avenue. She was killed at noon, and her body lay curled on its side for five to six hours. Extensive bruising to her throat, from jaw to collarbones. She's the only victim who was placed *on* the tracks. And her neck was arranged on one of the rails so that the train would cut through the evidence and destroy it. The only victim without blood and skin under her nails. The only victim whose outer clothing had been removed. The only victim killed in the daytime, and the only victim not living with a husband — who is excluded as a suspect, because from your case notes he is living in

California and was seen there by several people on the day his wife was killed.'

'Do you think she was killed by someone other than our man?'

'The thought occurred to me. Now, let's get to Georgie's mother, Mrs Miller, and Petey — your first suspect.' I paused and looked up. 'Have you released him?'

'A physician had him transferred to an asylum.'

I nodded, wiping away the images of McCurley's wife on the window sill, their newborn daughter in her arms.

'All right. So you summoned Mrs Miller to help with questioning Petey. Which was only half successful, owing to Petey not recognising Mrs Miller or anyone else who entered his cell. And with his general…state of mind.' I rubbed my brow. 'Dammit to hell and back! The one witness who might have seen the murderer has the memory of a colander!'

'Witnesses are often depressingly forgetful,' McCurley said. 'At least he was able to tell us that a man was with the victim. But his description can't be trusted.'

'It isn't even much of a description. "Wore a topper and an old-fashioned silk necktie."'

'He's not the only one who saw him. Remember—'

'Yes, the photographer. But he described a man with a bushy beard and thick glasses. Anyone could hide behind those. He could not say what colour the man's eyes were or what clothes he was wearing. He only remembers that his client was of normal height and had a pleasant voice. Nothing that could help identify him.'

'Let's focus on what we have.' McCurley sat down and poured more tea.

I moved a chair and propped a foot onto it. 'According to Ms Munro, who shared rooms with the victim, Mrs Hyde was having a secret affair. Although Ms Munro and Mrs Hyde seem to have been friends who talked about many things, Mrs

Hyde kept the identity of the man secret. This is important because there are only very few reasons to keep an illicit affair from a friend who works as a prostitute. There was enough trust between the two that they talked about Ms Munro's clients. So why did Mrs Hyde not talk about her lover?'

'He asked her not to tell anyone.'

'Yes.'

Slowly, McCurley nodded. 'Because he is married? A known criminal? Or…known to Ms Munro.'

I'd never considered that last point. Struck, I sat down and stared at McCurley. 'What if he is one of Ms Munro's clients? Most of them are married men, I'm sure. But if she knows him she…may be in grave danger.'

Absently, he fingered his moustache, said, 'Huh!' and pulled out a notebook. Scribbling in it, he mumbled, 'I'll send Boyle to get a list of the names of all her clients.'

'Now, the second victim,' I continued. 'Elizabeth Hughes, found near the New England Railroad on June 7. She, too, had extensive bruising to her throat and neck. Faint bruising was found on her forearms, and her fingernails were broken, bloody, and dirty. Her clothes were in disarray. Clearly, she put up a fight. And her body was used to convey the first message to you. A photograph of my portrait was pushed into her corset. The murderer begins to communicate with you, using *this* body, but not the first. Why?'

'I see only two reasons. One, the first killing was unplanned. Two, the first killing wasn't his doing.'

'My thoughts precisely. To make absolutely sure the first victim is his, you have to start talking to him.'

McCurley raised his eyebrows, bunched them together, and said, 'Ah. The newspapers.' He went back to his note-book, leafed through it, and wrote a note on a corner of a page. 'I'd thought about it and then dismissed it because it felt too…queer.' Slowly, he placed his pencil next to the book and looked at me. 'Why are you so keen to live inside a murderer's mind?'

'*Keen?* I'm not *keen* to do this.'

He raised both hands in a gesture of apology. 'I'm just puzzled by all this.' He motioned toward my notes scattered across the table. 'People usually run away screaming or show a sickening form of sensational curiosity. But you seem…to love the examination of every small bit of this tragedy. You are fascinated by it. Why?' His voice was rough, as though his throat was too sticky to let words slip through his vocal cords.

'Fascinated? No. I am a scientist. I gather data and analyse them.'

'I've never met anyone who would willingly put herself into the mind of a killer.'

'Odd. Don't *you* do exactly that? Put yourself in the mind of a killer, or a thief, or whatever kind of criminal. So you can predict his next step and catch him.'

'Yes, but…' He inhaled. 'Very few detectives do that. It's not a…pleasant place to be.'

'No. It's not. But it's necessary.'

'Where did you learn this?' There was a gentle curiosity behind his question.

'There was a time when I needed to be able to predict my husband's next steps. He regarded lives as nothing but things to be used and discarded at will. Knowing what he would do next kept me alive.'

'What about the man who hacked off your finger?'

'My husband's henchmen are all in prison now. Or dead. Except the one who took my finger.' My hand strayed to the scar on my shoulder. I massaged the tender spot that ached whenever the weather was turning. 'He shot me. Nearly killed me and my daughter. She was only a few minutes old then.'

McCurley said nothing for a long moment, and then spoke softly, 'Is he the murderer?'

'No. Not him.'

'Explain, please.'

'I know for a fact that he is in France. I trust my source absolutely. Let's get back to victim number two. More importantly, her connection to me. She was my patient for a day. How did the killer know that? How could he *possibly* know?'

'Why are you so sure that he knew? That it mattered to him?'

'Because of this.' I nodded to the small photograph. 'And my portrait, of course.'

He rubbed his neck. 'If your assumption is correct, then… He must have known the second victim, and she must have mentioned to him that she saw you. Or he saw her entering or leaving your practice because he was already watching you.'

'But there is no connection between the first victim and me. None while she was alive, that is. The papers did not mention my name. The only people who know that I examined the first victim are my housekeeper, my gardener, my closest friends, the post-mortem surgeon and his assistants, the coroner, and the police.'

'Yes,' he answered. 'That's the reason I keep insisting you know the killer.'

'Which brings us to the third victim.' My voice trembled, and he must have noticed the change, for he cut a sideways glance at me that was sharp and knowing.

'Her death is very similar to that of the second victim. She, too, was used to sending a message. This time, the killer wrote you a letter. The letter tells us that he loves what he's doing. And that he won't wait long until he strikes again. Because he needs it. The power. The ecstasy a kill brings.'

McCurley said nothing. If my assessment shocked him or surprised him, he did not show it. His expression remained neutral, almost relaxed.

I continued, 'Throttling someone is an intimate way of killing. Much more so than shooting or poisoning. To wrap your hands around a throat to kill, you have to look into your victim's eyes. You have to watch how her life slips from her body. You have to watch her pain, her terror, her struggle to stay alive, to fight you off. In order to keep at it, you need an extraordinary urge to kill.'

I paused and observed. His gaze drifted across the notes, from the first one I'd shown him, to all the others, the lists and schemata, and then got stuck on the photograph he'd brought.

He tore his attention away from it, and asked, 'Judging from the letter, do you think him intelligent? Educated?'

'The text is free of errors. But it's brief, not much to go by. He might have written it several times and corrected it. But yes, I think we can conclude that he is educated and not of low social standing. He might have an official function. A man in uniform.'

'Why would you think that?' McCurley asked.

'The second and the third victims died in the late evening hours. Soon after nightfall, to be precise. For a man to approach a woman in the dark — without her striking out, screaming for help, running away, or otherwise drawing attention to herself and her attacker — he must either be known to her or appear trustworthy.'

'He could have surprised her. Jumped out of the shadows.'

'Yes, he could have. But the post-mortem reports say otherwise. The only signs of a struggle that were found on the bodies must have occurred when the victim was already prone. None of them had been knocked out. None of them were given chloroform or similar substances. Picture Sergeant Boyle, for example. A kind man in uniform. He creates a situation in which he clearly needs help. A situation where — when his chosen victim approaches to assist him — she will position herself so that he can easily put his hands around her throat, throw her down, and strangle her. She won't even get a chance to make a peep.'

'But you said earlier that it's impossible to strangle someone without having them fight back,' McCurley pointed out.

'I did. But now I know how he kept them from fighting back.'

Warren had given me the idea. How he'd sat on my stomach and pinned my wrists. 'All three victims had faint bruising on their lower arms. He sat on them with his legs holding down their arms. He must've sat on the abdomen. High up. His legs would have trapped their arms by their sides, his ankles and shins pinning their wrists. There would actually be very little weight on the wrists when he sat like that. And he wouldn't need to put his full weight on their abdomen, either. Rather, he leans with full force on the windpipe. And crushes it.'

McCurley picked up my copy of the killer's letter. 'And he is arrogant.'

'Yes. He fancies himself smarter than you, or anyone, really. And that's why he will write to you again when you tell the reporters that the first victim, Mrs Hyde, was not killed by the Railway Strangler.'

McCurley smiled coldly. 'If our assessment of him is correct, he might even explain to me how he did it.'

'That's what I hope for. But more importantly: He won't see that we are baiting him.'

Shoulders sagging, he sat back. 'You plan to be the bait.'

'I already am, whether I want it or not. Anyway. You would do well to let him believe that he leads you around, and not the other way.'

'You seem to be very sure of all this.' McCurley cocked his head.

'I am. Because I know precisely what he wants.' I pushed the small photograph to McCurley. 'He's laid a trail. He wanted you to find this. But only to tease you, because you cannot possibly know what this photograph means to him. And you have to keep pretending that you don't know what I'm about to tell you. In fact, you can't tell anyone what I will tell you now.'

He dipped his head in assent.

'This man is your connection,' I said, tapping my middle finger on a young lad's face. A pale, fine-boned man I knew all too well.

'A friend of yours? Or an acquaintance of the murderer?'

'This man has no friends. He is harsh, arrogant, and knows only his work.'

McCurley drew back. 'But *you* know him?'

I nodded, and the movement made me feel nauseous. 'His name is Anton Kronberg. He is a German physician and bacteriologist.'

He narrowed his eyes at me. 'He means something to you. I can see that. Do you hate him? Love him?' He shook his head. 'I don't understand. Why are you so certain that he's connected to the killer, but not the killer himself?'

'He is not…innocent. But I know for a fact that he did not kill these three women.'

McCurley worked his jaw. 'Why are you so sure?'

'Kronberg left Boston years ago.'

He squinted at me, knowing full well that I was holding back information. Slowly, he slid the photograph closer to himself. After a long scrutinising moment, he said, 'Are you two related?'

I stared at the picture, feeling as though I were already falling, falling… I leaned on the tabletop. Opening my mouth and getting my tongue to work took an amount of energy and willpower I didn't seem to possess. I croaked, 'That man… That man is me.'

McCurley opened his mouth and shut it. Blinked. Shook his head. 'I don't understand.'

I squeezed my eyes shut and made myself say, 'The killer knows that Anton Kronberg and Elizabeth Arlington are one and the same person.'

19

*Y*ou are a spy for the British Empire.' McCurley cupped his mouth. He shook his head from side to side, then burst out chuckling. 'I should have known the moment the Chief mentioned the Crown, hinted at diplomatic relations, and ordered me to stop digging into your past. How stupid of me.'

'I'm not a spy. I infiltrated a criminal organisation. I'm a witness. I've told you the truth.'

'I doubt the British government protects all their witnesses the way they protect you.'

I lowered my head. 'It's how a potential spy is being courted, I expect.' Clearing my throat, I turned back to the matter at hand. 'There's more you need to know.'

'I sincerely hope so. Because so far, you've raised more questions than you've answered.'

'Patience, Inspector. My mouth doesn't fire as fast as yours.'

'That depends on who you ask.'

'It's late and I'm exhausted. Let's get this over with. The timing of the messages the killer sent you is important. Elizabeth Hughes was killed on the evening of Tuesday, June 6. The following day, her body was found together with a photograph of a drawing of my portrait. The photographer stated that only a day earlier the client had picked up that photograph. Two days before that, the client had brought it in and asked him to make a copy. That means the drawing was in the killer's procession on Saturday, June 3 at the latest. I know for a fact that the portrait has been drawn on Friday, June 2. Two portraits, in fact. And both disappeared that same night or the morning after. In a matter of only four days, the murderer put a plan together and executed it. It was the portrait that raised his ire.'

As I spoke, McCurley placed his mug aside and bent forward as though he wished to jump into my skull and dig up all that I knew. 'And you know who drew the portrait?' he asked.

'Yes. Warren Amaury.'

Blinking, he sank against the backrest. The chair produced a pop. I told him about the Freaks, our Friday afternoon meetings at the music hall, which always ended in Warren's townhouse. Only, on that Friday I hadn't joined them. Warren had drawn me from memory and then his sketchbook disappeared. I told him about that night's drop-in at Warren's, which ended with a black eye, a shot to pale-eyed Joey's heart, and a short visit to McCurley's apartment.

McCurley said, 'Huh,' stood and paced the kitchen.

'Don't walk too close to the curtains,' I reminded him, and received an absent wave of his hand as a reply.

'You told me earlier that your closest friends know that you examined Mrs Hyde's remains. Now you tell me that one of them drew the portrait which was pinned to Mrs Hughes's body. That makes them prime suspects.'

'I know.' I turned my gaze to the small photograph of bacteriologists. How young I looked. How fragile. I couldn't find any courage in that young face. None of the courage it had taken to betray each and every one of his peers, superiors, and neighbours.

'Wait a moment...' McCurley came to a halt. 'Where is the connection to the third victim? And to you? I still don't understand.'

'When I worked as Anton Kronberg at Harvard Medical School, Millie was a nurse. She fancied me. Everyone knew about it, while I pretended to be oblivious. Well...until she kissed me. I told her to stop being ridiculous, and that was that.'

McCurley grabbed a chair and sat down. 'I still don't see what you are seeing. The connections. And why you believe this is all about you.'

'I realised it only after I saw this photograph and learned about Millie's death.' I pointed to the group of bacteriologists. 'The killer knew me. Knew Anton Kronberg. The problem is that... The way others saw him...Kronberg was a brilliant, arrogant scientist. There was envy. Plenty of it. He was the youngest. He rarely talked to anyone if it wasn't about work. He never went to social events. Because he couldn't. *I could not.* Whatever Kronberg did, he was better than anyone before him. It caused...consternation among his peers, to put it mildly. The killer must have known Kronberg and he must have known about Millie. The killer must have hated Kronberg — me — for a long time. And when he saw my portrait he must have believed he was seeing Anton Kronberg, because it shows only my face in detail. My hair and my clothes were merely hinted at. If you have always believed a person to be a man, then it is a man you will see. Imagine the shock when he learned that Anton Kronberg was the doctor who examined the body of the woman he'd killed. Imagine the shock when he learned he was bested by a woman, and that she is now dabbling in his affairs.'

'So we are looking for a man who studied or worked at Harvard Medical School when you were there as Anton Kronberg, and who is connected to your friends or might be one of them.'

'You are a quick.'

Groaning, he rubbed his face. 'I need time to think. We should meet again and discuss your friends. Getting the Amauries to talk will be a problem.'

'I'm Hattie Heathcote's physician. I can go in and out of her home as she chooses without causing suspicion. And there's a plan on how to get into the Amaury mansion. Oh, by the way, one of the men who could have taken the drawings was Mr Stone. The flower grower. I have a list of the people who had access to Hattie's purse and the drawings. I'll make a copy for you.'

'Send it to my office.'

'I'd rather not let anyone know we are working together.'

He pinched the bridge of his nose and shut his eyes for a moment. 'As you wish.'

'My mind keeps returning to the first victim. That she did not fight. Or rather…it appears that she didn't. What if she was killed exactly like the others, but the killer didn't wear boots but—'

'Slippers.'

We looked at each other, our theories circling wildly in our skulls.

'She couldn't have broken her nails on felt slippers,' I said.

'But there would be fibres under her nails.'

'Under her short-trimmed washerwoman's nails? I've seen them and doubt much would get stuck under them.' I shook my head.

'Well, it's an idea. Let's keep it in mind, and proceed on the theory that she knew her killer intimately.'

'The child was his,' I said.

'Probably. And someone *must* have seen them together. Even if they were being secretive, they couldn't have coupled in a shack. They rented a room in a boarding house.'

I grabbed McCurley's sleeve to stop him. 'There are boathouses by the shore. Near the Glass Works. One could be his.' The thought chilled me to the bone. He could have seen Zach, Margery, and Klara sneaking from our boathouse to our new apartment.

'I'll have them watched.'

'Let me talk to Georgie. He could take a look without raising suspicion.'

McCurley lifted an eyebrow. 'You think that I or my men would raise suspicion?'

'A policeman peeking through the windows of all the boathouses isn't precisely inconspicuous, is it?'

'Why the bloody hell do you think us all blockheads?'

'I don't think *you* are a blockhead.'

'But an arrogant ass.'

I coughed. 'You haven't been an arrogant ass for about an hour. Out of several weeks. Your most recent behaviour might be an outlier.'

'An outlier?' Incredulous, he threw himself back in his chair.

'When one or two measurements fall outside the main body of data.'

'I *know* what an outlier is. You truly have a rare dislike for police.'

'I learned that I cannot trust them. They are either too dumb, too arrogant, or too corrupt.'

'They are just men. With all our faults.'

I crossed my arms over my chest. 'Why did you give me your case notes? Why take the risk? I could have destroyed them.'

'A calculated risk. I knew you were trying to find the

killer. Not giving you my notes would have meant leaving you unprotected. And there was a good chance you would share what you knew if I offered you my insights first.'

I placed a palm on the table and made a wiping gesture. 'Back to the case. What we need are the names of Ms Munro's clients.'

'Well…' He raked a hand through a mop of unruly hair that seemed unable to decide whether it wanted to be blond or brown, or in which direction to point. 'They wouldn't give her their real names, so I'll have to put a tail on each of them. Meanwhile, I'll be going through the list of staff and students of Harvard Medical School during your time there. God Almighty.' Groaning, he shook his head.

'What? Too many men to interrogate?'

He looked up. 'No. Yes. I was just wondering why you did it. Why you pretended to be a man.'

I snorted. 'How else would I have studied medicine? There was absolutely no other way. Women are still not permitted to enrol at German Universities.'

He dropped his gaze to his boots before cutting a glance at me through lowered lashes. 'May I ask what crime it was you witnessed? What criminal organisation you infiltrated? And why…you married a murderer? Did you know what he was?'

'I did. He abducted me. I told you that. And he abducted my father. I was Britain's foremost bacteriologist, and he wanted me to develop weapons for germ warfare. My experiments would have killed thousands. Tens of thousands. To stop him, I had to make him trust me first.'

'And getting with child was part of that plan?' There was no harshness in his question. He simply wanted to know what I had been willing to do to take down a criminal.

'I believed I was barren. To discover myself pregnant was…a shock.'

He nodded once, and said, 'Thank you.'

'I owed you. For what I made you tell me.'

Silence fell. It didn't feel uncomfortable, and I was glad he had no urge to fill it with useless conversation.

'Do you think she told him she was pregnant? Mrs Hyde? And that sent him into a rage?'

'Perhaps,' he said and scratched the back of his head. 'Impossible to tell. They could have been lying together when she told him, and he lost control and strangled her. Or she might've said something different that set him off. Or nothing at all. She might have been fully dressed, and he undressed her when she was already dead. Hum… He didn't seem to have a habit of abusing her. Ms Munro never saw bruises or signs of distress when Mrs Hyde returned from her lover.'

'Maybe it wasn't her lover who killed her.'

'Hum. Let's get back to what we know. The third victim had soil and cow manure under her fingernails.'

I sat up straight. 'She did? Why wasn't that in the post-mortem report?'

'It wasn't? Strange. I could swear Professor Goodman said it was cow manure. I'll ask him, and make sure.'

'If it was… It's hard to step in cow manure by sheer accident. Especially here in Boston. Dog turds, horse manure, and pigeon droppings — yes. But cow patties? If it really was from a cow, and not a horse. Hum. Could he be a farmer? But then… It makes no sense. A man who attended Harvard Medical School turns to farming?'

'The farmer could be a family member,' McCurley suggested.

I shook my head. 'A farmer can't afford to send his son to Harvard Medical School. Except his son is brilliant enough to earn a scholarship. And a brilliant surgeon or physician will certainly not allow his son to turn to farming.'

'Hum... Another matter that needs to be clarified is the transport of the bodies. How does he do that without being seen? He must be using a carriage. A closed carriage.'

'Or a carriage no one pays attention to,' I muttered. 'A grocer's cart.'

'He could have wrapped the body and covered it with wares.'

'You could ask a naturalist to identify the soil found under the fingernails of the second and third victims.'

'I did. Loamy soil. Nothing extraordinary.' McCurley put his head in his hands. It wasn't a gesture of exhaustion or defeat. It was more to shut out everything that surrounded him. To silence the world. I waited until he mumbled into his palms, 'There's a lot I'm not seeing.' He dropped his hands and exhaled. 'I need to leave. I'll send a note.'

With that, he stood, grabbed his revolver from the table, and slid it into his holster. Without another word, he made for the backdoor.

20

I'd had only two hours of sleep before we trudged through the tunnel back to our house. Zach carried a sleepy Klara. Margery eyed the ceiling for fat spiders, keeping her lantern aloft to singe away any and all webs that dared get in our way. I asked them to wait outside the antechamber while I unlocked the secret door to my bedroom, revolver cocked and ready to put a hole into whoever dared attack from the other side.

The house was empty and quiet.

I waved the others forward and went to check all doors and windows for signs of an intruder, but found nothing.

'Breakfast,' Margery announced with a huff and set to work.

We gathered around the table, a little stiff with sleep, and clasped the cups of coffee as though the brew could resurrect our spirits. I inhaled the aroma and said, 'I'll quit my lecturing post.'

'Hmm,' Margery answered. 'You don't seem to have the patience anyway.'

Zach snorted. 'Surprised you kept it up that long.'

Open-mouthed I looked from Zach to Margery, and dropped my gaze back into my coffee cup. 'I used to be good at it. But I can't bear watching all those girls dropping out as soon as a wedding looms on the horizon. As though higher education means nothing but mental gymnastics. Gah!' I slammed my hand on the table.

Klara also cried, 'Gah!' and hammered the table with both hands.

'Sounds like a good idea,' I said and drummed a rhythm.

My daughter laughed and drummed along. Zach whistled a tune, and just like that, the fears the night had brought blew away.

Before we were done eating, Mr Cratchitt delivered two letters with the morning mail. One was from McCurley and contained the first few names of Ms Munro's clients, asking if I knew any of them. I didn't but wondered if McCurley ever slept. He must have questioned her late the previous night.

The envelope contained something solid. I tipped it onto my palm. It was a key. A note was attached to it:

IF YOU NEED *to talk to me, but don't wish to be seen at the police station, come to my home. This is a key to the house. Also: We need to make a list of potential victims. Former and current colleagues, acquaintances, friends, and patients. Send a note whether you have time to meet with me tonight.*

Quinn McCurley

THE SECOND WAS FROM WARREN.

. . .

Come as soon as you can! You won't believe what I found!

Warren.

'Gods, Warren. A tad more drama and mystery is exactly what I need right now,' I mumbled and slipped both notes into my pocket, told Zach to find Georgie for me, and Margery to send in the first patient.

Around noon, just after Mrs Cratchitt had left with the newest addition to her family tucked into the bend of her arm — a son who'd shot into the world after only ten minutes or so of labour, and, as her husband had predicted, delivered entirely without my help — Georgie showed up in the frame of my office door. His chin was dotted with blueberry jam. He chewed on what suspiciously looked like one of Margery's muffins.

I bade him sit and placed a nickel on my side of the desk. 'Do you know the tenants or owners of the boat houses by the Glass Works?'

With a grimy finger, the boy swept remnants of jam from his chin into his mouth. Then he wiped his hands on his trousers and gave me the names of six men. None sounded familiar to me. I wrote them on a piece of paper.

'I keep wondering who Mrs Hyde's lover might have been. Have you heard any rumours?'

His nose began to turn red as his gaze dropped to the nickel. He produced a small cough and said, 'He was a masher, that one. Heard he had pots of money. Fat lot of good it did her.'

'Who told you that?'

'Freddie. One of me chums. Said the bloke was a smarmy piece of work.'

'This Freddie, does he know the man?'

Georgie shrugged. 'Freddie likes telling stories, he does.'

'Has anyone else mentioned Mrs Hyde's lover?'

'Nah. But everyone talks about the Railway Strangler. Everyone and their dog says they've seen him.'

'Do you believe any of it?'

Georgie rolled his eyes and shook his head. 'Can I have another muffin?'

I pushed the nickel toward him. 'I want to talk to Freddie. Can you ask him to come today at...' I checked the time. 'What about the two of you come by at six. Margery will have stew and fresh bread ready.'

Georgie snatched the nickel and pocketed it. Then he tugged at his ear. His tongue darted out to catch a crumb that was stuck to the corner of his mouth

'Tell Margery to give you two more muffins. Oh, and Georgie?'

The boy screeched to a halt in the doorway.

'Could you take a message to Pemberton Square and another one to Beacon Hill?'

LATE IN THE AFTERNOON, I went to see Warren. A maid admitted me and took my hat and jacket. I was worried about my new bicycle, but the sun wouldn't set for another three or four hours, so it should be comparatively safe. Even though it was chained to exactly that lamp post that had treated my old bicycle with so little regard.

'The master will see you shortly,' the maid said and indicated a chaise longue in the parlour.

I thanked her and went to a large window to peek out into the street. Entering Beacon Hill was like taking an excursion back in time. Warren lived in a part of town into which one could not enter without a thorough examination of respectability, where wealthy families occupied an entire house apiece, and musicians, painters, and authors found accommodation in old lodging houses. It was the only quiet part of Boston, removed from the noises of steam engines, cable cars, and dense traffic. At night, the cobbled streets and narrow alleys were thrown in flickering gaslight from old-fashioned lamps.

I always felt a bit removed from real life when I entered those streets. But the illusion was wiped away as soon as I stepped into Warren's house, which sparkled with modern appliances.

I turned when I heard footfalls. Warren and Owens entered the parlour, the former bouncing on the balls of his feet with excitement, the latter composed and entirely unruffled by whatever had occurred.

'Liz!' Warren rushed up to me, snatched my hand and tugged me toward Owens. 'Listen to this.'

Owens cleared his throat and clasped his hands behind his back. He seemed to grow a little discomfited. The corners of his mouth turned down. 'I must apologise, Dr Arlington, for any misfortune that my silence might have caused. What I did was only with the best of intentions. You see, Mr Amaury and his friends often play pranks on one another, and so I did not think anything amiss when I saw Mr Crocker place a small booklet into Mrs Heathcote's purse. I did not wish to spoil the fun. And after all, he did not take anything from her but rather gave her something. Had I known he had, in fact, torn two pages from her diary, I would have told Mr Amaury at once.'

I felt the pain before realising that my nails were digging into my palms. 'Uriel Crocker put a booklet into Hattie's purse, you say?'

'Indeed. It was on Friday, June 2, just before everyone left the house. Except for Mr Amaury, who remained at home, that is.'

'Can you describe the booklet?'

'It looked just like the ones Mr Amaury uses for his drawings.' Owens's gaze slid to Warren and back to me. 'Mr Crocker did not strike me as nervous. He slipped the booklet into Mrs Heathcote's purse as she was being handed her jacket and hat by one of the maids, and then he made a joke. He did not appear to be meaning any harm.'

I managed a nod, and a 'Thank you, Owens,' before finding a seat and putting my backside on it.

After Owens left the parlour, Warren sat down next to me, and huffed, 'This is not good. Not good at all.'

'I'll talk to Uriel.'

'That'll be difficult. He took his wife and children to Cape Cod. Two days ago, according to his housekeeper.'

I BARELY MADE it home in time for supper. Margery stood behind Freddie and Georgie, her arms akimbo and chin lifted as she watched the boys scrubbing their hands, nails, and arms up to their elbows. She produced a satisfied grunt and jerked her head toward the table. They didn't need telling twice.

Klara eyed the new arrivals with curiosity as they shovelled stew into their mouths with an enthusiasm that didn't even fade on a third helping. Margery was happy enough, and so were the boys. When one pressed a fist to his mouth to stifle a burp, I said, 'Let's go to my office for a moment.'

They shuffled through the door, Georgie aloof, with his hands in his pockets, and Freddie somewhat nervous, his glance bouncing from floor to ceiling and wall to wall.

Once everyone was seated, I took in Freddie, who was

scooting about on his bum. 'Tell me what you know about Mrs Hyde's lover.'

All colour drained from his face. 'I know nothing.'

'I see. Why did you come here, Freddie?'

'Free supper.'

Georgie glared at his friend, elbowing his side. 'You lied to me, you pig!'

Freddie muttered, 'Sorry, Ma'am,' and stared at his boots.

'Hum.' I leaned back in my chair, wondering what it was that was making the boy so nervous. Surely, this cloak-and-dagger operation to get a free serving of Margery's stew wouldn't gnaw on his conscience all of a sudden? 'I assume you are both clever enough to know that others have heard you talking about Mrs Hyde's lover, and that you've seen his face. Should word of that reach the killer, you will be in great danger.'

Freddie turned white as a sheet. Even Georgie was struck.

'Catching the killer rather sooner than later will remove said danger. You do know that, yes?'

The boys looked at each other, and then Freddie mumbled. 'Don't know the gent's name. Just that he always wears these ridiculous, old-fashioned cravats.' He drew a finger from the base of his throat up to his chin.

'Describe him as best as you can,' I said.

'Dark hair, dark eyes. Always dressed nice, except for those horrid high collars without the wings. And the yellow neckties, er…I mean scarves. Or whatever.' Freddie shrugged.

'How tall is he? Is he fat? Skinny? Does he walk with a stick or without one? How old is he?'

Freddie blew up his cheeks. 'He's old. Like…your age.'

Georgie elbowed him again.

'*What?*' squeaked Freddie, and scooted farther away from his friend. 'Normal figure, I guess. Bit on the heavy side, maybe. A head taller than Mrs Hyde. And he walks with a stick. Like all the gents do. But his has a funny knob. Looks like a head of a dog from afar. Made of silver, I reckon.'

I WAS EXHAUSTED and trembling with tension when I slipped McCurley's key into the locked front door. Three flights of stairs had me huffing when I reached the landing to his apartment. I knocked, and he opened a short moment later.

One glance at my face, and he announced he would make strong coffee.

To my surprise, the window of the sitting room was ajar. Ms Hacker was sitting by the table, mending a shirt. Upon seeing me, she retreated to her chamber. I checked the time. A few minutes past eleven. I felt like I hadn't slept in days.

'Coffee will be ready in a few minutes,' McCurley said. 'Sit. I have news.'

'I have news, too.' I placed my briefcase on the table, sat down and rubbed my burning eyes.

We went through the names of my former colleagues at Harvard Medical School, but I couldn't pinpoint anyone who might be in particular danger from the Railroad Strangler. My friends, the Freaks, were an entirely different matter. They were potential victims as well as suspects. When I talked about Owens' observations, McCurley fell silent. He moved the coffee grounds around in his cup and clinked the spoon against the rim.

At that moment, Líadáin woke with a cry. McCurley went to his bedroom and returned with his daughter. He sat and bounced her on his lap. Her blue eyes were large and curious.

I continued, 'And then there's Freddie, one of Georgie's friends. He claims to have seen Mrs Hyde with her lover. He describes him as dark-haired with dark eyes. He was well-dressed but wore old-fashioned collars and neckties. He had a walking stick with a silver dog's head as a knob. The man was about my age, he thought, but he wasn't sure. Adults all look old to children. Normal figure, perhaps a bit heavy, and a head taller than Mrs Hyde.'

'Does this description fit Mr Crocker?'

'No. Uriel is lanky. He has fair hair and blue eyes. And I've never seen a walking stick or old-fashioned clothing on him.'

Slowly McCurley nodded. 'Which does not exclude him as a suspect. Mrs Hyde's lover isn't necessarily the killer, and Mr Crocker could have worn a wig, and a false beard and glasses when he visited the photographer.'

'Yes. But there is no connection between Uriel and Harvard Medical School.'

McCurley paused, sniffed at Líadáin's bottom, and decided it was time to change her nappy. I watched him undress the child, and said, 'May I take a quick look at her hips?'

His hands froze.

'If she has hip dysplasia, she will have problems as soon as she starts walking.'

A brief nod.

I picked up the half-naked baby, sat on the floor with my legs outstretched, and placed her on my thighs. I tickled her belly button until she giggled.

McCurley began pacing the room. 'Explain the procedure to me,' he said, his tone overly authoritative.

Too tired to wonder what had changed his mood so suddenly, I braced for yet another session of policeman versus suspect. 'To examine a small child's hips, one flexes her legs, gently compressing her hips posteriorly as they are circumducted. A displacement of the femur signifies dysplasia.'

'Excuse me?' he shot at me.

'Stop running about like a like a rooster with its tail on

fire. You are distracting me.' Líadáin gifted me a gummy smile and stuffed a fist into her mouth.

McCurley growled with frustration. 'I want to see how *you* deal with pain inflicted on your daughter.'

Stunned, I looked up. 'You think I'm hurting her? How can you even... Just look at her, will you? She's smiling.'

He raked his fingers through his hair, and sat on his haunches by my feet, his gaze stuck to my face. 'When the physician set her bone, he hurt her so much that she passed out screaming. He fancied sounding the expert, so that no one could understand him and question his judgement. Is that what you are trying to do?'

I dropped my head. My hand settled softly on Líadáin's stomach. She waved her arms and burbled. 'I am so sorry,' I said to her, and then to McCurley, 'Sit here, next to us, and I'll explain what I'm doing. I won't hurt her. I promise.'

After a pause, he moved to my side.

I began flexing Líadáin's legs again. 'Do you hear the click when I do this?'

'Yes. That sounds...bad.' He scanned his daughter's face for any signs of distress. But there were none.

'That's the ball slipping out of the socket,' I explained. 'You will notice that she doesn't feel pain when that happens.' I rolled her hips from one side to the other, which seemed to entertain her greatly. She squeaked in delight.

'In a newborn, the hip joint is mostly cartilage which is gradually replaced by bone during the first year. The ball component of the joint grows faster than the socket, and the correct development of the hip depends on the ball remaining in the socket. In a typical case of hip dysplasia, the socket is underdeveloped, not holding the ball properly fixed. And it keeps slipping out. But this here...feels different. Only the right hip joint is affected, and severely so. And the femur…I can feel where the fracture was.' I looked sideways at McCurley.

His fingers were digging into his thighs, and his jaw was clenched. He flexed his hands and said, 'Will she be limping?'

'Perhaps slightly. But not because her leg was broken. What I think happened is that no one checked whether her hip was damaged. The bones of newborns are soft and easily broken. The collarbone, for example, is prone to fracture during birth. Your daughter's thighbone has healed properly. But her hip joint needs attention. How was she splinted? With her legs spread?'

McCurley shook his head. 'With her knee bent and thick bandages around the length of her leg.'

'Nothing that held her thigh fixed at an angle?'

'No.'

'Hum.'

'Can anything be done?'

'Well, if I were to listen to my colleagues, I would insist on a hip brace. And Líadáin would give us an earful for using such a horrid contraption on her. It forces the legs apart and bends them at the knees. Very uncomfortable. Let us first try something gentler. Pass me the nappies, please.'

He did as asked, and I showed him how to fold them so that her legs were farther apart.

'And when you lay her down to sleep, make sure her femur isn't displaced. I'll show you how. Give me your hand.'

I brought his hand to Líadáin's thigh and showed him how to flex and fold her legs, wiggle her bottom and roll her hips. I pressed my fingertips on top of his, led them to her hip joint and said, 'This is how it feels when the ball is in the socket. Do you feel this groove? It's very narrow.'

He nodded, all his attention on his daughter.

'Now we will dislocate the hip.' I flexed and compressed her hip gently. McCurley's hand twitched when we heard the dull clicking sound of the femur displacing. 'Feel her hip joint. Do you notice the difference?'

'It's…remarkable. Can you put it back in, please?' He looked nearly desperate.

I smiled and said, 'You do it. Flex her knee like this, very gently push at the femur in this direction — yes, like this — and straighten her leg. Do you feel how it slips back in?'

McCurley's expression switched from concerned and pained, to beaming. The brilliant smile changed the entire man. It left me dumbstruck. Our physical proximity became awkward.

I placed the baby into his lap, brushed off my skirts, and went back to the table with my scattered notes. 'I need a few hours of sleep before I think about…well, everything. Is there a way to contact the Cape Cod police to find out where Uriel Crocker and his family are staying?'

McCurley was putting clothes on his daughter. He paused, then said, 'It might not be a good idea to contact Mr Crocker. It would give away what we know. I'll give an official statement to reporters tomorrow morning. I only hope it doesn't provoke the killer into murdering another woman.'

I pushed my notes back into my briefcase. 'He doesn't need provocation. He will kill again very soon. He's hungry for it.'

THE FOURTH VICTIM

21

or three weeks, we made very little progress. McCurley's men completed the list of Ms Munro's clients, but none of the names rang a bell. Georgie helped identify most of the tenants of the boathouses by the Glass Works, but they were all fishermen or members of a small rower's club. Not one of those people had a connection to Harvard Medical School.

And I spent my time investigating the disappearance of *Hattie's diary* because we couldn't be sure that Uriel had indeed taken my portraits. Neither McCurley nor I thought it a good idea to travel to Cape Cod because that would reveal that he and I were cooperating, that the police knew more about the murderer than they should.

It would foil our plans for a trap.

McCurley should be able to masquerade as a client and visit Uriel in his office without the murderer's notice — if, in fact, the murderer wasn't Uriel — but he would have to wait for Uriel's return from Cape Cod. Until then, we had to explore all the other possibilities.

Every day I anxiously awaited the morning mail — one

part of me dreading a message from McCurley telling me about a new victim, and the other — a small and dark part of me — hoping a strangled body would be found before Uriel returned.

But there was no victim and no Uriel.

McCurley had contacted the Cape Cod police and was able to confirm that Uriel arrived with his wife and two children for an extended holiday. His brother-in-law had accompanied them with his wife and child. Warren had also confirmed all this with Uriel's housekeeper.

Waiting was maddening. I wanted to take a train to Uriel, shake him, and demand answers. Unfortunately, that wasn't how an investigation worked.

'You can't wear this!' Hattie squeaked, pulling me from my thoughts.

'My goal is not to socialise or be seen.' I hung the black gown back into the wardrobe.

'Well, I don't care. You'll be among my people, as my friend and physician, and I don't want half the town talking about you. I'll send over my tailor with one of my gowns. It won't be the latest fashion, but at least it won't be *that*.' She waved at the shut wardrobe with horror.

'I'm not at home tonight, as you well remember. In fact, you and I have to leave soon.'

A grin spread across her face. 'Even better! We'll ask Mother's tailor to fit a gown for you.'

I SURVIVED the gown fitting without so much as a small dent to my patience and trailed Hattie down to the kitchens where the first deliveries for the ball were being made. I'd already met and talked to the coachmen Peck and Howe, as well as to Ms Brophy, who seemed eager to help because I was privy to her secret affair with Mr Towers. Regrettably, she knew nothing beyond the daily gossip that Miss Trattles and Miss Sowerby shared. The gap-toothed boys Billo and Alfie, who polished boots, honed kitchen knives and hatchets, and shovelled horse manure, were an entirely different matter. They'd read a well-thumbed detective novel once and were eager to catch the culprit singlehandedly. Their wild speculations ('Deductions, Ma'am! They are deductions!') were amusing. The only bit of useful information they'd managed to provide was the correct name of the fruit grocer — a Mr Crow, not Cow. But I could have learned that from any of the maids.

Mr Crow was just retreating through the backdoor when Hattie marched into the kitchens and called him back. Pretending not to eavesdrop as she asked him about fresh strawberries, I scanned his face for any familiarities but found none. I hadn't expected much else. A man who'd worked at Harvard Medical School wouldn't end up a grocer, would he?

Cold poured down my neck. Why had I not thought of it earlier? Had McCurley? The murderer didn't necessarily have to be a medical man. He could as well be a janitor.

'Are you quite all right, Liz? You are pale as a cheese.' Concerned, Hattie touched my elbow.

Shaking off the chill, I pulled myself together. 'I need to send a message.'

'You could use the telephone.'

And have half the house hear what I would be yelling at it? No. 'Billo or Alfie will do. And I need an envelope that I can seal.'

Hattie raised her eyebrows but complied with my wishes. A few moments later, my note was on its way to McCurley.

~

I KEPT WIPING my hands on my gown, and Hattie kept frowning at me from wherever she stood. Only minutes ago, she'd instructed me how a lady had to hold her fan so as to not accidentally signal to all the men in the room that she was feeling flirtatious. But I couldn't remember what precisely was supposed to attract male attention. The rapid opening and closing of the fan…or chucking it into one of the large vases by the windows? I let it dangle limply on my wrist until I found a statue in a far corner of the hall and stuffed it between the wall and the marble buttocks of a mildly amused Adonis.

One of the servants would surely find it and return it to Hattie.

The place made me nervous. It felt like everything there was a museum piece. The corridors alone were so richly appointed, I dared not skid my shoes on the carpets. The walls were panelled with wood that shimmered a warm golden yellow. The stucco on the gently vaulted ceiling was gold leaf on turquoise. The many paintings went back to the 16th century. The people seemed to as well.

But the great hall was…a picture of arrogance. I found no other word for it. The walls were covered with either gold leaf or silk tapestries. Several crystal chandeliers, each half as large as a horse carriage, were hung from the ceiling. I felt sorry for the maid who had to keep them dust-free.

As I made my way through the crowd, I caught snatches of conversations. One man with greying temples attempted to pull me into a discussion about the weather. 'Isn't Boston rain like a hundred shower baths? All the Englishmen I know insist they'd never seen *real rain* until they came to Boston.'

'Probably,' I replied and pretended someone across the room wanted me. Which, in fact, was only half a lie.

Warren was leaning against a pillar, arms crossed over his chest, and nodding at the three ladies who surrounded him.

When he spotted me, his expression lit up. He excused himself and took me aside. 'Please put a hole in my head. I can't *stand* the torture,' he groaned.

'But it's just started.'

'As if I don't know that.' He exhaled loudly, then bumped my side with his elbow. 'That's my intended over there. What do you think?'

A radiant girl of perhaps sixteen stared at us from the centre of the room. She was accompanied by an older woman. Probably her mother. 'Hum. Pretty, I guess.'

Warren guffawed. 'Beautiful, rich, and the daughter of a very influential family. And very traditional family. You won't find a women reformer among them. All they do is talk about raising money for furnishing newsboys with an extra pair of Sunday trousers, without ever donating anything themselves. The most progressive among them are board managers of charitable institutions. Which translates to Saturday afternoon tea spent with other rich women, who have nothing to do but gossip. Shall we dance?'

'There's no music. And I didn't come to dance.'

'Ah, yes, I remember. But look who honours us with *his* presence.' Warren nodded to a young man strutting toward us.

'Is that…' *Margaret? In men's clothes again?*

'Yes.'

'Good evening, my dear fellows.' Margaret dipped her chin and theatrically twirled a fake moustache.

'Outrageous!' Warren whispered, grinning. 'I'm so glad you could sneak in. Be a good chap and lift my mod. Liz here has only one thing on her mind.'

'Oh? And what might that thing be?' She eyed me from head to toe, then proceeded to run her gaze over Warren's attire. 'Oh, *I know* what it is. It has crossed my mind once or twice. Its perfect shape…rather hard to come by these days.'

Warren blinked. 'What the deuce are you talking about?'

She bent forward and whispered, 'Your perfect behind, of course. If I weren't so interested in the fairer sex, I would have taken you to bed long ago.'

Laughing, he boxed her chest. 'That's my boy!'

Coughing, Margaret grabbed her ribcage.

The two began to banter about the varying physical qualities of the men and women present, while I scanned the room for the Wray brothers. Warren — who knew what I was looking for — bent close to my ear and said, 'You won't miss them. They'll be announced when they arrive.'

Hattie pushed through the throng, beaming. 'I've decided to write pieces for the Pud!'

'The what?' I asked.

'The Hasty Pudding Club of Harvard College. It's a literary club. They accept papers on the changing role of women in society. And I'm going to interview *you* first.' She poked her fan at me.

I shook my head. 'I prefer privacy.'

'No problem. I won't publish your name.' She winked with both eyes and grinned expectantly.

'All right. As long as you keep my name out of it.'

She produced a happy nod and then caressed her stomach absentmindedly.

My gaze dropped to her hands. 'Is your uterus contracting?'

'Elizabeth Arlington!' she hissed. 'Your manners are unbelievable! You can't say that word in society!'

'Dear God, my intended is approaching. Can someone please tell a joke? Or stage a kidnapping?' Warren said.

'You want me to kidnap your bride?' Margaret perked up.

'No. *I* want to be kidnapped,' he said, keeping his voice low. And then to the approaching girl and her mother, 'Dorothy, Mrs Auston, it is a pure pleasure to see you.' He inclined his head, slipped his fingers around Dorothy's and pulled her knuckles in for a kiss.

Margaret, Hattie and I stared mutely at each other as Warren began to sweet-talk the two women. After a moment, he sauntered off with Dorothy. Mrs Auston remained and joined the staring contest.

Everyone else seemed perfectly comfortable, but I felt like a foreign object. Sometimes I couldn't help wondering why the Freaks wanted me for a friend. I didn't fit into their social circles.

Perhaps it was because I was a physician? Despite the progressiveness of the Bostonians, women doctors were still a curiosity, and hotly discussed in newspapers and drinking halls. Women like me even inspired stage plays and divorces.

But then, Eliza and Margaret didn't fit in either. They were performers, hot-blooded suffragettes, secretly married to each other, and partners in crime. The contrast between each and every one of us was stark. Where Margaret was dark and rather ill-mannered, Eliza was a fairy sprung directly from the woods with curly chestnut hair, grey-green eyes and a sprinkling of freckles perching high on her cheek-bones. No one would suspect that she and her wife were flouting social conventions and getting away with it.

Uriel was the Freaks' cool mind, and Jerome our brute force. Margaret and Eliza were our passion, and Hattie was our heart. She poured affection over us like a hummingbird over a tulip tree. And perhaps all this was what made us the Freaks. Our differences brought us together.

'Uhmpf.' Warren sidled up to me. 'I got rid of her. By the by, Uriel has returned.'

'Is he here?' I had a thousand questions for him.

Warren shook his head. 'Of course not. His housekeeper sent a boy over this evening with the message. Before the ball opened. I forgot to mention it. Gods, could someone please tell a joke? This...*thing*...is boring me to death.' He threw out his arm, motioning at the hall and all his guests.

'Ugh. Warren's jokes. *That's* where real boredom starts,' muttered Margaret and strolled off to talk to a pretty lady who'd kept smiling at her from beneath a flower garland.

'I'll start. Then it's your turn,' Warren said, and sucked in a breath. 'A newspaper reporter asks a woman: "Excuse me, Miss, do you believe that the American woman has any sense of humour?" She answers, "Your question has horribly tragic implications! Any woman attempting to answer it would suffer an immediate attack of nervous prostration. Ask me something easier."'

Hattie snickered.

'Did that really happen?' I asked and got a nonplussed stare in return.

'Err...' Warren scratched his neck. 'In fact, it did. But it doesn't seem to be your kind of humour. Which is acceptable, I guess. Anyway. I have another one, about Germans. Shall I? All right. Here it is: A German roundsman says to an English policeman: "Why don't you run in that man who's creating the disturbance?" The policeman answers, "I'm afraid it could be the emperor travelling incognito."'

I waited a few moments longer, but it seemed Warren was finished. 'Was it supposed to be funny?'

He rolled his eyes. 'I admit, I never found it amusing, but I've been told that Germans find it hilarious. You grew up in Germany, so I assumed...' He shrugged, and then his eyes lit up. 'But here's a *really* good one. Listen: Jasper says to Jumpuppe, "Nothing exceeds the insolence of the average German soldier. One time when I was in Berlin I saw a civilian riding a bicycle, and he bumped into an officer. The officer promptly drew his sword—" Jumpuppe interrupts, "And killed him?" "No," Jasper answers, "He punctured his bicycle tyre."'

Hattie giggled. For Warren's sake, I smile a bit.

He threw up his hands. 'Aw, dammit, Liz! You have no humour whatsoever.'

'I do, but you wouldn't understand it. People who work in the medical field have a very...dark sense of humour. Besides, one joke is all I know.'

'Well,' an elderly man pushed between Hattie and Warren. 'Everyone knows the American people *are* noted for their keen sense of humour. But the women of our nation,' he clicked his tongue, '...are entirely wanting.' Grinning, he stuck his pipe between his teeth and sauntered off.

'That was funny,' I said, pointing at the man's back.

'Let's hear your dark medical establishment joke,' Warren said.

I shook my head. 'You would hate it. And I *swear* someone is going to be sick if I tell it.'

That piqued Hattie's interest. She smiled expectantly. Warren leaned close to me and pressed through the side of his mouth, 'I have to announce my engagement tonight. I *need* a good laugh. Don't you see how desperate I am?' He wiggled his fingers at his face.

Hattie nodded until her perfectly coiffed curls bounced.

I groaned. 'You have all been warned. All right, here we go: Two lady post-mortem surgeons—'

Warren nearly choked. Wide-eyed, he filled his lungs with two hasty gulps, and then burst out braying with laughter.

'That's a good one!' Hattie squeaked with delight.

'Actually, I was just getting at the funny part,' I said, a little discomfited. 'May I continue?'

Hattie wiped away the tears that leaked from her eyes and flapped a hand at me to go on.

'Two lady post-mortem surgeons are performing an autopsy.'

Subdued laughter ensued.

'The first post-mortem surgeon says, "Do you remember that fellow from yesterday?" "Of course I do," says the second. "Strangely enough," the first post-mortem surgeon says, "His prick reminded me of a gherkin." "Oh, really? Because it was greenish and wrinkly?" "No — because it was sour."'

As soon as the word "prick" fell, Hattie blushed a fiery red. But when I got to "sour" she turned several shades of green and white. She clapped a hand to her mouth and burped softly.

Shrugging, I looked up at Warren in an *I told you so* fashion.

He stared at me. 'That was *disgusting*, Liz.'

'Did I miss something?' Margaret had reappeared, her expression alight with curiosity.

'No, you did not!' hissed Hattie.

Warren bumped my shoulder, and nodded toward Margaret, 'There's someone who'd enjoy that particular joke.' He looked up at the ceiling and began to snicker. 'Gherkin,' he muttered, and then his shoulders shook. 'Ew!'

'I've had enough.' Hattie turned and disappeared among the guests.

'Now I *have* to hear it!' Margaret said.

'You tell her.' I waved at Warren and followed Hattie. I hoped she wasn't too upset with me.

Behind me, Margaret and Warren guffawed. I looked back. He was grinning and wiping his eyes. She was covering her face with both hands and rocking with laughter. I wasn't sure if they were laughing about the joke, or about me believing it was hilarious. When I first heard it, I'd nearly died with laughter.

I drifted through the crowd, not quite sure what I was looking for. A familiar face? A man who looked like he wanted to choke me, or one with a sign saying "I am the Railroad Strangler" attached to his back? The more time passed, the less certain I was about the usefulness of my endeavour.

When, finally, Warren came up to me to tell me that the Lords Wray had arrived and would be announced shortly, I breathed a sigh of relief. I would take a look at them, and then go home.

Warren moved us a little closer to his parents, near the entrance to the hall. His father was an imposing figure with a booming voice. A man who believed the world was his for the taking. His wife was a slender and beautiful woman. A mother who lived solely through her children, according to Hattie.

'Is your mum happy you are actually attending your own bachelor's ball?' I asked.

'My *mom* is completely beside herself. As you can well see.'

I looked over at Mrs Amaury, who slid a hand through her husband's elbow bend. 'She looks rather… stone-faced.'

'She's nervous. There is so much to go wrong with a son like me.' Warren clicked his tongue.

Three middle-aged men entered, effectively hushing the crowd. Grimshaw announced them loudly. He had to pump his lungs several times to get out their long names and titles.

'Are you going to interrogate them now? Shall I get the thumbscrews?'

I laughed and waved my lids prettily at Warren.

'Ah, I see, your main goal is to torture me. Is that why my sister asked you to join the Freaks?'

'Of course.' I shifted my focus to the Wray brothers who were in polite conversation with Mr and Mrs Amaury. The men looked…faintly familiar. Hattie told me that they'd had spent time at Harvard. But I couldn't place their faces. Where had I seen them before? 'Warren, would you introduce me, please?'

Only when I heard a faint croak, did I take my eyes off the group and look up at Warren. 'What?'

'Are you looking for a husband or something?'

I opened my mouth, but nothing came out. I couldn't go into detail about what McCurley had told me, could say nothing about our conclusions and suspicions. So I cleared my throat and answered, 'Yes'

Warren straightened. 'Well, I must disappoint you but two of the Wrays are already married, and the youngest is infamous for...buggery.'

I snapped my fingers. 'Damn.'

'By the gods, Liz. Sometimes I don't know whether you are joking, or not.'

'I'm just curious about them.' I nodded toward the Wray brothers. 'Somehow, they look familiar.'

Warren pulled up his eyebrows. 'A lot of people say that. That the Wrays look familiar. I think all they look is too smooth.'

Then he offered his arm to me and tugged me along. 'Mother, Father, Lords Wray, may I introduce my sister's best friend, who is also her physician, Dr Elizabeth Arlington?'

I'd met Warren's parents briefly before. They had taken as much notice of me as they had of their servants — none. Now, though, they looked me up and down, plastered perfectly courteous masks on their faces, and enquired about my husband.

'He passed away two and a half years ago,' I provided, which was answered with profuse apologies.

My gaze slipped over to the Wray brothers. 'Warren's told me you all went to Harvard. I was wondering if one of you studied medicine there?'

One of the older two laughed mildly and shook his head. 'We are barristers.'

'I see. But…do you think the Harvard Medical School will one day open its doors to women?'

The youngest of them — a swarthy man of perhaps thirty-five — cocked his head. 'They will drag it out as long as possible. As a rule, males do not like to share power. We compete for it. As well, we compete for domination over females. Allowing women into a man's domain would destroy our long-established power hierarchy. Knowledge is power. We view females aspiring for power as an existential threat.'

Mr Amaury's jaw muscles bulged. 'Darwin and his honourable colleagues have proved time and again that women are less evolved than men, and hence, they do not have the mental capacity for medicine. Or any other form of higher education for that matter.'

Mrs Amaury nodded severely, snapped open her fan and fluttered air at her chin.

I said, 'Darwin also told his wife that she was, and I quote, "an object to be beloved and played with — better than a dog, anyhow." Isn't it strange how many people are happy listening to themselves spout off about women not being as good as men?'

Mr and Mrs Amaury bristled with disgust. But certainly not directed at Mr Darwin's faulty statement.

I turned my attention back to the youngest Wray brother. 'Yours is one of the aptest observations I've heard. I like your directness.'

A slow grin spread over his face. He gifted me a small bow. But before he could say more, music began to play.

I thought back to the dances I'd shared with Garret in tumbledown warehouses in a London slum. There had been no faked smiles. No one was made to strap herself into a corset or had worn a gown so expensive the price would have fed a hundred street urchins for months.

I didn't take notice of the people moving around me in waves. The younger Wray brother asked for a dance, but I only shook my head. I had wasted enough time. It was time to go.

Margaret whirled a young lady with long golden hair over the dance floor. Her cheeks were shining and her eyes glistened mischievously. I wondered if the young woman was aware that Margaret was lacking a certain few — but crucial — physical attributes of a gentleman.

Warren was dancing with his bride, but he didn't seem wholly present. Slowly, I took a step back and wove my way toward the exit. This parade of spoiled upper-class individuals was entirely unpleasant. I stopped myself. Wasn't I getting there myself? My wealth had to be greater than that of half the guests. The same I had just deemed spoiled.

Was I all that different?

A hand came down on my shoulder. 'Why did you not ask the Lords Wray about the sketchbook?' Warren was a bit out of breath. He smoothed back his hair. His light-blue eyes glittered with an emotion I couldn't decipher.

'I got all the information I needed.'

'Oh. Did you, now? Hum. Care for a dance?' He placed a hand on my waist, cocked his head, and breathed in mock horror, 'No corset! Dear me!'

I pushed his hand away. 'I don't dance.' Which wasn't entirely true.

'Why ever not?'

'Because dancing is…an idiotic…' I looked around, trying to catch the right words. 'Stylised mating behavioural display.'

Warren sputtered, 'It is *what?*'

'Never mind. I don't dance. Don't ask me again.'

He laughed. 'Is that so? I wonder what all the sweet young ladies think about your theory.'

'It's not a theory. And I wish to leave now. By the by, I am relieved you did not include *me* when you talked about sweet ladies.'

He clapped a hand to his chest. 'Oh, I would *never* dare insinuate such a thing! You are not sweet. Your personality is bigger than one would think would fit your frame. No, you are not sweet, you are beautiful.'

I snorted. 'Warren, don't be ridiculous. I'm not beautiful. And why are you flirting with a woman who is nearly a decade older than you?'

'Are you? And is that all that can be said about you?'

'Yes. And that I need to leave now. I wish you an entertaining night.' With that, I turned and made for the door.

Warren followed me. 'You don't want me to flirt with you?'

I came to a halt. 'Indeed, no. Although I must admit I find it quite pleasant. But I do not want to raise false hopes.'

'Aha! So you have thought about the possibility of me flirting with you, and then came to the conclusion that nothing is ever going to happen between us.'

'What? No! Or…yes?' I shook my head and resumed walking. At least I'd made it to the first corridor.

'Hum. I see. Whatever it is, you did come to your conclusion very quickly. So, either you find me entirely hideous — which I am not — or, you thought about flirting and then decided I was not flirt-worthy material, for whatever reason that might be.'

Groaning, I stopped and grabbed his elbow. 'Warren, I hate to say it, but you are about to get married.'

He lifted an eyebrow. 'Am I now?'

I threw an arm toward the hall. 'Well, this is a bachelor's ball is it not?'

'Precisely. Which means it is not a wedding.'

'What are you planning, Warren?' I narrowed my eyes.

'Several things.' He smiled mischievously, shrugged, and continued walking.

'You'll probably end up breaking her heart.'

'Fortunately, she is not interested in marrying me.'

'Are you entirely blind? Did you not see how she ogled you most of the evening?'

'I know for a fact that she loves another man. And her parents won't allow her to marry him.' He produced an impatient growl, and flapped his hand over his shoulder, indicating the merry crowd in the hall far behind us. 'And I know for a fact that all those girls have only one thing in mind: To marry me for my name, my wealth, and my influential family. I am nothing but breeding material, Liz. A means to an end. Do you think that's romantic?' He strode through the entrance hall, nearly at a run now.

I'd never even considered that a man could suffer the fate of a woman. I caught up with him and told him I was sorry.

He nodded once. 'You judge fast and harsh, my friend.'

He accompanied me outside and down the marble steps. The walkway crunched under my feet as I walked to Hattie's carriage.

'Allow me to bring you home,' Warren said. Upon my frown, he added, 'I insist.'

We climbed into his calash and sat opposite one another.

'Why can't you say no to it all?' I asked.

'Because Father has power. He has threatened disinheritance.'

'So, it was money or freedom. And you choose money.' I couldn't feel sorry for Warren. Many people had to live on less than a nickel a week.

'Isn't money freedom? But…it isn't just the inheritance that's the problem. If I refuse my father, he'll make sure I never find a post. Not in America. Not even in England. He'll make sure I'm not taken on even as a chimney sweep's help. I even toyed with the idea...' He trailed off, frowning.

'Which idea?'

'To fake my death. But I can't do that to Mother.'

'You'd need an excellent forger to start a new life.'

He shrugged. 'No problem. I have...friends.'

'The mysterious McConaughey?'

'How do you... Oh, I told you about him.'

'Of him. Not about him.' As the carriage pulled up to the gate of my house, I realised that I had forgotten something essential. 'Warren, it seems I do need your help.'

He bent forward. 'Finally!'

I smirked. 'I don't want to wake up my housekeeper, so, if you please?' I turned and presented him with my back.

'Oh, you mean...'

'Just down to my shoulder blades. I should be able to reach the rest.'

Warren coughed.

'Just do it, for Christ's sake! I won't bite.'

'All right.' Swiftly, he unbuttoned the top of my gown. He made to say something, but I blurted, 'Thank you,' and yanked the door open before the coachman could do it for me.

I jumped out, but the hem of my gown had got tangled around Warren's ankles, effectively tipping me face-first onto the walkway. Swearing, I scrambled up and inspected my bloody palms. 'Gods, how I *deplore* gowns!'

Warren's feet hit the pavement. He hurried to help me up. 'Are you hurt?'

'No,' I bit out.

He took my hands in both of his and gently blew on the abrasions.

'It is unhelpful to blow germs on an open wound.'

'Is my breath offensive?' He cupped a hand to his mouth,

exhaled and sniffed. 'Champagne. Sweetmeats.' He narrowed his gaze at me. 'How do germs smell?'

'There is no need to keep holding my hand.'

'No medical need. I see that.' He gazed down at my hand in his, held it up to his mouth and kissed my wrist.

'What…are you doing?' A stupid question, but nothing useful would form in my mind.

'I am applying my lips to your wrist. Do you wish me to stop?'

'I…'

He turned my hand and kissed my knuckles. His light-blue eyes were black in the night. He took a step forward until his chest touched mine.

'Two dozen beautiful and well-bred ladies are salivating over you, but you flirt with a woman who is older than you, who hails from the working class, and who runs around in knickerb—'

His lips touched mine. A soft brush of butterfly wings. Then he slowly pulled away.

'—knickerbockers.'

He grinned. 'Yes.'

'Why are you flirting with me, Warren?'

'Isn't that obvious?'

'Your motivation? No.'

He paused, turned my right hand and caressed what was left of my index finger. 'You are beautiful and untamed.'

I wrenched away from his grip. 'Neither do I aim to be decorative, nor have I *any* desire to be tamed.'

He opened his mouth and snapped it shut, shook off my words with a jerk of his head. 'Why do we suddenly need a dictionary to understand each other? I tell you that I find you beautiful, and you hear me say I wish you were my pretty accessory. I tell you that I find you untamed, and you hear me say I wish I could tame you.'

I took a step back and crossed my arms over my chest. 'Like you, I don't wish to be a means to an end.'

'Whatever do you mean?'

'You are looking for a way out. I understand that. Your parents are insisting you find a wife and have children. You feel pressure to comply because you don't want to lose the luxuries provided by the wealth of your family. Your way out is to openly court a working-class woman. Your father might suddenly find that an unmarried heir is better than an heir courting the wrong woman and causing a scandal.'

'Do you believe *that's* my motivation?' He straightened his shoulders. 'Did you love your husband so much that no one compares to him?'

I sucked in a hiss.

He blinked as it dawned on him. 'No. You hated him so much that every man now is likened to him.'

'This has *nothing* to do with my late husband.'

'Then why do you explain away what I feel for you? Wouldn't it hurt you if I rationalised your emotions?'

He was right. But it did nothing to change my mind.

I lifted my hand and ran my fingers along his jaw. 'I'm sorry. But I'm not the right woman for you. Good night, Warren.' I turned away.

22

*E*arly the following morning, Hattie all but broke down the door. Her first words were incomprehensible. It took her several attempts to convey that Warren had been attacked by a gunman.

I snatched my doctor's bag, and she hurried me to the waiting calash. The two horses were sweaty and foam dripped from their bits. The coachman must have whipped them like the devil.

I stopped. 'Have you not summoned a surgeon yet?'

'Of course, we have. Father called for a doctor as soon as Warren appeared!' She shoved me into the carriage. The door was shut, steps folded up, and we dipped to the side as the coachman climbed onto the driver's seat.

Unsure whether my skills would be needed at all, I asked, 'What happened?'

Hattie was puffing with agitation. She flipped a disorderly lock of hair from her face and clamped it behind her ear. She squeezed her eyes shut for a moment, filled her lungs, and exhaled slowly. 'Last night, as he was returning from your home, someone shot him.'

Gingerly, I took Hattie's hand in mine. 'How serious is it?'

'He…' Tears welled up her eyes. She pressed a hand to her mouth to muffle a sob. 'He will lose his left eye.'

'A shot to the head?' No. That can't be. How would…

'The attacker missed him by inches. Thank God! But the window shattered and the shards flew directly into his face, and…' She turned away and pressed a handkerchief to her face. I moved to her side and wrapped an arm around her. Weeping, she collapsed against my chest.

No words of comfort would come from my lips. All I felt was fury. It boiled under my skin and screamed for revenge. 'I'm done. I'll kill this prick.'

'Wh…at?' She sniffled.

'I have an idea who might have attacked Warren.'

She looked up. 'You do?'

'Maybe.'

Her tear-streaked and reddened face suddenly lost all colour. 'You don't mean… The Railway Strangler? Is this some personal vendetta against you? Is that why he left your portrait with one of the bodies?'

'I believe so.' I didn't tell her that McCurley and I were working together, and had reached the same conclusion. That needed to remain a secret. For now.

We reached the Amaury mansion, stormed into the house, up two flights of stairs, and into a bedroom that seemed as large as my entire house. It was as richly appointed as the rest of the mansion. The bed was an enormous, hand-carved, mahogany contraption. The wastefulness of it all was sickening.

Warren lay half propped up on the bed, one side of his head wrapped in bandages. Next to him sat his father, smoking a cigar. His mother stood by the window, kneading the front of her gown into small dumplings. From time to time, she sniffled.

I dropped my bag next to Warren's bed and turned to his parents, who had yet to acknowledge our presence. 'Open the windows. Throw out that cigar, the smoke is doing your son's injuries no favour.'

At my sharp command, Mr Amaury snapped upright and eyed me with disgust. 'Aren't you the common wench—'

'Don't you *dare!*'

Stunned, I turned to Hattie. I'd never expected her to speak with anything but respect to her parents. She stood in the centre of the room, fists propped against her hips.

'None of this is Liz's fault. She is here to help. Step out of the room and let her work.' She was practically growling. Then, she said with less grit in her voice, 'Please.'

Nostrils flaring and without ever looking at his own daughter, he left. Mrs Amaury sniffed once more and approached Hattie. 'He is upset, you know.'

'And *of course,* he is the only one,' Hattie retorted.

Her mother left without another word. Hattie threw the windows open, and I sat down on Warren's bed.

'She can be a harpy when she wants to be,' Warren whispered and winked his healthy eye at me.

'Tell me what happened,' I said.

'Someone… Someone shot me.'

I touched the healthy side of his face, pulled his lids apart and checked the reaction of his pupil. My fingers felt for his carotid and measured his pulse. Nothing seemed to indicate shock, pain, or blood loss. Odd.

'The surgeon must be excellent.'

'He's brilliant. But Father insisted on summoning a specialist from New York,' Warren bit out.

'A good decision. Why are you not happy with it? You could lose your eye, for all I know.' I threw a glance at Hattie. She leaned against the window sill, chin trembling.

Warren turned his head away. 'It's just… It's because

Father never listens to anything I say. He discounts my wishes and only sees his own. I am twenty-five, Liz. Twenty-five and he treats me like a small boy. Anyway. Don't worry about me. I'm all right.'

'Are you not in pain?'

'No. It's the morphia. I'm sure it will wear off soon.' He picked at his fingernails.

'Strange. The surgeon must have given you very little because your pupil reaction is normal.' I scanned his face. I knew he was not saying something. Or, in fact, that he'd been lying. But about what precisely, I couldn't tell. 'Have the police been informed?'

'Yes,' Hattie said from across the room. 'A sergeant took Warren's statement earlier. Father asked him to send their best detective. So far, no one has come, but it's only been two hours or so.'

'Hum. Would you please telephone the police headquarters? I understand that Inspector McCurley is leading the investigation into the Railway Strangler. He questioned me about the first victim. And perhaps it would help if you told him that I asked for him? I'm sure he remembers my name.'

Warren's gaze followed Hattie as she left the room. Perplexed, he looked at me. 'Why are you... Oh. Oh! You believe the Railway Strangler might have done this?' Shock spread over his features. 'But that's nonsense!'

I stood and paced to the window, wondering what all this was about. Why I couldn't shed the feeling that Warren was lying. But why would he?

'Do you—' I broke off when Hattie came back in.

'Inspector McCurley will be here in a moment,' she said.

'Really? But that's entirely unnecessary!' Warren protested.

I said to him, 'You know that the Railway Strangler left a

copy of my portrait for the police to find. It's a far stretch but…I wonder if he saw us together last night.'

'What do you mean by "saw us together"?' Hattie asked. 'You said you dropped her off.'

'He dropped me off and then he…kissed me.'

'What? You did *what*? Warren! How could you? She's my friend!'

Warren groaned, shut his eye and leaned back. 'So? I *was* respectful, wasn't I?' He opened his eye and directed it at me.

'Yes. You were.'

'And you?' Hattie jerked a finger in my direction. 'Are you going to break his heart now that he has only one eye left?'

I opened my mouth but was interrupted by Warren. 'She's not interested. At least that's what she said. So there's no possibility of heartbreak whatsoever. Just a small dent to my ego.'

Hattie blew out a breath.

'What about your engagement?' I asked.

Warren levelled a cold stare at me. 'It's called off. And I don't expect Father will be able to find a one-eyed pirate princess for me any time soon.'

A sob erupted from Hattie.

'Will you allow me to examine your injury?' I scooted closer.

Warren threw up his hand. 'I am in enough pain already.'

Puzzled, I drew back.

He continued, 'So far, all of our encounters have ended in pain. So, no, thank you, but I'll survive without you checking my eye.'

'What the deuce are you talking about?'

He lifted a finger. 'Your shifting of the broken bones of my poor nose was painful and entirely unnecessary.' He lifted a second finger. 'As was you breaking my nose before it had a chance to heal.'

'She did what?' Hattie cried.

Warren licked his lips. 'Would you care to explain it to her, Liz?'

Without turning my gaze away from him I said to Hattie, 'I broke into his house in the dead of night to confront him about the drawing. We had a…scuffle.'

'A *scuffle?*'

'I gave her a black eye, and she broke my nose,' Warren supplied. 'Did you know her gardener has been teaching her boxing?'

Hattie gasped.

'He doesn't…' I shook my head and waved the argument away.

'And then,' Warren said cheerfully. 'Then you have the guts to explain away my feelings for you, and the next thing that happens is this.' He pointed at the bandage on his face.

I couldn't believe it. 'You are blaming me for the attack?'

He dropped his gaze.

My shoulders sagged. 'Well, I guess in a way I drew you into this. *After* you drew me.' Slowly, I pushed away, too tired to continue the conversation. Too tired of not getting anywhere, of always limping ten steps behind the murderer. I needed to talk to Uriel. Right away. 'I'll see you later.'

I grabbed my bag, walked up to the door, and threw it open.

McCurley stood on the other side, fist poised to knock. 'Is Mr Amaury awake?'

I nodded. Neither of us gave the slightest indication that we knew each other from more than the brief meeting we'd had between inspector and witness.

'Would you mind waiting just a moment, Dr Arlington? I will need a statement from you.'

'Of course. Hattie, are you coming? Unless she is needed here?'

'Later, perhaps,' McCurley said and shut the door behind us.

Hattie and I waited in the corridor. It wasn't long until McCurley emerged. He announced that he would take my statement down in the stables, where he would also examine Warren's carriage. He added that Mrs Heathcote was no longer needed.

Unspeaking, I followed him. He inspected the shattered window, the frame, and the door. He looked inside the carriage and stared at the blood on the floor. 'He comes home with a bloody handkerchief pressed to his face. Hum…'

McCurley dipped a finger into the congealed blood on floor and bench. 'The spatter looks odd. I don't see any small droplets. If Mr Amaury told the truth, the blood must have fallen from a height of about four feet. When a drop hits the floor, it bursts. But there's nothing like that here.'

He examined the shards, their number and size, peeked under the benches of the carriage, and then climbed inside. With a soft grunt, he pushed his pinkie through the hole in the back wall. 'Very odd indeed.'

He unplugged his finger, squatted down and gazed up at the hole, and how the light fell through it. Then he looked back at the bench and at me. 'Does your friend have any reason to lie about the attack?'

23

*W*hen we returned to his room, Warren's eye shifted from my cold expression to McCurley's unfathomable one.

'Dr Arlington will remove your bandage,' McCurley said, his voice flat.

Warren swallowed and sat farther up. 'I c-c-can't allowed that. The surgeon ordered n-n-not to touch or rem-move the bandage under any c-circumstances if I wish to keep my eye.'

McCurley titled his head a fraction. 'Dr Arlington, in your expert opinion, is it possible to do further damage to Mr Amaury's injured eye by carefully lifting the bandage off the wound?'

'If a trained physician does it, someone such as myself, I believe it to be quite safe.'

'Go ahead then,' McCurley said.

Paling, Warren held up a hand. 'I c-can't allow it. Except you p-p-present me with a w-warrant.'

McCurley walked to the chair Warren's father had occupied earlier. He picked at a cushion, sat down, and regarded the large oil painting that hung above Warren's bed. A hunting scene. 'Well, Mr Amaury, you have two options. One, you can tell us the truth now. Or two, you can insist that I spend my time on this investigation. I will write notes, examine the rather odd blood splatter in the carriage, the even stranger angle of the bullet hole, and the queer fact that the glass shards cannot be arranged around a small point of impact — such as one would expect from a bullet.'

The longer McCurley spoke, the more fidgety Warren grew.

'You see, Mr Amaury, I never trust witness accounts. I trust evidence. And the evidence I've seen tells me that the bullet was fired from inside the carriage, and the blood did not come from a fresh wound. Were you keeping it in a jar? Did it clot so that you had to rub it hard into your handkerchief to make it look like it had come from your wound? But then, perhaps you were pleasantly surprised that clots do look like pieces of flesh from afar, do they not?'

'You show no signs of shock, pain, or blood loss, Warren,' I said softly.

'It appears to me that you have committed fraud,' Mc Curley cut in. 'Now you must decide if you also wish to obstruct my ongoing investigation into the Railway Strangler murders.'

A shudder went through Warren. Sighing, he shut his eye. 'She doesn't need to remove the bandage. I'm not injured. I haven't been attacked. It's like you said. I had a jar of pig's blood under the bench. I spread it on myself, the seat, and the floor, and I used the empty jar to break the window at the same moment that I shot a hole in the back wall of the carriage.'

I approached the bed and sat on the mattress. 'Why, Warren?'

He kept his gaze pinned to his blanket. 'I saw no way out.'

'Really? Have you *any* idea of the damage you have

caused?' Angry, I stood. 'You hurt your mother, your father. You broke your bride's heart. You pretend to be in love with me, pretend to be severely injured — about to lose your eye — and you don't think *anything* of it? Have you not for a moment considered Hattie's feelings? Your twin sister? Didn't you see her crying her eyes out? And all of this suffering just so you don't have to stand up to your parents?'

He looked up then, searching for words. 'Well, I…'

'I don't want to hear it. Look around you, Warren. All this luxury. You have been spoon-fed your whole life. Twenty-five years. No worries. No responsibilities. Of course, your father leads you around on a leash. He doesn't see you can walk without it!'

He was pale as a ghost when I turned away and strode from the room, the mansion, the majestic driveway and premises, to finally come to a stumbling halt in the street.

'Well, that was interesting,' McCurley said.

'Damn it to hell and back!' I cried.

'What was all that about?'

'His father is trying to force him to marry. I know I probably judge him too harshly, but this — *this* — is going too far. I believed the Railway Strangler did that to him. He even let me believe it!'

'It was an obvious conclusion. I wonder if he toyed with it. If deceiving you was part of his plan all along.'

'I don't care!' I kept stomping ahead, hoping to shed some of my anger.

'He will be prosecuted. As will his accomplice, the surgeon. If the man even was a surgeon.'

'I know. Warren deserves it. I don't have time for his nonsense now. Uriel is back and I want to talk to him about the portraits.'

McCurley grabbed my arm and brought me to an abrupt

halt. 'Mr Crocker is back? Why didn't you tell me that before?'

'I only learned about it last night. A lot has happened since then.'

'You will not talk to Mr Crocker. I will. Right away, in fact.' He looked back. 'We just passed the police carriage. I could ask the driver to—'

'You won't get far with Uriel. He is the most level-headed man I know. And he's a lawyer. If he gets the faintest inkling that he is being investigated for a crime, he won't say a word. You'd have to arrest him, or at least get a warrant. He is like you. He knows how to use silence to his advantage.'

Unconvinced, McCurley cut a sideways glance at me.

'You don't have anything to lose if you let me talk to him for a few minutes first.'

He gave me a single nod. 'Do you have your revolver with you?'

'No, I…didn't think I would need it.'

WE ALIGHTED A BLOCK from Uriel's office. McCurley walked with me to the entrance of the brownstone building. His revolver was hidden under my jacket that was folded over my arm.

'Fire a shot through the window if he threatens you, and I'll get there in ten seconds.'

'I doubt it will come to that.' I left him standing on the pavement.

When I entered Uriel's office and he looked at me in shock, my heart wilted. I wiped all emotions off my face and shut the door.

'I'm sorry, but…' He trailed off when I plopped down in a chair opposite him, a massive desk between us.

'You can't be here, Elizabeth.'

'No *Hello Liz* today?'

He folded his hands in front of him. 'My apologies, but I have to ask you to leave. A client will be arriving in a minute.'

'I was told your client is to arrive in about forty-five minutes. I will take only ten. You stole my portraits from Warren's sketchbook. Why?'

He sagged in what must have been relief, but...that couldn't be. As though having been discovered was making him feel better.

'I knew that she took the sketchbook,' he began. 'Hattie, that is. I wasn't sure if she just wanted to keep it away from Warren, or if she wanted to destroy your portraits. So I decided to make sure they were gone for good. I knew you didn't want them to end up in the hands of a stranger.'

'But they did.'

Uriel put his face in his palms. 'Yes, and with that, all the problems began.'

It felt like he had dumped a bucket of ice water over me. 'Explain.'

'My wife found them that same night. In my pocket. She thinks we're having an affair, for Christ's sake!' He dropped his hands flat on the desk, leaned back and groaned up at the ceiling.

'Go on.'

'I tried to explain, but she wouldn't listen, wouldn't believe anything I said. She threatened a divorce. So I took her and the children to Cape Cod. We hadn't had a vacation for a long time anyway.'

'What did she do with the portraits?'

'She destroyed them, of course.'

'Do you happen to have a walking stick with a dog's head?'

Puzzled, he drew back. 'What? No. You know me. I don't like running around like a masher.'

Funny. The same term had been used to describe Ms Munro's lover. 'Did you see your wife destroy the portraits?'

'Of course… Well, no. I didn't see her burn them, but why would she lie to me about that? She has absolutely no reason to keep them.'

I stood. 'I need to talk to your wife.'

Wild-eyed, Uriel jumped from his chair. 'No, I can't allow that. You have no idea what I've been through this last month.'

'No, I can't imagine.' With that, I left.

I met McCurley down in the street and told him what I'd learned.

He told me he would go on up to ask Uriel a few more questions, and then talk to his wife. I agreed because it seemed the best strategy, given that my appearance at Uriel's home would be seen as an affront. And Uriel's wife would close up like an oyster the moment she laid eyes on me.

We bade each other farewell after I extracted a promise from McCurley — that he would send a note as soon as he learned anything new.

IT WAS in the early afternoon when Margery entered my office to tell me I had a visitor.

I rose from my chair the moment Sergeant Boyle stepped into the room. He wasn't wearing his uniform. I knew immediately that something was wrong.

He shut the door and waved at his clothes. 'My apologies. I don't want anyone to know the police are here. Inspector McCurley sent me. He's talked to Mrs Crocker. As you know, she found your portraits. She was very upset and believes you are having an affair with her husband. She has consulted her brother on whether or not to divorce Mr Crocker.

During that discussion, she showed him the *evidence*, as she calls it. She did note, though, that her brother appeared oddly stricken by the drawings. He tore one to pieces before she could stop him. She found that very puzzling, but he explained that he was overcome with fury, that he couldn't endure the thought of his lovely sister being betrayed by her husband. Mrs Crocker told her brother she wanted to retain the second portrait as evidence. Interestingly, she was able to produce it upon the inspector's request. Meaning to say, it was put back after it was taken to the photographer. Inspector McCurley is certain that the portrait Mrs Crocker showed him is the original.'

With each of Boyle's words, I grew colder. 'Is he the murderer? The brother?' I croaked.

'It appears so. Mrs Crocker's brother — Mr Haywood — works as a hygiene inspector for two large dairy companies. According to his wife, he'd wanted to be a physician and was accepted to Harvard Medical School. However, he aborted his studies. The reasons are unclear, but hopefully, the inspector will find out more.'

'Where is he now?'

'Inspector McCurley?'

'Yes. No! Mr Haywood.'

Boyle sucked in a breath and his expression grew apologetic. 'That is the reason Inspector McCurley sent me. For your protection. Mr Haywood's whereabouts are unknown.'

I stood and paced the room. 'What do you mean, *unknown?*'

'The inspector enquired at the Elm Farm Company — one of the two large dairy companies Mr Haywood works for, the other being the Boston Dairy Company — but the suspect has not been seen since the day Mr Crocker took his family to Cape Cod.'

'But that would only be one day of—'

Boyle held up his hand. 'Mr Haywood did not ask to take a holiday. He left work without telling his employers of his plans.'

'That is…worrisome.'

'Indeed,' said Boyle, and dropped into a chair.

'Do you have a revolver?' I asked.

Boyle looked offended. 'Of course not! I'm a policeman, not some…Wild West dandy.'

'Well, good that I have one.' I left the office to fetch my gun and ammunition, and informed Margery to send away all remaining patients.

THE WAITING CLAWED at my nerves. Boyle seemed quite relaxed and to be enjoying the refreshments Margery had prepared for all of us. I didn't allow Klara to go out into the garden, so instead we read books and drew pictures. Zachary kept working outside, to keep an eye out for us.

Late that afternoon we received a note from McCurley. A photograph was enclosed that showed Haywood with his wife. I didn't find anything familiar in his face.

McCurley's note read,

MR HAYWOOD HAS NOT BEEN SEEN at either of the dairy companies, at any of the farms he inspects, or at the milk contractor's depots. All three railways where the Strangler's victims were found are used to transport milk to and from the milk depots that Haywood inspects. Mrs Haywood stated that her husband went to work on the mornings in question, and returned late in those evenings. She has no knowledge of his current whereabouts.

Boyle will remain at your house for your protection. Do not leave! I will come to you later this evening.

Quinn McCurley

. . .

I CRUMPLED the note and began to disassemble my revolver on the kitchen table.

'A Wembley Mark I,' Boyle remarked. 'British service revolver. Reliable.'

'Would you like more tea?' Margery enquired with a trembling voice.

When I'd finished cleaning and oiling my gun, I gave the photograph to Zachary. 'If you see this man, point your revolver at him. Sergeant Boyle will arrest him.' And then to Margery, 'Pack food and milk for tonight and tomorrow morning. And several books for Klara. As soon as darkness falls, you will all leave through the tunnel.'

'Inspector McCurley ordered me to protect you,' Boyle pointed out.

'And you will. I will lock up the house, and make sure it looks as if we're at home, and then follow shortly after.'

Frowning, Boyle scratched his neck but then nodded in agreement.

24

J walked about the house to draw the curtains, switch off lights, and lock all doors. From the outside, it would look as though we were retiring early. A deviation from the norm. But I didn't worry about it, for who goes to bed at precisely the same time every night, like an automaton? No one.

I went into the kitchen and found one of Margery's muffins. It was bone dry. I spread butter on it. Leaning against the sink, I ate and thought about Haywood. It was not an unusual name. I'd probably heard it previously. But his face…I didn't think I'd ever met him. Perhaps in passing, years ago. If he'd spent a short time at Harvard Medical School and we'd never talked, there was a good chance I would not have noticed him at all.

Margery, Zach, Klara and Sergeant Boyle had left an hour before. It was time for me to follow, else Zach would grow alarmed and send Boyle after me.

Despite the danger, I felt surprisingly calm. This case would soon be solved. All fears and worries would soon be gone.

I drank the last bit of cold tea left in the pot, brushed muffin crumbs off my hands, and picked up a candle. I held a match to the taper, switched off the electric light, picked up my revolver, and made for the dark corridor.

There was a sudden movement in the corner of my vision. The revolver was wrenched from my grasp. I couldn't even turn my head before something heavy wrapped around my throat and squeezed. As the candle dropped to the floor, my mind sent quick flashes of information: The first was the revelation of how the murderer was able to subdue his victims without a fight. The second was that the blood flow in my carotid arteries was reduced to a minimum and I would lose consciousness within seconds. Five, perhaps. The third was that I desperately wanted to live.

I kicked. My heel met his knee. He grunted. But the pressure on my throat did not slacken. Lights were popping in my vision. My ears began to sing.

I struggled against his weight. He was massive. The top of my head didn't reach his collarbone. My elbow sank into his gut, but he didn't even twitch. I tried to squeeze my fingers between my throat and his arm. He didn't budge. My limbs felt oddly detached. My mind began to float and darkness descended.

Something tugged on my consciousness: Had I in any way indicated that there might be a secret door in my bedroom? Had I in any way betrayed my family's hiding place? Had I in any way…

I woke to pain in my head and chest. Something was crushing my ribcage. Groaning, I opened my eyes and received a slap to my cheek. My ears rang. A face came close to mine.

He hissed, 'So, what do you think of me now, bitch?'

'Who are you?' I croaked. My throat felt raw. Words crept up my windpipe with reluctance.

'You don't even remember me? Ha! You've always been arrogant.'

'I can't see your face. It's too dark.' I tried to move my arms, but they were pinned.

'Colin Haywood,' he rasped.

I dug in my mind, but still, he was only a stranger. There was nothing familiar about his voice, his figure, his facial features — from the photograph and the few I could make out in the dark.

I needed a strategy. Fast. Something to bargain for more time. Because the longer I managed to stay alive, the greater the chance that Zachary would realise something was wrong. They *were* expecting me.

Sergeant Boyle would come.

Would Boyle even accept Zachary's gun? Probably not. And where was my gun? Still on the floor? Or had Haywood grabbed it?

'I don't know you,' I said.

A chuckle. 'Oh my. But I know who *you* are. The games you played. For years! I could get you behind bars for fraud. You'd be stripped of your license.'

I said nothing.

He waited for a moment. 'Come now. There is no need to deny it. You are an abomination.'

A snorted. 'And *you* are not? You took Henrietta's life. And then you killed Elizabeth. And then Millie—'

He boxed me hard. The side of my face fell numb, and then began to pulse with pain. 'You believe you can distract me? Ha! I never forgot your arrogant face. That self-important scowl. You've always been so full of yourself, Anton Kronberg. Or should I say, Elizabeth Arlington? Your Judgement Day has come. Death is spreading his cloak for you.' He threw out his arms, pausing for effect, and then lowered them to slowly draw a finger along my jawline.

My body vibrated with fear. It took effort to keep my mind focused. I couldn't buck him off — he sat too high up my chest. I couldn't drive my knees into his kidneys — they would merely tap his shoulder blades as ineffectually as a friendly clap. I wriggled my arms again, but they were trapped so tightly under his shins, I could as well have been manacled.

There was only one thing I could do.

'I think… I think I remember you. But it's too dark to see your face.'

He lifted his hand from my neck, and sat up straight, putting his weight fully on my chest. I gulped for air.

He fumbled in his pockets, extracted a small something, and then struck a match. He held the flame close to his face. 'Remember now?'

I studied his features. 'I…I'm not sure.'

He bent lower. The flickering light painted his right iris red and yellow. The heat crept too close to his fingers. He flicked the match aside and struck another one. 'How could you forget me?' he hissed. 'You threw insults at me. You broke my nose.'

'Don't be ridiculous! I'm a woman. I was never involved in fistfights at Harvard.' Was he mad? Or did he confuse me with someone else?

Snarling, he bent even closer. I felt his breath and the heat of the match on my face. And I struck. My forehead crashed against the bridge of his nose. There was no crunch, but he reared back with a cry. He dropped the match on my chest. The flame died. The weight on my wrists disappeared. I yanked back my arms, landed a right hook and a straight left punch in quick succession. I boxed his chest, aiming for the solar plexus to cut off his air.

But failed.

Grunting, he threw his weight forward. His hands came around my neck like vices, setting my throat on fire. Cutting off all air. I clawed his face, his wrists, his arms. But he didn't seem to register the pain. He kept squeezing and I felt my windpipe collapse. My eyes nearly popped out of their sockets. Blood screeched in my ears. My only thought was Klara. That I could not — *would not* — allow this man to make her an orphan.

With a last scrap of consciousness, I lifted my hands from his face, angled my arms, and wrapped the fingers of my left hand around his wrist. With the other palm, I struck his elbow. A satisfying *pop*, and the bones dislocated. He cried out and slapped at me wildly. I struck his chest again and again until I heard the telltale screech of air freezing in his lungs.

I pushed him off of me. His arms flailed, his legs kicked out and hit my side. Gasping, I scuttled backward and nearly fainted from the exertion and the lack of air. My trembling fingers flew over the floor, searching for my gun, but came up empty.

I jumped as the backdoor shuddered in its frame. Once. Twice. And burst open with a splintering crack. A silhouette rushed into the corridor, and hollered, 'Stop! Police.'

McCurley. I could have hugged him.

Haywood rolled aside and flung an arm out at McCurley, who took a swift step back. There was the metallic snick of a hammer pulled back. And a steady voice, 'I'm arresting you for the killing of three women, and the assault of another. Put your hands flat down on the floor, Mr Haywood. Now!'

The last word was shouted with such force, it made my ears wilt.

McCurley took a step closer to Haywood. But Haywood didn't want to go down quietly. There was a flurry of movements. Sounds of dull impacts. McCurley cried out. Haywood grunted.

I had no wish to get between McCurley's gun and Haywood's fists. I saw only one option. My arm shot forward, my fingers curled around Haywood's testicles and squeezed with a violent twist.

A high-pitched screech nearly drowned out the gunshot. The large man's legs jerked straight out and threw me on my rump. Then Haywood fell silent. A burbling and hissing betrayed the hole in his chest.

'Are you all right?' McCurley asked, his breath coming in short bursts.

I wanted to say yes, but all my throat was able to produce was a faint croak. He ran his hands over Haywood's prone form, and muttered, 'He still has a pulse. Faint, though.' Then stepped over the man. There was a scraping noise as he searched for a light switch. A *click* and electric light pierced my eyes and hurt my brain.

I groaned.

McCurley knelt at my side, touched my hands, arms, shoulders, and brushed his fingers along the bruises on my face. 'How badly are you injured?' he asked.

I shook my head.

'That pig.' He muttered and touched my throat.

A memory flashed past my vision: That of Colonel Moran and his footman Parker. One pressing an arm over my throat, the other sitting on my chest and hacking off my finger.

Panic struck. Fast and hard. I flung out my arm and smacked McCurley's chin. My throat seized. I couldn't breathe. All I managed were small gulps. *Hap-hap-hap.* In a distant corner of my mind, I knew that I was hyperventilating and that I needed to put a damper on it. To breathe slowly. But I couldn't. Terror had its claws in deep.

McCurley was saying something I didn't catch.

'Tilt up your chin!' His sharp command cut through my haze. All I wished to do was fill my caved-in lungs, but nothing would slip past my clenched teeth. Only the tiniest sips of air. My vision was dimming again, my heart racing.

'Up with it!' He repeated loudly and put a single finger under my chin to lift it. 'In through the nose. Out through the mouth.'

The sips grew bigger. Half a mouthful. And then another. Air began creeping down my windpipe. I could have wept.

'Good. You are good. In through the nose. Out through the mouth,' McCurley spoke in a soothing voice. 'Lean on me. I won't touch you, I promise. Slow now. Take your time.'

Leaning back against him, I kept fighting the fear. His knee touched my side, and I slapped it away. I couldn't stand anything near my chest or throat. With every fibre, I pulled my focus toward breathing. In through the nose. Out through the mouth. Chin up. And little by little, I regained control. It was agonisingly slow.

'That's good. You're doing well. Breathe.' He was breathing with me now. He pulled in air through his nose when I did, and pushed it out his mouth when I did. My back was pressed against the length of his torso, my head rested on his shoulder. His heart was beating with mine, our lungs filling in unison. Gradually, my airways relaxed and my senses returned to me as sweet air rolled through my body.

'There. There you are,' McCurley whispered into my hair. 'It's over. He's dying. He can't hurt anyone anymore. You did very well. I'm sorry I didn't come earlier. Did I ever tell you that I earned coin as a pit fighter when I was young? It's highly illegal so don't tell anyone.' He chuckled. A puff of air blew across the top of my head. 'I got kicked in the throat twice. The pain was unbelievable. I thought I would never draw another breath. I know exactly how you are feeling.'

He paused and looked over at Haywood, who had begun

to suck in short, hacking breaths, interrupted by wet noises from his chest wound and an occasional thump of his heel against the floor.

'It was strange. Suddenly he cried out and seized up. I wonder why. He must have pressed the trigger. But I'm not sure. We were both grappling for the gun. How stupid of me to get too close to him. He could have grabbed it and… Never mind.' McCurley shifted to look down at me, his mouth compressed, and said again, 'I'm so sorry I didn't come earlier.'

I tapped a finger to my chest, pointed at Haywood, then pantomimed grabbing my crotch and twisting.

He laughed. 'Ah, so *that's* what happened. Mystery solved.' And then, he pressed his mouth to my hair, groaned and instantly jerked back. 'You saved my life.'

I shook my head, tapped his side and then my chest. *You saved mine.*

'Maybe. That's up for discussion. Can you sit?'

I nodded, and he helped me lean forward. He moved around me and inspected my face. 'Your eyes are blood red. Bruises and swelling… Can you move your jaw at all?'

I opened my mouth and moved my jaw from side to side. It didn't feel fractured.

'The swelling here looks bad.' Gingerly, he touched my eyebrow.

I probed my face and skull with my fingertips but found no serious injuries. I put a smile on my face, to let him know I was all right. In some fashion.

His eyes flared in shock. 'You are in pain. I'll summon an ambulance.'

Well, that hadn't worked as planned. I shook my head at him, wondering how horrid my attempted smile must have looked. Or my face in general.

'No ambulance?'

I put my hand on his shoulder and slowly pushed myself up. I swayed on my feet and McCurley caught my arm, steadying me. I motioned toward my bedroom, and he helped me walk there.

Without thinking, I opened the secret door, snatched a piece of paper and a pencil from my nightstand, and wrote down the address of our hideaway. And below that:

Make sure my family is safe.

HE LOOKED FIRST AT ME, then at the black maw of the tunnel. A jerk of his head toward the man in the corridor. 'I don't think he'll ever move again, but…can you keep an eye on him anyway?'

I nodded.

He handed me his revolver, picked up a candle and a box of matches from my nightstand, and left.

Cocking McCurley's gun, I shuffled back to the corridor. Only then did I recall my own gun. I found its butt peeking out from beneath the splintery leftovers of the backdoor.

The bright ceiling lamp painted Haywood in a harsh light. The bruises on his face. The twitching of his limbs. Even the wet whistling emanating from the hole in his chest. Close to the heart. He must be drowning in his own blood, his lungs collapsed, unable to draw breath.

His eyes pleaded for mercy.

Exhausted and aching, I leaned back against the wall and sank to the floor.

I watched him die and felt no pity.

Death is spreading her cloak for you, I thought.

EPILOGUE

The sudden quiet was setting me on edge. A part of me was waiting for someone to emerge from a dark corner of the house and wrap his hands around my neck. I bit back a threatening shudder. I wished McCurley would say something. Anything. But he just sat in the wicker chair, his face tilted toward the darkening sky.

Margery had been hovering protectively the entire day. She'd found a hundred reasons to enter my office — either to bring us fresh tea or coffee, or to enquire if I or the gentleman were in need of anything. I would smile at her and shake my head. She flinched every time.

I looked horrible.

Klara hadn't left my side for most of the day. Only later in the afternoon had Zach managed to lighten her worries by taking her to the workshop to tinker with some wooden contraptions.

After helping Zach to reattach the back door, Sergeant Boyle and Mr Halverton had taken my statement — a slow process because my voice was a painfully small thing stuck to the back of my mouth. They left then, a mix of worry and relief was carved into their brow. McCurley asked if he could stay a few minutes longer.

That was more than an hour ago.

Since then, he'd said very little. He was concerned about something. Whether it was the beaten-up state I was in or the sketchy statement I had given, I wasn't sure. I doubted he was upset about the promise that I extracted from him and Boyle to never mention the secret tunnel. After all, it was a small omission and irrelevant to their investigation.

When McCurley finally spoke, I nearly jumped from my chair. 'Will you be all right?'

I nodded. He'd asked me that about a dozen times already, and my answer had been the same. After a heartbeat, I whispered, 'I watched him die.'

His gaze sharpened. 'There was nothing you could do.'

'I know. And I was glad of it. I wouldn't have wanted to save his life.'

I watched as his eyes lost focus. He opened his mouth, then shut it and turned away.

'What is it?' I asked.

He frowned at his hands. 'I keep wondering what death might be like. Have you ever had a patient who…woke up? After you thought they were dead?'

I shook my head. 'No, but I saw Death once. My own. She was not at all terrifying.' I huffed a bitter smile. Why was this memory coming back now? Hadn't I buried it deep, with the others? 'But dying… I don't know how it would feel. Perhaps to some, it might feel like falling asleep after a long struggle. To others… To others, it would be their worst nightmare. I didn't want to leave my daughter. Everything — *everything* — in me revolted at that thought when Haywood…' My voice faltered with a croak.

'Your courage is…' McCurley said softly but did not continue.

I took a sip of the honeyed fennel tea Margery had prepared for me in large quantities. 'To answer your question with a question: What did your death feel like before you were born?'

Surprised, he gazed up. 'I never looked at it from that angle.'

'When did you become alive? Or rather, aware? Was it not…a process more than just a sudden spark? So perhaps, death is not the sudden snuffing of that spark, but more of a…process itself. A fading from this life to whatever comes next.'

Shutting his eyes, he leaned back in his chair. Something was glinting in his lashes. 'Do you believe there is an…after?' His voice was husky.

I was about to say no. But then I couldn't help wondering if that was how his grief might abate — with forgiveness, and the hope that his wife might have found peace.

'I don't know. I think it's not for me to know if or what comes after I die. Because it would distract me from trying to make the best of the life I'm living.'

The sky blackened. Silently, Klara sneaked up on the porch, climbed into my lap, and nestled her face against my chest.

END

❀

Keep reading for a preview
of the next book in the series

RIVER OF BONES

PREVIEW

Prologue

*B*oston, September 1893

Had Mr Wilbur known that his two Dachshunds would resurrect a corpse, he certainly wouldn't have taken them for a walk.

He would have stayed in bed.

It was a crisp Sunday morning when Mr Wilbur strolled down Middlesex Avenue and into the marshes of Mystic River. The grass stood high. Dew was rubbing off on his new trousers, moisture creeping through cotton, weighing them down. He should have taken the time to put on his wellingtons, he told himself. Or his gaiters, at the very least.

A thin sheet of fog hovered above the water, tickled by rays of sunlight. Mr Wilbur thought of fairies. He shook his head. Ridiculous. He turned, his eyes searching for his dogs. Their sleek bodies were hidden by the grass, their tails pointing straight up, flicking like whips. When they began yipping in excitement, he wondered what they'd found. He would have to ask the maid to wash them upon his return — they were surely rolling in something revolting.

The yipping grew more frantic as Mr Wilbur stepped out onto the bank. He regretted the move instantly as his shoes sank into the soft mud. With a curse, he took two steps back, and skidded his mucky soles over clumps of grass. Then he lifted his head to call his dogs back.

And paused.

There was a big lump lying on the bank, fifteen yards or so away. The dogs were doing…*what* precisely? Tugging at something? Eating it? What was it, anyway? He narrowed his eyes. It was large. As large as a fat man. Shaped like one, too. No, that was impossible.

He would make an appointment with his ophthalmologist. Yes, right away. No, it was Sunday. That would have to wait until tomorrow.

Mr Wilbur lifted his fingers to his mouth and whistled. The dogs didn't even look up. They were entirely focused on…whatever that thing was.

He felt anger roll in his belly. Disobedience would not be toler—

A sharp, aggressive bark — like a small cannon shot. The dogs scattered like fleas.

The lump gave a violent twitch.

A wail cut through the fog.

The Boston Post, *Tuesday, September 5, 1893*

CORONER'S NOTICE - *Body of a man found two days ago at Mystic River near Middlesex Avenue, Somerville: about 45 years old, 5 feet 9 inches in height, stout build, dark hair, smooth face; had on Kentucky jean pants, brown vest, light calico shirt, blue*

cotton socks, and congress gaiters. Body at City Morgue for identi-
fication. Henry Millers, M.D. & Jacob Rubenstein, Coroners.

BY MIDSUMMER 1893, the recession had begun to grind people down. The census reported surging unemployment rates, and panic was beginning to stir among the working class. Housing prices notched up every other week, and the slums grew more and more crowded.

During that time of economic upheaval, only three things kept Margery from fearing the four of us would surely fall into poverty: her ability to preserve nearly everything she found at the farmer's market, a rather extensive root cellar for storing unfathomable amounts of food for months (never mind that this wasn't a root cellar at all, but a tunnel and secret escape route), and my inheritance that was mostly in gold.

I had told Margery and Zachary that I had inherited more than seventy thousand dollars, which they trusted would be enough for a lifetime. Had I told them the truth of it, Margery would have fallen over in shock.

Now, with autumn approaching, Margery, Zach, and Klara were going to the market almost daily. They would set out after breakfast and return before lunch, their small handcart laden with whatever was being sold at the best price that day. Then they'd sort their loot in the kitchen. Our tunnel was equipped with two rows of shelves down its considerable length, holding jars of fruits, jams, tomatoes, applesauce, artichokes, casks of sauerkraut and pickles, and even wheels of cheese sealed with cotton cloth and butter. Come winter, our larder would be stocked with ham, bacon, smoked sausages, crocks of lard, and other delicacies.

Margery seemed to be preparing for war. Or the apocalypse.

When the others went to market, I would make my way to Wards Six and Seven. It was a world of stink, grime, rats, dead goats, and drunkards. For that stink, I'd quit my lecturing post at the medical school for women. I'd closed my practice for these drunkards. And I hadn't been happier in years.

If anyone had asked what had compelled this choice, I'm not sure I would have found a satisfying answer. Slum life isn't pretty; everyone knows that. But what I found nearly impossible to stomach were the countless drunken children and babies.

In the slums, alcohol makes life bearable. In stale beer dives, the dregs from old casks were gathered and rounds of beer were sold at two cents. The recession hadn't changed that in the least, and the slum dwellers kept on drinking savagely. To them, alcohol was an anaesthetic. It lifted any and all inhibitions. It wiped away worries. Consequences no longer existed. People coupled, made babies. Pregnancies were a mere afterthought. Births happened nearly accidentally for mothers so stone drunk they didn't even feel the contractions. If both mother and child survived, the father or one of the older siblings would often wrap up the newcomer in some dirty rag to dump it in a park or an alleyway, or on the doorstep of some fashionable house.

Most of those babies ended up in squalid almshouses, with paupers, drunks, and the insane for company. They slept and cried and shat in small cardboard boxes lined with cotton wool, their lifespans measured in days.

My daughter seemed to have inherited my impulse to try to fix hopeless situations. She kept bringing home dying animals. Songbirds and their chicks that she'd wrenched from the maw of a cat, horribly chewed up but still twitching. Sickly kittens that were only skin and bone, and much too small to survive without their mother. And once, a small dog that must have been purposely set on fire. They all died. It was heartbreaking to watch Klara trying her best, and failing. I did all I could to help her care for them, but she needed to understand that sometimes, all one could do was to make a passing more bearable.

She had a thousand questions but asked none of them. She rarely spoke a word.

Margery couldn't fathom why I frequented Boston's worst slums, why I wanted to help the dregs, the ignorant, the shiftless. Zach, though, understood without me ever needing to explain.

Once you open your eyes to the suffering around you, it's nearly impossible to ever shut them again.

But one day, my trip to the slums was forestalled by a knock at the front door.

'Good day, Dr Arlington.' Inspector McCurley ripped off his hat and straightened his mop of unruly hair with several impatient flicks of his hand.

It took me a moment to process his appearance. I hadn't seen him for three months. Not since shortly after he and I killed Haywood — the man who had murdered three women and was known as the Railway Strangler.

McCurley looked healthier. Happier. A light shone in his blue eyes that hadn't been there before.

'Is your daughter well?' I asked.

He smiled broadly. 'She's crawling.' And then his eyes flared with a mix of pride and fear. 'She's horrifyingly fast.'

I chuckled. 'Ha! Wait until she starts walking. *That* is most terrifying. They wobble around on chubby legs and their huge head seems to take aim at every pointy bit of furniture nearby.'

His shoulders dropped. I regretted my words a little. As a

police inspector, he must have seen enough blood and gore to know how a toddler with a head wound would look.

Clearing his throat, he pushed his hands into his pockets. 'I've come to ask a favour. For your help, really. You'll be paid for your time, of course...' He trailed off, glanced over my shoulder and spotted Klara, who was getting ready to leave with Zach and Margery. 'She has grown so much.'

'Sometimes I could swear she grows half an inch overnight. Why don't you come in, Inspector?' I said, stepping aside.

We walked toward the sitting room, but he said, 'I'd like to talk to you in private. In your office, perhaps?'

'Of course.' Steering us into my office, I wondered what he might want.

He shut the door and cleared his throat. 'Early this morning, a body was found on the bank of Mystic River in Somerville.'

I propped my hip against the edge of my desk. 'And you've been assigned the case, which allows only one conclusion.'

He inclined his head. 'First evidence points to homicide. An autopsy is scheduled for...' He looked around the room, then pulled a watch from his pocket. 'An hour and a half from now. But that's not why I'm calling on you. A boy was found huddled with the corpse. Maybe six or seven years old — we're not sure. He's malnourished. Skittish as a cornered rabbit. The police surgeon described him as disturbed and unresponsive.'

'He examined the boy?'

'Well...from a distance. More or less. The boy wouldn't let the man touch him. He began screaming when the surgeon tried to pull him up. It was the strangest sound. Like a tortured animal.' McCurley shrugged helplessly. 'He's covered in grime and reeks of decomposition.'

'Did he say anything?'
'Not a word.'

find it in my bookshop:
https://anneliewendeberg.com

ACKNOWLEDGMENTS

This is to the lovely people who have supported the making of this book:

Gloria Horton-Young, Heather Lopez, Lou Valentine, Therese Webster, A. Zecha, Linda Koch, Carrie Pandya, Linda Koch, Steve Howard, Sandra Stehr, Gudrun Thäter, Michael Morrison, Rich Lovin, Caroline Wolfram, Kim Wright, and Victoria Dillman.

And to my beta readers Kim Wright, Sabrina Flynn, and Rich Lovin, and my proofreader Tom Welch.

THANK YOU ALL!

A quick note on the jokes Warren tells in chapter twenty-one: Yes! That's real Victorian humour found in 1890s newspapers.

The gherkin joke is from this century, my absolute favourite and the only one I am ever able to remember. Need I mention that I'm the only one who finds it hilariously funny? So you see, the author has inserted herself into her character. Tsk!

Printed in Great Britain
by Amazon

47708387R00159